Country of the Heart

Sharon Butala

A Phyllis Bruce Book

HarperPerennial
HarperCollins*PublishersLtd*

This book has been published with the assistance of the
Saskatchewan Arts Board.

http://www.harpercollins.com/canada

HarperCollins books may be purchased for educational, business, or sales promotional
use. For information please write: Special Markets Department, HarperCollins Canada,
55 Avenue Road, Suite 2900, Toronto, Ontario M5R 3L2.

Canadian Cataloguing in Publication Data

Butala, Sharon, 1940–
Country of the heart

"A Phyllis Bruce book".
ISBN 0-00-648158-2
I. Title.
PS8553.U6967C6 1999   C813'.54   C98-932567-9
PR9199.3.B87C6   1999

98 99 00 01 02 03 04 HC 10 9 8 7 6 5 4 3 2 1

Printed and bound in the United States

To Peter

Chapter One

LANNIE PEERED OUT the rain-streaked window of the cab, trying to see the river far below them. It was an opaque green today, pressed into flat ripples by the wind, dissolving here and there into fringes of greyish foam. She had heard that if you jumped from such a height the impact would kill you before you had a chance to drown. She doubted that, not that it mattered. She was not the jumping kind.

They were crossing the bridge in heavy traffic, the wet, gleaming bodies of cars hissing past them. She leaned back and closed her eyes. The taxi smelled of cheap face powder and some unidentifiable rubbery odour. The tires sizzled on the pavement, splashing through puddles. When she felt the car leave the bridge, Lannie opened her eyes. They were downtown, moving through the traffic, braking to a stop while pedestrians crossed in front of them, the driver humming and tapping his fingers on the steering wheel. Behind the stolid rows of glass and masonry, purple thunderclouds rose silently, billowing and receding. Late afternoon, late April, and she was going home.

At the bus depot she got out, the wind rippling her plaid poncho, whipping her long hair around her face. She paid the driver, took her suitcase from him, slipped her big tan leather bag over her shoulder and went inside.

As she pushed open the heavy glass door, the smell of coffee, french fries, diesel fuel, and damp, massed humanity rushed over her, suffocating after the light fresh scent of rain on the pavement. A few months in the city and she stopped noticing how evil it smelled—until she was unexpectedly assailed by a concentration of it like this.

She set her suitcase down, while she brushed her hair out of her eyes and shifted her bag back onto her shoulder. The book inside thumped against her ribs and she welcomed the solid, reassuring feel of it. Everywhere she looked there were people, standing in groups or alone or sitting on the orange plastic benches, their bags leaning against their legs. A frail old lady, clutching her ticket in white-gloved hands, too poor to travel any other way, stared at her.

Lannie considered her own appearance—five feet seven, reddish hair, thin, pale and haughty, in faded beige corduroy pants, narrow-legged, the pointed collar of a beige checked shirt protruding over a brown, crew-necked pullover, the neckline and cuffs of which showed from under her old tan and olive poncho, with the inter-mittent inches of fringe missing like teeth from a comb. Young straggly-haired mothers, fat or too thin, in cheap, damp wool coats, stared at her, oblivious to the toddlers stretched from their hands, too numbed by the brilliance of the lights, the unfamiliar red tile floor, the crush of people, to do more than hang wide-eyed from their mother's grip. Indian women in dark dresses and moccasins sit-ting apart sullenly, their hands on their laps, looked blankly at her, their malevolence carefully hidden. Teenaged Indian girls, going nowhere but to trouble, dodging among the people, laughing, their black hair swinging, their cheeks red from the cold outside, threw glances like bitter arrows at her. Expensive shiny boots, their eyes said, the fine-grained smooth leather only the rich can have, college girl going home for the summer they concluded, with contempt, or envy, or boredom, before their eyes slid away.

Lannie lifted the suitcase, the weight lowering one shoulder, and went to buy her ticket. She would not let Uncle Barney buy her a car. Clearly, this was foolish. Uncle Barney could afford it. He was baffled by the sums of money accumulating in his bank account. It made him uneasy, nervous, to have more money than he knew how to spend. Often Lannie had seen him standing at the window staring out over his neatly summerfallowed fields, jingling the coins in his pockets, rising onto his toes, then lowering his heels rhythmically, staring at nothing, his mouth twitching restlessly, a worried crease in his forehead. She knew he was thinking about the quantities of money he couldn't spend, that he perhaps felt guilty for having, and that puzzled him endlessly, his imagination not taking him beyond a house and a car and a fur coat for Iris.

"Come on, Lannie," he'd say. "A college girl should have a car. Just think, you could come home weekends and not just on holidays. You could take more of your things with you. You could give your friends rides . . ."

"A car is just a nuisance in the city," Lannie would reply in her clear, firm voice. "I don't have a garage. I don't know how to change a tire." Which was true, although not the real reason she refused. Without a car, she would tell herself, she never had to worry about an oil change or a funny noise or a place to park. She was never stranded, as she sometimes would have been with one, when it wouldn't start or had a flat. Without a car she was free.

But when she had once allowed herself to think of the real reason, she knew that she was actually fighting to keep free of her uncle's feeling for her, which he would call love, but she registered as humiliating and unbearable kindness. She couldn't take anything more from him. Already her debt was so large that she despaired ever repaying it.

"One way to Chinook," she said. The man behind the counter cradled the phone against his shoulder, talking into it, pushing her ticket toward her without looking at her. She slid her salmon-coloured suitcase toward the counter where the baggage tags were.

Another present from Aunt Iris and Uncle Barney. Too expensive for the bus depot, it stood out among the yellow tweed suitcases made of cardboard and held together with worn leather belts, the duffel bags and the bulging plastic garbage bags dumped on the floor. It was a neat, compact suitcase that a casually smart girl like herself should carry. She could imagine the pleasure picking it out had given Aunt Iris.

The suitcase contained another pair of corduroy slacks—sage green, two more shirts—one gray-checked, the other pale blue flannel, some underwear—all white, a pair of moccasins, and Proust in three volumes. She had sent everything else as freight. Iris would smile at her single suitcase but concern would glimmer in her dark eyes. And she would notice that Lannie was wearing the same outfit she had worn the day she left on the bus the previous fall. Lannie had few clothes, all of them good, and she wore them over and over again while Iris's closet bulged with colourful, briefly-worn garments in shiny silks and rough linens, fur-trimmed, beaded, frilled. Lannie needed to feel at home in her clothes. She thought of her clothes as the only things she had. And it seemed necessary to her to keep it that way. She stooped and tied the 'Chinook' label onto the suitcase.

Going home. When she straightened, this thought piercing her with its immediacy, she thought she caught the scent of the house in the morning, remembered Iris's blue dressing gown in the yellow kitchen. For a second she thought it might have been her mother who wore a blue dressing gown. She saw her room, hers since she was ten, when Iris had showed it to her and asked, "Can I do anything for you, sweetheart?" and Lannie had said, "I'd like it rose, please." Iris had gone out and bought the paint the next day and painted the room a deep, rich rose colour for her. Lannie could not to this day remember why she had asked for such a thing.

The other home, the true home, lingered in the back of her mind, as though she had been taken from there only yesterday. The kitchen floor sloped, its linoleum worn down to the floorboards in the doorway and in front of the sink. On the kitchen table was a blue and green flowered oilcloth that was cracked in the corners and was always sticky with jam and egg yolk. The blue flowered wallpaper had turned brownish and greasy with age and under the window by the table there was a brown stain from the rain that leaked in under the badly fitting window sill.

"These windows are worn out," she heard her mother say. Lying at night in her new white bed with the thick, pink chenille spread covering her, surrounded by the deep rose walls, she had tried to remember every word her mother had ever said to her. She repeated the ones she could remember over and over again until she fell asleep. But the words that had once come clearly had, through repetition, lost their certainty, so that Lannie no longer knew if she imagined them or if she truly remembered them. Now they had a reality of their own, divorced from what they had once meant to her. And, of course, the voice was gone. Once in a long while, in a dream, she would hear it again or sometimes when she woke in the night she thought she could hear her mother speaking to her. Then she remembered at once the sound of her mother's voice. And for a moment, she would feel better. She had a mother like everyone else, and then she would throw herself over onto her stomach or onto her back, noisily, sighing and kicking at the bedcovers hurriedly, before the familiar pain of loss could catch up and sweep through her.

She had shared a room with her little sister, Misty; her single iron bed against the wall on one side, Misty's worn wooden crib—that all of them must have slept in—across from her, the rag rug in between. And her father, she felt a pang just remembering him that she no longer felt when she thought of her mother, her father and her brother Dillon, they had been there, too.

She shoved her suitcase along the floor toward the lineup for her bus and fell in at the end, glancing at her watch—the flat gold watch with the narrow, brown lizard band that Barney had given her for Christmas. She reached into her bag and pulled out her book: Edith

Wharton's *The Custom of the Country.* She used her ticket as a bookmark and, straddling her suitcase, lifted it to begin reading. Ahead of her in the line a fat young mother in a brown wool coat, faded unevenly as if it might have been left out in the rain all summer, was holding an infant over her shoulder. Its wool bonnet was twisted sideways. It stared solemnly at Lannie with flat eyes, unblinking. Lannie stared back, then looked down to her book.

Out of the corner of her eye she caught a glimpse of a green and black lumberjack shirt moving toward her through the crowd. Something familiar about it made her risk a quick look. She saw a lanky blonde boy excusing himself politely as he slid between the passengers standing in long lines that snaked around and almost touched each other in front of the glass doors that formed the platform wall. Tim. She should never have told him what day she was leaving. Confused, she lifted her open book and bent her head toward it, hoping he wouldn't see her.

"Lannie." He had known where she was, came straight to her. His voice wobbled slightly, as though he was unsure what his reception would be. "I hoped I hadn't missed you." Tim was always late for everything. She looked up at him, carefully keeping any expression off her face.

"Hello," she said, closing her book with the air of a teacher who'd been asked the same question too many times. It always seemed to her that if she were cold enough, if she held him far enough away from her, he might at last give up and leave her alone.

"Going home, eh?" he said, although the way he said it, gently, softly, it was just another way of saying that he loved her. Lannie held herself still without replying, trying not to let him know that she heard him. She looked up at him unflinchingly, without smiling. His jacket was too big for him. It looked as if it might belong to his broad-shouldered father. His clothes were rumpled, mismatched; he was too tall, too thin, and he needed a haircut. She waited. She wanted to reach out and re-button his shirt, smooth his twisted collar. "I'll miss you," he said, leaning toward her.

"At least until you leave the bus depot," she said, almost gaily. It was as if a shadow had fallen across his face, darkening it, and then passed by, leaving the luminosity of his expression behind. Lannie dropped her eyes. She always regretted hurting him, only did it because it seemed necessary. She wished he would go.

"Can I get you a drink to take on the bus?" he asked.

"No thanks," she said.

"Will you write to me?" he asked. "I'll be in town all summer. Same place."

"I . . . oh, maybe," she said, shrugging her shoulders impatiently. He pulled one hand from his pocket, took a breath, reaching for her, trying to kiss her cheek. She turned her head abruptly so that his kiss caught her hair above her ear. When she looked at him she saw that his blue eyes were shiny with tears.

"Don't be so sentimental," she hissed, wanting again to hurt him, shaking her head so that her hair fell back from her shoulders and her pale face lifted toward him. He only looked at her. The steady gaze seemed to see past the hostile look on her face, past her fine, translucent skin to the girl inside. She could feel herself colouring.

"Write to me," he said again and closed his eyes so that she could see his thick white lashes, lying against the delicate flesh under his eyes. Then he opened them, and before she could say anything (what would she have said?), he turned away. She watched him taking long steps across the depot, brushing people as he dodged by them without the caution he had shown only moments before, his unkempt blonde head bobbing above the crowd. Her heart was beating too quickly, and she could feel that the blood had risen to her cheeks. For some reason she felt like crying. Taking her book from under her arm, she opened it and held it as though she were reading.

He was so easy to hurt, she did it now almost as a hobby or a compulsion. She did not want him to love her. If only he would laugh when she insulted him, like Armand did, or better still, just go away like the others did. She moved her shoulders irritably, making her poncho ripple.

She could not get over being ashamed of sleeping with him. When he brought her home from a movie or walked her home from the library after an evening of reading across the study hall from her, not daring to sit at the same table with her, he would kiss her with such love that she felt her heart would break with not loving him; she could not refuse. She would open her door and he would come in behind her. They would walk, she first, he behind, across the room to the bedroom, where they would undress in silence. Then Tim would kiss her and touch her with such tenderness that she would lie trembling under his fingers, suffering his caresses for reasons she couldn't give but that brought her to a pitch of misery for her unworthiness, for Tim's mistake, for her losses.

When it was over, she would lie with her back to him, he knowing better than to touch her, and think how the world was too sad a place for life to be possible. Then she would make Tim go home, and promise herself that this would never happen again. Better to sleep with strangers than with someone who loved you.

Her arm was jostled, and Lannie almost dropped her book. An Indian, short, heavy-set, walked past her to the front of the line. Watching the solidity of his tread, the impassivity of his back, she realized that he had bumped her deliberately. The passengers he passed pretended not to notice him. She stared at him as he stood at the front of the line facing all of them, his back against the glass wall where the bus driver would soon be taking tickets. Both fists were shoved into the pockets of his leather windbreaker. His legs in their faded jeans were crossed at an insolent angle. His face was set in creases that looked as if they had been there since he was born, as though there might no longer be anyone behind the blank mask he wore. Lannie watched him. To dare so much and not show by so much as a flicker of an eyelash whether he felt the hostility and fear of the people he had passed or not. That was what she needed. She needed to learn such control.

The line began to move. She extracted her ticket from her book and slipped the book into her bag. The line moved slowly past the driver and up the steps of the bus. The four front seats were occupied by children. Lannie found a seat halfway down the aisle. As she sat down she noticed that the Indian was sitting in the seat behind her. He stared at her without blinking as she slid down out of his view. She allowed her poncho to spread onto the seat beside her and set her bag on top of it. Then she tried to look as unfriendly as possible so that nobody would sit beside her.

An elderly woman sat down heavily on the double seat across the aisle, holding a bulging net shopping bag and a large black leather handbag on her lap. Her fat legs were stuffed like sausages into their support hose and the buttons of her too tight coat strained open over her mountainous breasts and rounded stomach. She puffed, rested a moment and then shifted and spread herself out on both seats. Lannie opened her book quickly, sensing that the woman was about to speak to her.

After a moment, the driver swung himself on board, arranged himself and his papers, pulled the door shut, and backed the bus out of the terminal. Splatters of rain hit the windshield and he turned on the wipers. They stopped at a traffic light and Lannie watched the pedestrians crossing in front of them, bent over, holding their coats together against the wind. The city was cold and heartless, melancholy in the blue light of late afternoon. She liked it best that way.

They were humming along the highway. The murmur of voices filled the bus, an occasional laugh rising above the rumble of the motor. Lannie drifted, her eyes on her open book, not reading. Suddenly a cry pierced the murmur, high-pitched, short, unreadable. Lannie felt her heart lurch. There was another deeper, shorter cry. Nobody stopped talking. Nobody moved out of his seat to see what it was. The driver sat looking at the road. He didn't even glance up into his mirror. Lannie strained to hear something, anything that would explain those heart-stopping cries but there was nothing but the sibilation of the tires on the pavement, the babble of voices embroidering the steady drone of the motor, the beat of the wipers. It must have been one of those peculiar distortions of sound you sometimes hear that is not what it seems to be, but a collection of different noises combined by chance to produce something terrifying. Lannie's stomach slowly unknotted.

Barney and Iris would be waiting for her at the bus stop in Chinook. Or rather Iris would be waiting and together they would cross the street to the cafe, where Barney would be drinking coffee. His face would light up when he saw Lannie. Lannie felt a small surge of pleasure at the prospect of seeing the two of them—Barney, jolly, going to plumpness, and Iris, small, dark and pretty—but she quickly dampened it.

Later, after crossing Diefenbaker Lake, silvery-white in the moonlight, when they were climbing the smooth shadowed hills on the far side, she thought she heard the cry again. This time she ignored it, as everyone else on the bus did. She assured herself there was a rational explanation for it, although she might never know it. There was so much for which there seemed to be no explanation: mothers dying, families breaking up, people loving one another. She could tolerate one more mystery.

Now when she peered out the window she could see only the reflection of the fat woman across the aisle from her, who had put her seat back and lay like a beached whale, sleeping, snoring with soft precision. The driver turned off the wipers. Someone had turned on a radio and she could hear snatches of rock music and the staccato voice of a male announcer.

Lannie thought of Misty and Dillon. Misty staring at Lannie, her face frozen like a kewpie doll's over her grownup cousin Dick's shoulder when they took her away. That chubby child transformed into a strange twelve-year-old, too tall for the cotton dress she was wearing, her tangled hair looking as though someone had tried to bleach it—Lannie had seen them both the summer before for an hour or so. Their new parents had been driving to Winnipeg for a holiday and stopped in at the farm, without notice, refusing even to stay overnight. It was the first time in four years that Lannie had seen her brother and sister. She watched the van leave, her heart pounding in her chest, her throat constricted with rage and sorrow, watched a trail of dust down the grid grow thinner.

She had begun walking. She had walked and walked and then run till her lungs were on fire and her muscles refused to lift her legs. Then she had stumbled to a walk and walked some more until finally she saw with less appalling clarity the girl who had looked at her with such sullen hatred and the big dark boy with the bruise on one cheek who looked just like their father, Lannie had seen that at once, who had not spoken at all during the whole visit.

Misty's eyes had returned again and again to Lannie's boots, which were new then and shone with a burnished brown glow below her slacks. She had lifted her eyes to Lannie's face briefly, wonderingly, and when Lannie's eyes caught hers she hung her head stubbornly and a barely perceptible stiffening came into her shoulders and long thin arms. Lannie shifted uneasily. She shouldn't think about Dillon and Misty, those stupid names. And Lannie, which meant nothing, was, in fact, a boy's name. What a nitwit their mother must have been. Lannie switched on the light above her seat and began determinedly to read her book, at first word by word, until finally the words began to flow and form ideas and she abandoned herself to Edith Wharton's calm and ironic lines.

Ahead of her in the darkness Iris and Barney waited. The bus sped down the highway, past deserted shabby towns and lighted farmyards, past empty fields lying dreaming under their weight of snow and water, past hidden places where deer, coyotes and rabbits lay and watched and shivered at the swiftly passing roar and the sickening smell that drifted across the coulees and flats behind it.

Chapter Two

IRIS WAITED ALONE in the dark cab of the half-ton. It was parked on the main street in front of Chinook's shabby, only cafe—not counting the diner in the old Gulf station on the way into town or the concession in the skating rink—across from the new Esso station, where the bus would stop. All day the air had felt like spring and even tonight with the day's accumulated warmth radiating upward off the earth, it was still not cold. The night had that soft, purple darkness that it only had in spring or during a chinook, and the stars seemed larger than usual.

Barney had shut off the motor when he went into the cafe and she hadn't felt the need to turn it back on. She was wearing the black wool coat that Lannie said suited her. The narrow black mink collar formed a ring around her neck and kept her chin and ears warm and she had put on the silver earrings that James had given her (she told Barney she bought them in Calgary), that emphasized her dark hair and eyes and heart-shaped red mouth.

In a few moments Lannie would be home. Iris imagined her stepping down from the bus like a foreign princess among the blunt heavy farmers and their wives, the pale freckles across her nose and in the hollow of her throat looking blue in the unnatural light from the mercury vapour streetlights, the trace of eagerness in her eyes while she searched the waiting crowd for them that she would quickly dampen when she saw Iris holding out her arms. Always it was this way. Ever since Lannie had come to live with them.

Lannie in the too-short cotton dress in early December holding Howard's hand in Iris's kitchen, it had been painted in shades of turquoise in those days, walking so quietly it almost seemed there was no one beside Iris on the way to her new bedroom. Even then, a week after her mother's funeral, Lannie carried herself as though her limbs were frozen. A fine chill emanated from her, making the air around her seem cold; Iris shivered even now to remember it. Iris had never seen anyone so forbidding, and in a child it was especially intimidating. So she never tried to force Lannie into unbending, not only because she respected Lannie's right to be the way she was, but also because the wall Lannie built between them seemed impenetrable and it baffled Iris and sometimes frightened her. For the most part she left Lannie alone and waited humbly for any thawing or offerings from her.

From the darkness in the truck she could look through the windshield across the narrow shadowed strip of sidewalk through the big plate glass window into the yellow lit interior of the cafe. She could see the wet streaks the waitress's cloth left on the yellow countertop, shining in the light from the dusty globes that hung in an evenly spaced row above the gleaming red vinyl booths. It would have been like watching a silent movie if everybody inside hadn't been so familiar. She had gone to school with most of them.

She had dated Hank Osborne, even let him make love to her once after a summer dance up in Cypress Hills Park. She could still remember lying on a scratchy gray blanket he found in the cab of his pick-up, probably carried for just this purpose. Could remember how it smelled of cigarette smoke and dust, how the red wool stitching along the edges was unravelling. And his urgency, he had held her too tightly, frightening her. She hadn't liked his need, hadn't liked the feel of his long sinewy body, or the way he fell away from her when he was done and lay on his back staring up at the stars that blinked through the swaying trees, smoking, as if she had not had a part in what just happened, was no longer lying there, getting cold and nervous from the sound of the wind, like the distant humming of a train in the tops of the pines.

She watched Barney sitting at the counter with men he had known all his life. He had been especially cheerful all day, knowing he would have Lannie in the house by nighttime. She was so glad Barney was there to provide the steady, good, male influence that Lannie needed. If only Howard were dead, she thought. But to promise he would be back for her—she had heard him—and then to gradually stop writing, to deliberately fade. So that Lannie couldn't forget him, couldn't plan her life, but felt she had to wait for him. I'm no psychologist, Iris thought, but there are some things you don't have to be a psychologist to see.

She supposed she ought to go inside and sit with the women who sat facing each other in the red booth. She could imagine the squeak of the vinyl when one of them moved, the smell of their coffee in the heavy, greying china cups with the thin green line around them; Greta hardly bothering anymore to cup her hand over her mouth when she coughed her rough cigarette cough; Marge pushing up her thick glasses every once in a while, the flesh of her plump hand rounding over her wedding band. But for now Iris liked being alone in the cab in the warm darkness, watching the occasional passerby and looking through the window at the men and women laughing together in the bright interior of the cafe.

Barney spun around on his stool, presenting his other side to her, to call to a farmer sitting in one of the booths on the far wall of the cafe. He was four years older than Iris and she could barely remember him as a child. They had gone to different one-room schools, Iris on foot to hers only a half-mile from the farm, and Barney, five miles to his, riding one of the district's infamous, stubborn old school ponies. His father was a small rancher up on the bench, one of the tough, old-time ranchers, and her father was a farmer, a big farmer, on the profitable flat sweeps of land to the south of town. There was no reason why they should know one another.

She and Barney were at Chinook High School at the same time for one year. Iris in grade nine, Barney in grade twelve. Barney's sister Fay was still in elementary school then and his older brother Howard hadn't gone to high school. And of course, Wesley. Wesley had never been to school at all.

Nobody was surprised when Iris Thomas went to high school. She was, after all, the only child of the respected Thomas family, but it was a surprise when Barney Christie stayed on in school and got his grade twelve. Christie men were respected, too, but it was a grudging respect for the tradition they represented and a fear of offending their thin-lipped pride.

Barney was tall and in those days had the lean, narrow-hipped, heavy-shouldered look of a rodeo cowboy that made blood rise to Iris's cheeks inexplicably whenever she saw him. He used to come to school in cowboy clothes—the tight levis, tooled leather boots and plaid or checked western shirts, as if he'd just arrived in a cloud of dust on a bronc and checked his spurs at the principal's office. Iris smiled, thinking of her crush on him, how she had smiled at him whenever he happened to glance her way, how she had contrived to stand near him at the water fountain so that he would notice her. Till years later, that one trip to the Christie ranch, when they were de-horning, and she finally got over her fascination with ranching and cowboys.

Barney rose from his stool and strolled over to the women. For a second, as he passed behind a pillar, he disappeared from her view. Then he was leaning against the booth across the aisle from them, talking. He was wearing a hockey jacket over the sort of sportshirt that any city businessman might wear to relax in, and matching tan slacks. He didn't even own a pair of levis or a western shirt anymore. She noticed how his stomach had begun to bulge over his belt. Too little work, she thought, too much time on his hands. And his cheeks were too red since he had been putting on weight. Could it be high blood pressure? She should see that he have that checked. But she noticed too how his hair was still thick and golden brown, not a trace of grey, and how his eyes still glowed with life.

Sometimes she could almost believe that he was what he now appeared to be. By an effort of will he had become cheerful, good-natured, unselfish Barney Christie. Only his family knew that he was not as uncomplicated as he seemed to be, that darker forces worked inside him, that he struggled with them, pushed them down, pretended that they weren't there. Barney's father was as angry over this new personality as he was over Barney's defection. She supposed that Luke resented in a way that Barney's life was easy now, that he no longer needed to set his jaw and narrow his eyes till that was the only expression he had, so he could stand up to feeding cattle day in and day out all through the bitter winters, to the losses, the bad prices, the physical rigours of ranch life.

Greta Osborne was gesturing with her cigarette, pausing to cough. It seemed to Iris that she could hear the sound. The other women were laughing and Barney's head was thrown back, his even white teeth shining. The waitress, a skinny, brown woman from an outlying farm, whose husband was said to have left her, had come over with the coffee pot, steam rising from it, and was leaning over the table pouring more coffee.

Iris stirred and said to herself again that she should go inside but something in her mood held her back. The night was fragile. The air felt light on her cheeks, her whole body felt light as if she could stand up and float away. She liked the feeling. Usually she felt so solid in her skin, so firmly her own earthbound self. She liked watching Barney without his knowing it, she liked thinking about James, she liked sitting quietly alone. Soon Lannie would be home and she wouldn't have a chance to sit and feel herself alone. And how would she get away to visit James? It was the first time she had clearly articulated the thought, although it had been perched in the back of her mind ever since the day she looked at the calendar and realized it was only a month till Lannie's return. She couldn't neglect James. He needed her.

"We have to go see old Jake Springer," Barney had said, and she was surprised because usually it was she who said to Barney, after a death, "We'd better go visit the McCormacks," or the Longmans or the Sproules. Barney always agreed; he had been raised in the district too. He always smiled through the visit, remembering to wipe the smile off at appropriate moments and then forgetting again, so that it crept back when his mind was on something else. That is how habitual it has become, she thought to herself, and shook her head. He would offer the bereaved family help in the form of money (he did not care about repayment), or he would offer to come and feed their stock for a couple of days till they were, "on their feet." She knew Barney would have taken Misty and Dillon too, if Howard hadn't been determined to pay some obscure debt to his wife's cousins by giving them two of his children, as though they were puppies in a litter to be divided up among those who had no pets.

So they went to visit Jake Springer after his wife's death. They found him sitting in his armchair, his large square hands, veined, thick-fingered, nicotine-stained, resting solidly and incongruously on the crocheted lace covers on the arms of his chair. He had answered their knock by calling, "Come in," and didn't get up during their visit.

Jake's head reminded Iris of a bull. Below the prominent cheek-bones were sloping, flat planes and two deep lines from his nose to the corners of his mouth. His hair was thin, glittering silver in the overhead light. The waves on each side of his head emphasized his profile with its large straight nose. Even in his old age and his grief, she thought, he was a handsome man.

His wife's picture hung on the wall behind them. She was gazing with spirited eyes into some 1930's world that Iris couldn't imagine. Looking at the picture, Iris could understand why the old man was taking his loss so hard.

He sat in his armchair, barely moving, not stirring the air around him, his expression immobile and sad. His eyes seemed dark and sunken under his heavy white brows. Speaking seemed an effort, as though he had to pull the words out of an almost forgotten part of himself. His voice was gravelly and without inflection. Iris could remember him striding around town or riding a bucking horse in the Chinook rodeo when she was a child. He had seemed very big to her, black-haired and powerful. He had exuded a vitality that made her remember him over other men. The women had all shot him glances which Iris even as a child knew how to interpret.

When the visit was drawing to a close, Barney, unable to think of anything to offer this old and self-sufficient man in his bereavement, offered Jake his wife. Or rather, he said, "Iris'll drop over and give you a hand with the housework for a while, or whatever it is that women keep themselves busy doing." And he gave Jake that knowing smile that Iris had seen men do when the exclusive activities of women were mentioned, expecting Jake to return it. Jake said only, "No need for that," and didn't bother to answer Barney and Iris' protests.

There was a loud bang. Iris jumped. Hank and Ray Johnson had come out of the cafe and were crossing to the bar on the other side of the street. Seeing her sitting in the truck one of them had banged the hood to make her jump. Both men laughed and waved. Stifling her irritation, Iris waved back. Inside the cafe, Barney was at the counter, sitting on a different stool, talking to a couple of farmers from down the valley. She pushed the light button on her watch. A few more minutes. She would hear the bus before she saw it. She felt a quick flutter of excitement in her chest. She leaned her head back and looked at the sky through the side window, luminous night blue pinpricked by stars.

She had found him alone, sitting in his armchair as though he hadn't moved since they'd been to visit him. He smiled when he saw it was her. Iris was pleased that he seemed glad to see her. She took off her jacket and sat down across from him. She was wearing a brightly flowered, blue silk blouse and matching slacks.

"My wife had a blouse like that," he said, "when she was young." Obscurely, Iris felt pleased.

"I like bright colours," she said. "I like cheerful things." He looked at her silently, then exhaled and bent to flick the ashes off his cigarette. There was a softness in the air that Iris couldn't identify, as though the old man gave off warmth in the way that Lannie gave off cold. She looked at him thoughtfully. He continued to look at her.

"You're a pretty woman," he said. Iris was surprised. Before she could speak, he added, "I can say that. Nobody minds what an old man says." Then he laughed, a short, deep laugh. Iris had a sudden picture of him as a young man. His curly black hair. Cigarette smoke curled in the air around him. Iris felt as if she could sit forever in this warm, dim atmosphere, in the silence laden with the dreams, memories, ghosts of his well-lived life whispering around them. She leaned back on the couch and fingered the buttons of her blouse.

"I came to clean your house," she said languidly, not moving.

"It don't matter," he said. They sat for a long time, not speaking, the old man smoking.

"Is your name Jacob?" Iris asked, looking at the picture of his wife above his head.

"James," he said. "My old man called me Jake." He was leaning forward, his elbows resting on his knees, his palms touching each other, the cigarette extended from between his fingers. "His name was James too." Iris looked around the room. There were cigarette ashes and flecks of mud on the carpet. The room was dusty, the ashtrays full. She began to move around the room, collecting ashtrays, running her finger through the dust on the TV.

"Now," he said, "leave that." He caught her hand as she passed him. She stopped, surprised. They looked at one another. His eyes glowed blue through the haze. Iris caught her breath. The haze dimmed the deep lines of his face, softened the wrinkled skin. She thought again of his face as a young man.

"When I was ten," she said, "you were already in your forties. I remember seeing you then. At the rodeo." He laughed again, the same ironic laugh.

"Yeah, I was a cowboy then," he said. He had dropped her hand and was sitting back in his chair, smoking. Iris moved around the house quietly, dusting, sweeping, washing the dishes, changing the sheets.

It surprised Iris to see what a pretty woman his wife had been. Iris couldn't remember her at all from the same period that Jake stood out in her memory. But she and Iris had both been at a tea a week or so before her death, Iris serving, Aurora attending. Iris had stopped to speak to her and been struck by the brilliance of Aurora's eyes, blue like her husband's, but paler. Aurora, on touching Iris's hand, had looked into Iris's eyes and held them with a look of such intensity that Iris had been disconcerted. But she looked back calmly, the fingers of her right hand touching Aurora's palm, accepting what seemed to be Aurora's favourable judgement.

Then Aurora's eyes had changed; she let go of Iris's hand and inquired politely if her husband was well, as though nothing unusual had happened. Iris knew Aurora was a woman of extraordinary personality, and she wondered why she had never noticed it before. A week later Aurora had died of a heart attack and Iris had forgotten the incident at the tea.

She was pulling up the quilt on the double bed when a thought occurred to her. She dropped the quilt and went into the living room. She stood across from the old man and looked up at Aurora's picture. After a moment she dropped her eyes to him. Hesitantly she said, "Do I . . . do I look like her?" She nodded her head upward toward the picture of Aurora. The old man's voice, after a pause, came back softly through the haze.

"Yes," he said, "same hair, same figure. You even dress the same.

Your eyes are a different colour, though." He drew on his cigarette.

Iris was touched, confused. She sat down on the couch, looking at the picture and then at him.

"You smoke too much," she said, surprised at herself.

"Sound like her too," he said. He smiled briefly. Iris felt tears in her eyes, she had no idea why. Suddenly she stood up and before she understood what she was going to do, put both hands on his head, against his ears and kissed him lightly on the mouth. Her tears overflowed and lay on her cheeks. She started to take her hands away, but Jake caught her by the wrists, held her bent over him and kissed her firmly, his mouth open. Then he let go of her wrists and said as she rose, "I'm sorry . . . it's just that . . ." He put both his hands over his face. His head trembled. She touched the silvery hair gingerly and then brushed it back with her palm.

"It's all right, it's all right," she said, as she might have spoken to a child. She wanted to put her arms around him and hold him, but allowed herself only to kiss his forehead.

Iris sighed, still looking out the truck window at the stars. She touched the fur of her coat. Barney was standing up, walking to the cash register, feeling in his hip pocket for his wallet. There was a distant hum in the air, growing louder. The bus. Excitement leapt in her and she fumbled for the door handle. She climbed out and hurried across the street to the service station. The bus came down the main street of the town, breaking the silence with its roar, and pulled to a stop with bursts of expelled air and a short, mechanical screech. Barney was beside her. He squeezed her elbow without looking at her. They were both smiling.

The door opened, the bus driver stepped down and waited by the door, while his passengers began to climb down. First the children, making noises like a flock of birds, then one by one the farm wives, the old people, one young Indian (what would he be doing in town?), and then Lannie, pausing for a second, blinking before she descended, the driver touching her elbow carefully. She looked so exactly as Iris had pictured her that the smile Iris was already wearing stretched a little further, and she could feel the start of tears but blinked them back. She hurried forward with her arms outstretched. Lannie bent forward and allowed herself to be hugged, first by Iris and then by Barney.

Lannie stood, blinking under the unearthly light from the streetlamps. There was a sharp noise, a cry like a bird's.

"What is that?" she asked, drawing back and looking around.

"It's the children," Iris said, pointing to them. They had clustered like nestlings around a tall woman Iris didn't know. She looked like a mother bird dropping worms into her babies' open mouths as her fingers moved rapidly. The small faces were turned up to her. Lannie saw then that hearing aids glinted like exposed bone in each child's ears. "The Sawchucks are taking in some children from the School for the Deaf for a farm vacation." Lannie looked relieved.

"It's good to see you," she said. Barney picked up her suitcase and laid his arm across her shoulders. He pulled her toward him and smacked her on the forehead. Lannie smiled faintly as the three of them walked across the street to the truck.

"Want some coffee before we go?" Barney asked.

"No, thanks," Lannie said. Iris knew Barney would be glad she had refused. He didn't want to share her just yet with the people in the cafe, who would feel compelled, partly out of politeness and partly out of curiosity, to cluster around her and ask her about school and her trip, tease her about being home just in time to do Barney's seeding for him.

They settled into the truck, with Lannie in the middle, and drove out of town. Iris suddenly kissed Lannie lightly on the cheek and patted her knee. Lannie dipped her head, embarrassed.

"I painted the kitchen," Iris said.

"Is it still yellow?"

"Yes," Iris said. "But I put up new curtains. They're yellow too, with big white flowers and just a touch of turquoise."

"You have such good taste."

"I think it's pretty. First thing in the morning, a room should be cheerful."

"Right," Barney said. "So, how's school? Did you pass all your exams?"

"I think so."

"We know you work hard," Iris said. "I admire you so much, the way you study. When I went to college, that one year, I just couldn't get interested. I guess I just wasn't cut out for it. You'll probably get all A's." Lannie was silent. "I try to imagine your life in the city. You know, what your day is like. You get up in the morning, and . . . what do you have for breakfast?"

"Usually nothing." Lannie said. "I think of you on the farm often." Barney said solemnly, "Iris on the phone. Me watching TV." He and Iris laughed, glancing at each other in the light from the dash. Iris turned to Lannie.

"I imagine you going out with your friends to movies and having pizza afterward, or going out dancing with a boy, like I used to do." Lannie laughed. Iris heard something out of place, a falseness in the sound, and she wondered what it meant.

"You can't imagine," Lannie said.

"I suppose life's not like it was when I was twenty." Iris said. "But I hate to be reminded of when I was twenty." She sighed. "Here I am a twenty-year old trapped in a forty-two-year-old's body."

"You can still pass for thirty," Barney said. "You're still as pretty as when I married you." Iris touched one of the silver earrings, then quickly withdrew her hand.

Chapter Three

THE LIGHT ON THE DASH glowed a soft orange. It illuminated Barney's big brown hands on the steering wheel, dissolving into darkness past his elbows, lighting up a patch on one of Lannie's knees, leaving Iris by the window in shadow. They rode quietly, their bodies trembling with the vibration of the truck as it droned toward the farm through the sapphire-coloured night.

The moment, and Iris's words, made Lannie remember other nights—lights glowing in a warm moment in the dark, a cigarette lit, a light from an opened car door flaring up, a face lit, then swallowed by the darkness, the smells, the touching.

Music, crashing meaninglessly around her ears without rhythm or tune, lights around the bandstand blinking off and on, now green, now purple, now magenta, catching the faces of the dancers like masks, momentarily. The welcome weight, the heat of an arm across her shoulders, the blur and tilt of the sidewalk, the crushed cigarette packages lying crumpled in the dirt, the rough brick wall in the alley, the chrome and enamel gleam of cars shining in the cold light in the parking lot behind the club. His car, red, gleaming. The smell of leather when she leaned back. The coloured lights flashing through her closed eyelids, her head forced back into the seat by the speed.

He poured her a drink. She drank it quickly. In the bedroom, moonlight gleamed through uncurtained windows, the bed was unmade, the room cold. He had thrown the covers up quickly and kicked some twisted clothes under the bed. He had laughed, embarrassed, and held her by the elbows, pulling her toward him.

"You don't smile much," he had said. She pulled back, lifting off her t-shirt, kicking her feet out of her sandals, beginning to undo her slacks.

When he offered to drive her home, she lied to him about where she lived.

"The Park Towers," she said. It was only two blocks away.

"Okay," he said, yawning, stretched out lazily on the rumpled sheets, the smooth, tanned skin of his chest glowing like copper or brass in the light from the lamp by his bed, his eyes already drowsily closing, dismissing her as if she no longer existed. She had closed her eyes wearily and touched her fingers to her forehead. Then she turned, left the apartment silently and walked the mile and a half across the city, putting one foot in front of the other, crossing the bridge, moving like a shadow down the tree-lined streets of the university district. Across the river and below her she could see the lights from downtown glowing like fireflies in the night, while she walked alone in the darkness under the heavy, still branches of poplars.

How did it happen? Time and time again she came to this, to the long silent walk home, to the shock in the morning, and the other things that came later. She knew it was the yearning for her mother, whose loss would never be replaced, for her father who had left one freezing winter day, bending over her, saying, "I'll be back for you, honey, just as soon as I can," for faint memories of things that were never right even before she had lost them, "You be a good girl," for the impossibility of her being a good girl, of ever being good enough, of being, instead, hopelessly bad, for being an unasked-for weight on Iris and Barney's lives. But knowing didn't help.

She wished they would have given her a bare room in the attic, a diet of porridge and hand-me-down clothes, while she waited for him to return for her. They ought to hate me, she thought over and over again. They ought to make me leave now that I'm almost twenty. Hating herself because she didn't have the courage to leave and take nothing with her.

They had reached the farm. In the violet light from the yardlight, the big, white-trimmed, brown house looked eerie and unwelcoming. The three went inside, Iris first, turning on the lights and talking as she opened the closet by the front door.

"Come into the kitchen." Carelessly hanging up her black, mink-trimmed coat, Iris started down the blue-carpeted hall past the silent, cavernous living room on the one side and the stairs leading to the second floor on the other, past the long, seldom-used dining room where the heavy, silver tea service, that had been Iris's mother's, sat like an anchor in the centre of the big oak table, past the china cabinet full of cut glass and thin white dishes from France and England, that tinkled as they walked by, and the long buffet on the far wall, whose long narrow mirror framed them passing and whose drawers were lined with dark red plush and were full of silver that sang when someone picked a piece up or set it down.

At the end of the hall on the left was the kitchen. It was a big room, too, as if the women of the house still had a threshing crew to feed every fall and six children the rest of the time. Although the walls, the ceiling and the floor were a bright lemon yellow, the room was still somehow not quite warm, as though it were secretly melancholy without a big noisy family to fill it.

"I thought you'd be hungry," Iris said. She tried to hide the apologetic note to her voice. She hadn't really thought that. Lannie was never hungry, but Iris wanted to make some celebratory gesture for the three of them, but especially for Lannie because that was the only way she dared to try to show Lannie that she was loved and that this was her home. "I made us a bedtime snack." She pulled a warm pizza out of the oven with a half-uncertain, half-merry gesture and held it out for Lannie to see. Lannie looked at it, trying to hide her dismay at both the act and the garish lumpiness of the food resting on the cookie sheet.

"I love pizza," she said, swallowing and trying to smile. She did not love pizza. She did not love anything, but she pulled out the flowered vinyl-covered chair, where she had sat at mealtimes since she was ten, and sat down obediently. Iris went to the row of mahogany cupboards and took out the blue and white china plates that she used for everyday and set them down on the table. She turned on the burner under the pot of coffee she had made before she and Barney left to meet the bus, and then sat down in her place. Handing Lannie a piece of pizza, the hot cheese pulling and then springing back onto her fingers, she glanced at Lannie's face and thought, there are blue patches under her eyes, they must come from sleeplessness and worry, and then, lowering her eyes back to her plate, said to herself, it is only a trick of the very fair-skinned to look so delicate. No doubt she's fine, only tired from her trip.

Barney ate quickly. Between bites and sometimes during them, he told Lannie all the local gossip he could think of.

"That Wolfe kid? The older one with the long hair?" Lannie nodded, watching him. "Just got six months for car theft—guess whose car it was?"

"Yours?"

"That new caddy of old man Tremblay's." He laughed and swallowed. "Imagine! Just wanted to try one out, I guess." Iris got up and brought the coffee pot to the table and filled their cups.

"Did you know that your cousin Gloria graduated from nursing in Calgary this week?" she asked Lannie.

"My cousin?" Lannie asked.

"Well, Barney's cousin," Iris said. "I get who's related to who mixed up." There was a silence. Barney helped himself to another piece of the pizza, dropping squares of green pepper on the table and scooping them up with his fingers and popping them into his mouth.

When they had finished their coffee and there were only crumbs left on the tray, Iris and Lannie gathered the few dishes and put them in the dishwasher, while Barney yawned and stretched and wandered around the kitchen. Then they started up the stairs to the bedrooms together, first Lannie, then Barney, then Iris, who had made a last check around and turned out the lights.

Barney watched Lannie climb the stairs ahead of him. Iris was a little behind and he could feel, as always, the warmth of her body near him. He tried not to watch Lannie, the way she climbed the carpeted stairs lightly, straight-backed as if she weighed nothing, the way she lacked the pendulum motion most women made, walking or climbing. Like Iris, he thought, who was all woman: she curved, she was soft to touch, she couldn't walk without swaying. Even now, half-behind him, he could imagine the sway of her hips as they flowed outward from her small waist, the slight bounce of her breasts as she climbed the stairs. Lannie moved upward ahead of him, so slender that she reminded him of the stately grace of a field of ripe wheat. Or like a fine Thoroughbred that nobody could ride. Abruptly he took his eyes off her body.

Lannie turned at her room, the first to the left at the head of the stairs.

"Good night," she said, and he said, "Good night," listening to the depth of his voice after the sweetness of hers. He didn't kiss her anymore, had stopped when she was almost seventeen and that accident, he thought of it as an accident, had happened.

She shut the door to her room quietly. Iris caught up with Barney and they turned together to their own bedroom, which looked out over the front of the house, the gravel driveway, the long mysterious row of pines leading out toward the road. Behind them, all around them, lay his empty fields, waiting for his tractor and drills to roll over them, cultivate, lay seed in them. He thought with satisfaction of the work ahead, of the long days in the sunlight.

"Did I turn off the outside light?" Iris asked. He pushed back the curtain and looked down to the darkened front door below him.

"Yup," he said. He stretched slowly and began to undress. Iris went into their bathroom and closed the door. He listened to the water running as he lay on the bed barefoot, shirtless, waiting for her to come out. Her scent filled the room. Lilacs tonight. Iris always smelled like flowers, always had, as far back as he could remember her, which would have been when she was about twenty and he was twenty-four.

He'd seen Iris one night, going into a movie with the town's new pharmacist. Just the sort of guy who'd get to take her out. He'd been with Alana Sproule, whom he figured, without really giving it serious thought, he would probably end up marrying. Then he'd seen Iris, caught a glimpse of the tops of her full, white breasts as she half-turned in the lineup to say hello to Alana standing beside him, and felt a sudden ache. Alana never looked like much after that. Not that there was anything the matter with Alana, but she had sun-bleached brown hair and a year-round tan and long legs, hard with muscle from barrel-racing and riding with her father. Iris's hair was thick and dark. It rested on her shoulders, touched her collarbones, bare in the summer dress she wore. He had restrained himself from leaning down and lifting it off her bosom, sifting it through his fingers, smelling it. It reminded him of cotton candy, the way it seemed to be spun.

Gradually he'd found himself thinking about her more and more, imagining her riding beside him in his truck, dreaming about having her in his bed with him. And then he'd asked her out to the ranch to one of their brandings and just as suddenly as the night he'd first started to want her, everything changed again. He saw that Iris could never become a part of the world he inhabited—the worn houses of the ranchers, the outside toilets, the brandings and dehornings and caesareans, the trail drives, the fierce, unending work and cruelty of the life. Iris had never worked a day in her life. She didn't know what work was, didn't know what hardship was.

Iris came out of the bathroom in a long, sheer, pink nightie and began hanging up her dress. Her breasts moved under the gown as she lifted her arms and he felt a vague stirring. Lots of time.

He sauntered into the bathroom. It was another of Iris's rooms. Sometimes he felt like punching a hole in the wall to escape her sweet, powdery smells, her way of decorating a room so that it surrounded him, made him feel clumsy. The expensive little objects she set around usually pleased him because they stood for his success, but sometimes he wanted to knock them to the floor and grind them under his heel.

He thought with bitterness of the bare cold house he'd been raised in. His mother wasn't much of a housekeeper, but then she'd worked outside like a man until she got too old for it. Didn't have time for housework and decorating like Iris, even if there'd been the money, which there wasn't. And Fay, his younger sister, was the same as their mother. Poor housekeeper. But then she had four kids and a no-good husband to look after. He thought of Fay for a moment. Hadn't heard anything for a while. Hoped Barry was home with them and working. Hoped Quinn was staying out of trouble. He'd have to call his mother and ask.

Sometimes he felt homesick for the smell of sage. Longed to go herding cattle in the cold spring up on the lease, to drink from the clear, spring pools of melted snow, to lie for shelter from the wind in the tall prairie grass. To feel free again, and a man.

He took his bar of soap from the shelf and stepped into the shower, pulling the plastic curtain shut. Lannie made him think of a cool wind. She made him think of the prairie, how it lay out there vast, empty, starkly beautiful.

He caught himself. That was no way to think about the girl. His niece, almost his daughter. He scrubbed himself roughly with the soap, trying to rub out the image that kept flashing into his mind when he didn't want it: the accident—Lannie, nude, stretched out over her bed, pulling up the covers, the door drifting open as he padded by in the early morning, the long slender line of her bare leg stretched out, the curve of her hip, the way her small white breasts with their pale tips had pointed to the bed as she knelt on one knee and reached to smooth the sheet on the other side. Thank god she hadn't seen him. He felt the surge of, could it be desire? For a moment he stood still, both hands thrust against the tile of the shower wall, his head down, eyes closed, the water pouring over him. Then he began to scrub angrily.

He twisted the taps violently and thrust back the curtain, stepping out as if he had a meeting to go to. Steam clouded the mirror. That goddamn Howard, he thought.

He rubbed his head with a bath towel, drying his hair, wanting to rub out the past, his big, handsome, half-brother Howard, the fights, Howard's rage, Howard leaving because the ranch would be Barney's since Luke was Barney's father, not his, Barney's growing but hidden dissatisfaction with the life, Luke turning his back on all of them.

Barney stopped rubbing his head, took a fresh towel and dried his body, leaving the wet one in a damp heap on the floor. When he was dry and calmer, he went back into the bedroom.

Iris had turned off the lamp on her side of the bed and left his on. She lay watching him, half-smiling, her brown eyes glistening in the lamplight, her dark hair, shorter now than it used to be, fluffed out on the pillow around her face, one pink nightgown strap drifting down her shoulder onto the plump, ivory flesh of her arm. He felt his heart slow down, felt himself able to smile at her. She smiled back.

"It's good to have her home," Iris said.

"Sure is," Barney said cheerfully, and climbed into bed beside her, without bothering to put on his pyjamas.

In the room across the hall Lannie lay awake. The pizza sat heavily in her stomach. She felt almost ill from it. She plumped her pillows and sat up in bed, without turning on the light. There was a little moonglow coming through the window, lighting the room enough that she could fix her eyes on the shadowy outlines of the furniture, the smooth, flat walls melting away into darkness in the corners. She thought about school, about Armand, about her life in the city.

Armand's chalk chattered along the blackboard, leaving a trail of symbols. He was short for a man and Lannie wondered idly if his ex-wife shortened his jeans to make the hems rest so perfectly along the line of his bootheels. He said he and his former wife had a good relationship, but Lannie couldn't imagine how two people who had fought so much that she tried to kill herself and he once blackened her eye, could possibly have any kind of a relationship at all.

Armand spun around and faced the class, the yellow chalk held at shoulder level, his fingers smudged with it, the light from the windows down the far side of the classroom striking his glasses, making him look blind.

"Did you get that?" he asked the twenty or so students facing him. Several of the students nodded or said 'yes.' A small girl with pale brown hair frizzed out like a medieval martyr's around her fine-boned face said, "But there is another proof, isn't there, Professor Bourque?" In the campus pub at night (he was only a junior lecturer working on his Ph.D.), they all called him Armand. Janice was in love with him and she took tacks with him that baffled Lannie. Now, before Janice could show him her proof, he was nodding vigorously, his black curls bounding, his wire-framed glasses sliding down his nose.

"You saw that," he said. "Good, good. I wondered if anybody would," and he was back at the blackboard, erasing, explaining, scribbling. Lannie slid her books shut. Symbolic logic was usually a delight because it was so exact, so unemotional and pure, but today she couldn't concentrate. It was hard even to sit still, with anxiety that would soon be fear rising in her again. The buzzer sounded.

Janice captured Armand at the blackboard as she did after nearly every class. She looks anemic, Lannie thought. There was a blueish tinge around her mouth and the fine skin under her eyes, and she was so thin she looked as though she might levitate at any minute.

In her crushed Indian smock and jeans she looked a sophisticated fourteen. Still, Lannie thought, one day Armand will look at her and he will feel like making love to that tiny, pale-skinned body, he will touch his fingers to the hollows that appear on the inside of each hipbone when she lies on her back. He will put his nose to her skin to find out what her smell is and the tips of his fingers will explore her from the soles of her feet to the delicate skin of her scalp. He will know all there is to know about her. He will eat her alive, if she lets him, and then he will digest her and find another woman. Always another woman to test and study till he knows everything about her, till she has no secrets left.

The rest of the class filed out in pairs or singly, silent and bored, holding their books at their sides, passing between Lannie and the pair at the blackboard. Lannie picked up her backpack from the floor under the desk and pushed her notebook and text into it. She dropped her poncho over her head and started toward the door.

Behind her Armand said to Janice, "Uhh, excuse me." Then, "Lannie." She stopped and turned toward him. He was wearing a sagging, blue turtleneck sweater with a hole in one elbow. Lannie thought suddenly, why, he picked that outfit deliberately. He wants to look scholarly and shabby, but rugged. She could imagine him pulling on the sweater and then standing in front of the mirror frowning slightly, and then running his fingers roughly through his hair to make it stand up more. She hadn't realized that about him before and for a second she saw him vulnerable. Does everyone do that, she wondered? Choose a persona and then just act the part? Perhaps that was what she had been doing wrong, trying to find herself. Perhaps this was the way to get through life. Immediately she thought of Iris and Barney, both of whom, she was sure, were simply themselves. Armand came toward her and she watched him curiously.

"You be at the pub tonight?" he asked. Lannie shrugged, not speaking. He looked irritated, half-turning to glance at Janice, who pretended to be studying proofs on the board.

"Depends how I feel," Lannie said.

"Are you sick?" he asked. He had a disconcerting way of abruptly emerging from his absent-minded professor role to come exactly to the point. He annoyed Lannie sometimes because she couldn't make him leave her alone, as she could other people, by being silent and vague and apparently uninterested in them.

"No," she said. "I just might not feel like going out." She wondered if she was pale.

"Okay," Armand said, shrugging as if whether she came or not didn't matter to him. "But if you feel like it, I'll be there. I'd like to see you," he added softly so Janice wouldn't hear. Lannie looked back at him for a second. There is something about the whiteness of my body, she thought, its length and slenderness that appeals to him right now. Ahh, she thought, my body, my silence, remind him of logic. He sees some kind of purity and that's what he wants right now. For a moment she wanted to laugh. Then, without speaking, she hoisted her backpack over one shoulder and walked out of the room. Behind her, she could hear Armand walking back to Janice. She would check the calendar before she decided whether to go out or not.

There was still snow on the ground but the sun was warm and before long there would be puddles on the walks that criss-crossed the campus. She walked slowly, enjoying the sun's pale spring rays and looking about at the grey stone buildings grouped around the still snow-covered oval, called 'the bowl' by generations of students, where the grass was beginning to show. She had taken an art appreciation class in her first year and the professor had laughed at the imitation gothic architecture of the buildings; some of the earliest even had gargoyles. But Lannie didn't care what the prof said, she liked these old buildings, she liked their weight, their solemnity and permanence and the beauty of the stone of which they were built. She shifted her backpack and turned toward the library.

It was one of the new buildings, constructed of the same warm beige, pink and grey stone, but it was a modern building with walls of smoked glass and patches of rough grey cement, and she didn't like it as much as the old ones.

She had a paper to write, on satire, for her English class. Tim sat beside her in English and he had asked her to have coffee with him to talk over the assignment, but Lannie had refused. She never discussed assignments with anyone. Learning should be a hard effort done alone, in one's own head. There could be no collaborators.

She climbed the library steps. Armand was so different from Tim. He had thick, curly, black hair on his chest and he was exactly the same height as she was. Naked, he liked to stand face to face with her and look into her eyes.

"Why do you try to make yourself disappear?" he had asked. It was his prying, his need to be clever again. He was sitting on the end of her bed, watching her as she unzipped her cords and dropped them to the floor. She walked to the mirror and picked up her hairbrush.

"What do you mean?" she asked, as though she didn't care if he answered or not. She began to brush her hair vigorously until she could feel it crackle with electricity.

"You could be beautiful," he said. "But nobody would ever know. It's as though looking good makes you feel too conspicuous, so you don't wear makeup and you pick clothes that make you fade into the background, and you walk around with a look on your face that tells people to leave you alone." Lannie threw down the brush. If he knew her that well would he soon lose interest? Would he try to change her? She walked across to the bed and lay down on one side. Armand laughed. He had a nice laugh, masculine, sexy. "The maiden to the sacrifice," he said, bending over her.

Lannie watched the red light above the elevator click in a downward arc toward her. The elevator doors rolled open and she stepped inside. The library was crowded at this time of day but she found an empty carrel on the third floor in the English literature section. She hung up her poncho and got out her notebook. As she opened it to a fresh page and took the cap off her pen a feeling of calm began to settle through her. It was always like this. She felt most completely herself when she was working alone in the library, seated among strangers she could ignore and who would ignore her, the silence broken now and then by the squeak of someone's rubber-soled shoes on the tile floor, or the occasional thump of a book falling open or being closed.

She would stare at the page or the blank wall of the carrel until she stopped seeing what her eyes were focused on, until she found that uninhabited space inside her head and gradually she would fill it with clear, clean thoughts. She would plumb her own depths until the things she didn't know she knew crept into that room and formed themselves into words and sentences. Then she would write them down, and when she needed examples, dates, names, she had only to rise and walk along, the shelves of books to find the answers. The stillness of the library slowly filled her. She felt rich, satisfied and calm.

At five she put her notebook and pen into her backpack, slipped on her poncho and walked home. She made herself a cheese sandwich and turned on the television. Barney had insisted on buying her a television set. She used it to watch the news and sometimes, when she couldn't sleep, a late movie. Otherwise she never turned it on, as if by not using it she could deny the gift.

When the news was over, she read a chapter in her history text, underlining in pencil as she read. The next time she went over the chapter, she would make notes on the points she had underlined. It was not only because Barney and Iris were paying for her education that she felt obligated to do well, it was also because the only time she felt adequate was when she was studying.

Lannie washed her hair, blew it dry, and changed her clothes. It was nine o'clock. She felt well, not a hint of weakness, and she tried to dismiss the fear. She locked her apartment and walked the two blocks through the warm twilight to the campus pub.

It was in the basement of one of the original stone buildings. As soon as Lannie pushed open the worn oak door on the main floor she could smell the warm, yeasty smell of beer and hear a faint babble of voices and the thump of music. The sounds grew louder as she walked down the muddy, paper-littered marble stairs. The centre of each step was worn down so you had to tread carefully. Someone had just entered the pub from the bathrooms in the hall and the louvered half-doors were still swinging. She slipped between them and hesitated inside, waiting for her eyes to adjust to the dim, smoky air.

The campus radio station was playing rock and roll over the loudspeaker, but she could hear only snatches of the song over the laughter and voices, while its rhythm thudded against the walls and floor. It was a big, low-ceilinged room where the different-sized round tables were crowded in between poster-covered pillars. The one nearest her said "Music Recital, Adm" and the rest was obscured by a crookedly plastered-on poster of a clenched fist with "El Salvador" written beside it. Next to that was an old, yellowed sign that had once proclaimed "Sisterhood is Powerful." "Down with Engineers" was scrawled sideways down the pillar in black felt pen. Through the dim light and the smoke all the tables appeared to be full.

She looked over to the far right corner where the people she usually sat with would be. There they were—Armand with his back to her; Janice, holding an untouched mug of beer—Lannie was sure she ordered beer to show by contrast with the mug how small her hands were; Don, with his long blonde ponytail and moustache—out of place in Animal Science and spending his time with Arts students; Paulette's shiny brown head—a psychology major who liked to listen to people and always seemed to ask the right question or make the most tactful remark; and Ian and George—bearded and wild-haired and wearing wrinkled khaki shirts. They were both 'political' and couldn't talk about anything else.

She squeezed her way between the crowded tables toward them. There was an empty chair beside Armand and when he turned from his conversation with Janice and saw her, he smiled and patted the red leather seat. Lannie sat down between Armand and Ian. Somebody slid a mug of beer toward her. She slipped off her poncho and hung it on the back of her chair, bumping Armand by mistake with her elbow. After a moment she threw a couple of dollars onto the pile of dollar bills in the centre of the table and took a sip of her beer.

Armand slipped one arm around her waist and squeezed her. Then he took it away and went on talking to Janice. His glasses were smudged and she could tell by the way his head dipped now and then, listening to Janice, that he was drunk. She tried to concentrate on the voices at the table, so that she could slide into the mood, but so many voices were confusing, and Armand had his back to her and Ian was talking to a girl who had come from another table and crouched down on his other side. A guy from the table behind theirs stood up, pushed his chair back, and lurched against Lannie as he squeezed out.

"Sorry, babe," he said, grabbing the back of her chair to right himself. She was beginning to wish she had stayed home. The girl beside Ian got up and left, walking in the wake of the man who had bumped Lannie. Ian turned to her, his brown-black eyes snapping, his beard covering the entire bottom half of his face to his ears and down his throat, thinning till it met the thick black curls in the opening of his shirt.

"Those fucking bastards in Ottawa wouldn't know a principle if they fell over it," he said. Lannie didn't say anything. "No fucking guts at all," he said. "How many million blacks in South Africa?" He tried to pin her with his small, glittering eyes. "And how many fucking whites, eh?" Lannie moved and put her elbows on the table.

"How many?" she asked.

"What?" he said, putting his ear closer to her face. His beard tickled her nose. She pulled back, rubbing it. "Jesus fucking Christ," he said. He looked as if he was trying to poke a hole in the tabletop with his index finger as he lectured her. She allowed his face to blur. Behind him, around the frizz of hair and past the fringes of his beard, a collage of faces flashed in and out of her field of vision—headbands, hats, smooth sweeps of long hair, curls, laughing faces, open mouths, shoulders twisting, people standing, sitting down, walking by. Armand put his hand on her thigh and rubbed it. Then he took his hand away and went on talking to Janice. Across the table, Paulette was listening to George with a sympathetic smile on her face, nodding now and then. George had turned sideways in his chair, facing Paulette, and was leaning toward her. His jaw moved up and down. He looked as if he might start crying at any moment.

Lannie's body began to feel as though it were shrinking. The opal ring Iris had given her for her grade twelve graduation had slipped to her knuckle. She was shivering. Armand whispered something to her, but she couldn't hear him or she couldn't concentrate to make sense of the sounds he was making.

"What?" she asked, turning to him. Ian had stood up and walked away. Someone else was sitting in his place. Armand looked at her forehead. She realized she was sweating. Quickly she reached up and wiped her forehead. She had forgotten to check the calendar, not that it was much help, but still, she should have looked.

"You sick?" he asked, staring at her, his head bobbing drunkenly, his eyes not quite focusing. "I can take you home." He looked as if he would have trouble finding his own way home.

"No," Lannie said, wiping her palms on her cords. She was trying to think how to get away without any of them noticing. She could pretend to go to the bathroom and then just not come back. "I'm working on a paper," she said, abandoning the idea without trying it. She never knew how much time she had and she was getting frantic to get away before it struck. "I should go home." Armand leaned toward her.

"I thought we could spend some time together tonight," he whispered, trying to rub his nose against her cheek. She pulled back.

"No." She could feel the sweat on her face now and on the back of her neck. She had her poncho over her arm and she was pushing her chair back. She was afraid to even try to speak. He mustn't find out what was wrong with her, Armand who had to know everything. She knew how he would look at her, what would go through his mind. Quickly she stood up and without touching him, throwing a 'see you' from a parched throat, she began pushing her way out between the tables. She dodged between the louvred doors and started up the marble steps urgently, as if someone might pursue her. Realizing that this was absurd, and she had begun to sweat again from the effort, she slowed down. There was a couple standing, talking at the top of the stairs; when she reached the top, the man held the door open so she could go through. She turned sideways past him and was outside, in the sharp, clean night air. First it refreshed her, she stood for a moment breathing deeply, and then she began shivering. She fumbled with her poncho and finally finding the opening, draped it over herself. Its woolly folds were comforting.

Behind her, down below in the noisy bar, Armand would be leaning toward someone, studying her, his eyes roaming over her face and her hair, he would seem to be listening to her with his whole body, and his hand would raise itself of its own accord and touch her on the forearm, the cheek . . . Lannie knew it all. She'd watched him do it, let him do it to her. Sometimes she wondered why she let him, why she brought him home, when she didn't love him, didn't even like him. She understood him and knew she was completely safe from him. And sometimes she craved the warmth of another body, the comfort of male arms around her, the illusion of protection that came with having a man near her, concentrating on her. But even then the hollow feeling didn't stop.

Once when she was little, lying in her pretty bed, she knew

clearly what her body, her soul craved, knew why she ached in the hollow of her bones, the roots of her teeth, even the hair of her head, but now, years later, grown up, still afraid and lonely, she could hardly tell why she hurt.

Ah, the weakness had come. Miserably, she hunched under her poncho, shivering, a clamminess pulling her into herself. She walked more slowly, concentrating on moving forward. She couldn't bear to be found unconscious on the street again, and so it was imperative that she concentrate, that she will herself forward through the unnatural exhaustion that was taking over. Another block to go.

She stumbled up the curb of the last block, making a misstep sideways, suddenly dizzy. More steps, more steps, the grass appearing at the edges of the sidewalk through the snow. Her apartment sidewalk, the nausea rising, her teeth clenched, through the glass door into the foyer, holding on, holding on, she would not throw up in the lobby. Her key out, the door open, and the stairs, one step at a time, sweating, gasping, weak and ill.

The first cramp hit, a quick one, sharp but short. She bent over, gasping. When it slackened, she climbed two more stairs. Her hair was plastered to her neck and forehead, under her poncho her blouse was stuck down her backbone and against her chest. Another pain, this one longer, harder. She moaned, leaning against the wall of the stairwell, then pushed her legs up another step. When she reached the top of the stairs she leaned against the door, her head pressed against the wood. Wiping the sweat from her eyes with one hand, she tried to insert the key with shaking fingers. She wanted to scream. It was rising in her throat, but she gritted her teeth and it rose and folded over on itself and became only a grunt.

She stumbled inside. Oh, oh, oh, she repeated, but it was only her head. Pacing, dropping her poncho on the floor and stumbling over it, trying weakly to kick it away, unbuttoning her blouse with trembling fingers, trying to take it off. Suddenly she could not contain the rising bile. She staggered to the bathroom, fell to her knees and vomited into the toilet. The pain, the pain was worse and worse and worse. From her knees to her chest it gripped and squeezed and wrung her, and when she felt herself losing consciousness it weakened, then like a practical joker it grasped her again and jerked through her. When it paused, she looked at her watch. Midnight, another hour, two hours. She dragged herself to her feet and dropped a facecloth under the cold water tap. When it was soaked, she put it against her face, the icy water welcome, dripping down her bra and midriff, she could almost breathe again, but another cramp hit her and she dropped the cloth and fell over, hitting her shoulder against the toilet bowl.

When this spasm lost interest in her, she pulled herself to her knees, bent forward, dropped her forehead into the soothing cool nap of the rug and then she stood up, hugging her belly, her knees almost refusing to support her. She could feel tears running down her cheeks and although this always happened, it still surprised her because she didn't think she was crying.

The first time this happened, she tried to hide it from Iris. She could remember being in her room one night. The pains in her stomach got worse and worse, till she was crying with them. Why hadn't she called Iris? For a second Lannie sank back into that moment, into her fourteen- year-old self, felt her horror at vomiting on the beautiful rose-coloured rug, trying frantically to clean it so Aunt Iris wouldn't notice, the sweat and tears blinding her, on her knees on the floor by her bed, falling forward into the pool of vomit, it sticking to the side of her face when the cramp seized her, rising, gasping, the pain actually lifting her, she could feel her eyes opening with it, and then it loosened and she fell against the bed and instantly pulled away, the vomit in her hair smearing on the pink spread, trying to clean the spread, too, still on her knees, between cramps, sometimes stuffing the sheet in her mouth to stifle her moans so Iris wouldn't hear them.

But Iris had heard something and opened the door into Lannie's darkened room, the light from the hall falling in a rectangle over the pool of vomit, catching the vomit hanging from Lannie's hair as she sat on her heels, one arm up, clutching the pink bedspread for support. The other arm was posed above the vomit, holding the wet towel she was trying to clean with, tears, sweat, vomit on her face, her body . . . At that moment Lannie had wanted to die, simply to die, and it seemed to her that having once been overcome, steeped in that desire, she could never again fully shake it.

Then there were the doctors—the local one, puzzled and kind, then the specialist in Calgary and the examinations that went on and on and sometimes hurt and always shamed and humiliated her. The doctor's frown, the stare that made her shrink inside, want to crawl under his desk, hide behind the examining table, anything to get away from his accusing look.

"I can find nothing pathological, Mrs. Christie," he said, and Lannie felt her heart withering inside her. "You say her mother died when she was ten? Her father deserted her?" Then Lannie understood. This pain was hers to bear. It must be what happened to girls like her who were castoffs, who had no value. Lannie couldn't stand to think about the doctors.

Dropped to her knees again with pain, Lannie felt herself retreating into that dark cave where there was only sensation and she was alone. There she longed for her father, as if she would not suffer when he returned to her. Her pain, her pain, and here confusion would assail her and the two pains, the menstrual and the other, would mix and she could not tell the one from the other.

Iris soon learned that it was best to leave her alone during an attack, unless she screamed. It was an unspoken contract between them. The scream Lannie couldn't help meant that she couldn't stand the pain anymore, and Iris could call the doctor. The doctor would come and give her a shot that would knock her out, if she hadn't blacked out first.

Now that she was mercifully on her own, she told no one about her affliction. Sometimes she stayed locked in her apartment for three days before it came—pacing, reading, and watching television. She had no close girlfriends, it was safer that way, and men, men expected women to be mysterious, they expected not to understand them. Armand tried, but never understood anything; Tim knew more, which was why she had to be so careful with him and why she wished she could make him go away.

Lannie pulled herself around the room from table to chair to bookcase, one arm pressed against her abdomen, past the couch, the television, back to the table. She would never have a baby if this was what it felt like. Never. But then she thought, at least then you would have something for your pain. At least then there would be some point to it.

She had come to a stop in a corner of the room, her feet braced, pushing her backbone into the v, her shoulders curving together with the pressure of the wall on each side. Her hair was soaked, thick and heavy against her neck, her wrists crossed and pressed against her abdomen. Someone was whimpering and she knew it was herself. Slowly her knees gave out and she slipped down the wall to the floor.

In her bedroom on the second floor of the farmhouse, Lannie lay awake, staring into the darkness that was beginning to soften now with the first hint of dawn. A slight wind had come up and the light threw a web-like pattern across the wall, the branches swaying, touching like bony fingers rubbing against each other. Lannie watched drowsily, goosebumps rising on her bare arms in the chill from the wind. She had the sensation that the bed was floating like a great ship through space, lifting and dipping, the sky retreating from around them, the stars flickering coldly a millenia away. On and on and on they floated in the ringing silence and darkness of infinite space.

Barney had wakened when the wind came up. He lay beside his sleeping wife, thinking, the branches by Lannie's window will be rubbing against the house, I have to remember to climb up there and saw them off so they won't always waken her. But I mustn't think about her, he reminded himself, and turned to Iris, listening to her soft, rhythmic breathing. Iris, running his life in her sweet, persistent way. He smiled to himself in the dark. He was not sorry he had married her. He lay and listened to the sighing of the wind, heard his moist black fields whispering to him, smelled the earth's unmistakable tang as it drifted in through the open window, then he was cantering on a pretty sorrel filly with a mane and tail the colour of copper wire, feeling the warm sunshine on his back.

Chapter Four

LANNIE CAME SLOWLY DOWN the stairs and paused in the doorway of the big, yellow kitchen. A shaft of sunlight lay across the kitchen table making the cups and plates, the table, the floor look fragile and new. Iris was bathed in sunlight as she sat at the table wearing her yellow velour robe. She looked like a Renoir, Lannie thought, 'Woman at Table.' Her large diamond ring threw a rainbow across the ceiling and opposite wall and the sun even seemed to be in the bluegrass music, coming from the radio, that filled the room. Iris looked up.

"Hi," she said, and blushed. Lannie, noticing, thought, it must be the light. Iris closed the magazine by her coffee cup, smoothing the cover with her hand and riffling the closed pages. Lannie had forgotten how pretty Iris could be. Tender innocence sometimes shone from her face.

"Morning," Lannie said. Iris riffled the pages again.

"I'm slow getting started today. Barney went to town for some cultivator shovels. Spring work's starting." She watched Lannie pour herself a cup of coffee from the pot on the stove, then sit down at the table across from her. How transparent her skin looks in the light, Iris thought.

Iris stood up so quickly that her chair rocked. She caught it with her hand, not looking at Lannie. What's the matter with her,

Lannie wondered. Could she and Barney have had an argument? Were they talking about me? She looked up quickly at Iris, but Iris was looking out the window.

"Toast?" Iris asked. She was frowning.

"No thanks," Lannie said. Iris hesitated as though she couldn't decide whether to sit down again or go to the counter and make toast anyway. She patted her hair absently with one hand and sat down again.

"I . . . forgot to tell you last night. Angela's been asking about you. I saw her at the co-op last week and she wants you to phone her as soon as you get home." Lannie shifted her gaze from Iris to the wall across from her. Now what's she thinking, Iris wondered. "She's pregnant again," she said out loud. Lannie's face changed almost imperceptibly, taking on a brooding, hurt, puzzled look.

"Oh," Lannie said.

"I always liked Angela," Iris remarked. Now, she said to herself, now. "Lannie?" she asked. Lannie looked at her. "You remember Jake Springer?"

"Yes."

"Well, his wife died a couple of months ago, I think I wrote you, and I've been cleaning his house for him." She stopped, searching Lannie's face anxiously. Lannie cleared her throat.

"He should hire somebody," Lannie said.

"Oh, no," Iris said quickly. Then she could feel herself blushing. I should never have started this, she thought. "I mean, it's just that, he needs more than somebody to empty the ashtrays right now. He's very lonely. He's so sad . . ." Lannie laughed. It had a bitter ring to it.

"You've got the world's softest heart." Iris couldn't tell if this was praise or blame. For a second she wanted to defend herself, but then thought, careful, careful.

"But the thing is," she went on, "I go in once a week and give the place a good cleaning and today's the day I usually go." Lannie seemed hardly to be listening, she had that look on her face again as if she were listening to an inner voice. She pushed her chair back and walked to the counter where she put a piece of bread in the toaster.

"Oh?" She leaned against the counter, her hands in the pockets of her corduroys, looking down at her moccasins.

"I hate to leave you on your first day back," Iris said. "I won't go if you'd like me to stay." She waited for Lannie to say something. Lannie lifted her head.

"It doesn't matter," she said, sounding surprised.

"I feel guilty," Iris said, her heart speeding up with hope.

"I'd feel terrible if I thought I was keeping you from something," Lannie said. Iris thought with some sadness that this was true. Lannie couldn't stand people doing things for her.

"Okay, dear," she said. "I'll go in after lunch."

When Lannie had finished her toast and gone back upstairs to her room, Iris waited till she heard Lannie's door shut, then went to the phone and dialled James's number. When he answered, she said, "I'll be in just after one."

"Good," he said. When she put the phone down she looked at the clock and then went upstairs, changed to slacks and a blouse and began to do the housework. She worked from room to room, methodically, without hurrying, following a pattern she had worked out years before: make the beds, gather the dirty clothes, vacuum. While she worked she thought about James.

She had dropped in one evening when Barney was curling in a bonspiel. For several days he had hardly been home and when he did come in, late at night, smelling of whiskey, he dropped asleep at once, barely mumbling hello to her. She had been restless, but didn't feel like visiting friends, and didn't want to go to the curling rink to watch Barney. Then she thought of visiting James. She had begun to call him James when he told her that was his real name. It suited him so much better than Jake. He accepted it from her at once.

"Take your coat off," he said, as she came into the living room. She had been feeling excited in a way she didn't recognize. She slipped off her coat and draped it over a chair. She had put on a white georgette blouse with long full sleeves and a frill around the neck, and a slim, dark, wool skirt, and high-heeled shoes. Turning to study her reflection in her bedroom mirror, she wondered why she was dressing like this to visit him. Fluffing the collar of the blouse, she hesitated for a second and frowned at herself, knowing full well that, like a spoiled child, she would do it simply because she wanted to. He's a man who appreciates women, she said to herself. It will cheer him up.

"You look pretty," he said, and she knew she blushed, suddenly feeling shy. She sat down across from him. Neither of them spoke. He was smoking again.

There was something about the atmosphere in his house that calmed her as soon as she stepped inside the door. There seemed to be a warmth in the air, a serenity, and she could only think that it must come from the years James and Aurora and their children had spent happily in the house, that it was a residue left from years and years of love. She smiled at the thought. Her own house, by contrast, felt empty.

James had been studying her.

"I've got something that . . ." he said. He got up from his chair and went into one of the bedrooms. After a minute he came out again carrying something in his hand. He sat down beside her on the couch and held his hand out to her. Cupped in his palm lay two carved silver earrings gleaming in the lamplight. "They were Aurora's," he said. "I gave them to her, oh, years ago." Iris looked at them, not daring to touch them. "Traded a horse for 'em." he said, laughing that wry half-laugh of his.

"Oh, they're beautiful," she said, without touching them. They looked precious cupped in his hand. How she would love to own them.

"Take them," he said. She looked at him. He stared back at her. "Go on, take them," he said. "I want you to have them. They'd look just right with that blouse." Iris touched them with her finger. They were warm from his hand. She picked one up and studied it, a silver half-moon with a small drop of silver hanging at the bottom. They made her think of Winken, Blinken and Nod. "Go on, put them on," he said.

"They're beautiful," she said, "but how can I take her earrings?"

"Because I give them to you," he said. "She hasn't got any more use for them." He looked away. She heard the catch in his voice. The room was very still. Then Iris, holding the earrings in both hands, stood up and going to the mirror that hung on the wall above the table, put them on. She turned to him.

"I knew they'd look good on you," he said. She looked back in the mirror, turning her head this way and that. He laughed. "Just like her," he said. Iris was embarrassed. Impulsively she hurried back across the room and bending over, kissed him on the cheek.

"Thank you," she said. "I'll cherish them always. I've never had anything so beautiful." There were tears in his eyes. Suddenly he grasped her by the wrists and pulled her down until she was sitting on his knee. He held onto her wrists so she couldn't get up again, bent his head over hers and kissed her, open-mouthed, gently, but with passion. With the other hand he touched her breasts and then slipped his hand inside her blouse. She pulled her head away, thinking, I didn't know he was so strong, I didn't know he wanted me. She realized that part of her was waiting for his fingers to touch her in such a way that she, feeling the quivering starting deep within her abdomen, would not be able to resist. Part of her wanted him to make love to her.

"James," she said huskily, "James, don't." He let go of her wrists and quickly, in one movement, put both arms around her and pressed his face against her shoulder. He was trembling. She waited, passively, her heart thumping. Then he let her go. She touched his head gently before she stood up and walked away to sit on a chair on the other side of the room from him. He watched her.

"Let me," he said to her. "Let me, I love you." He seemed to tremble, his voice so deep and soft she almost thought he might not have said this.

"I don't know," she said. They looked at each other across the room. The air was warm and still, the light from the lamp limpid and golden. It did not seem strange in this atmosphere that he should love her.

"Let me kiss your breasts," he said. "You're so beautiful. I love you." His longing was palpable. It fell softly on her, touching her face, her shoulders, the skin on the backs of her hands.

"Let me think, I have to think," she said. She sat primly across the room from him with her knees together and her hands on her lap.

"I love you," he said again. "Let me love you." She didn't move. "If I were a young man," he said, "you wouldn't have to think." It came out of him with a broken sound as though his chest hurt. Suddenly Iris doubled over so that her face rested on her knees. You're wrong, she thought. If you were a young man I would never even be tempted.

"You're frightened," he said in a different voice. "I can see that, you're just frightened." She lifted her head.

"No," she said clearly, "but I'm married." She could imagine the curling rink, the lights, the shouts of the men echoing down the rink, the clear, cold air. He lifted both hands and dropped them again. They looked at each other. His eyes had darkened again, the way they were when she and Barney came to see him the week of his wife's death. He turned his head away from her and she knew he was crying. His passion filled her with awe and tenderness. Before knowing what she was going to do, she had walked through the still, hazy air and sat down beside him. She took his head in both her hands as she had done once before and kissed him on the lips. She could see the confusion in his eyes. He didn't lift his hands to touch her. She spoke to him, wiping the tears that sat in the wrinkled reddish skin under his eyes, with the tips of her fingers.

"James," she whispered. "Let me think about this. Let me think about it." She brushed his hair back and for a minute left her hand cupped against the side of his face.

"Don't leave me," he said. "Promise me you'll come back."

"I'll come back," she said. "I promise." He lifted his hand and touched one of her earrings, then he leaned toward her and kissed her. She kissed him back, meaning to be kind, but suddenly the quivering began again low in her abdomen and she knew she wanted him too. Then she stood up, put on her coat and went home.

It was time to fix lunch. She had just finished cleaning the half-bath by the kitchen door and was about to go to the fridge when Lannie came into the kitchen, blinking as though she had just set her book down but not yet found her way out of it.

"I'll . . . help," she said.

"You could set the table," Iris said. "It's only soup and sand-wiches." She was chopping broccoli for the soup and slicing beef for the sandwiches. The phone rang just as Barney came in the kitchen door, whistling, and slammed it behind him. He always seemed to bring the bustling, noisy world in with him. He picked up the phone before Iris could.

"Hello." He hadn't washed yet. Iris could imagine the grease he would leave on the phone. "Hi, Ma," he was saying. "How's the old man?" Silence. Iris began buttering the bread for the sandwiches. At the table Lannie straightened the salt and pepper shakers. "Yeah," Barney said. "Oh fine, Lannie's home." Hearing her name, Lannie glanced at Barney. Iris began to lay the thin slices of beef on the bread. "How's Fay and the kids?" This time it was Iris who looked over her shoulder at Barney. Barney was moving restlessly, fingering the yellow phone cord with one hand, turning to look out the win-dow in the back door, turning back again, looking into space as he listened, his gold wedding ring, on the hand holding the phone, glinting in the sunlight. "Honest to God," he said, moving his head angrily. "She should never have married that sonofabitch." The muscles of his upper arm bulged against the cloth of his coveralls as he tightened his grip on the phone. The receiver looked small and silly in his hand. Another long silence while he listened.

Iris stirred the soup and piled the sandwiches onto a plate. Lannie was standing with her back to them looking at the table as though she might have forgotten something.

Barney hung up the phone, unzipped his coveralls and stepped out of them, leaving them on the floor by the door.

"I'm starved," he said, crossing to the stove and grabbing Iris around the waist. He nuzzled her neck and she laughed and twisted her head to kiss him. Lannie had begun reading Proust, was thinking about the child Marcel frightened in his bedroom, waiting for his mother, wondering what it would be like to be so attached to your mother and so afraid . . .

"How's Fay?" Iris asked.

"Same damn thing," Barney said. He ran both hands through his hair roughly and turned away, crossing the kitchen to the half-bath. The sound of water running noisily into the sink. Iris could imagine it splattering on the tiles and the floor she had just wiped, and forgave him immediately. He was trying his best to keep his anger down.

She thought of Fay, Barney's younger sister. The wedding in the small white church up at Knox's Coulee. Fay barely seventeen, pregnant. At least the dress had hidden it. And Barry. Barry was a handsome boy. Wild as a coyote though, everybody said. Fay looking so thrilled and innocent. Later at the dance, crying in the kitchen with some of the women, looking for Barry, who was probably out drinking in somebody's car, or worse, necking with a girl somewhere. The lace train of Fay's dress grey with dirt from dragging on the hardwood dance floor, torn in one place, the women shaking their heads at one another behind Fay's back. A sad affair. And four kids later things weren't any better.

The times Barney had tried to help Fay out. Once he had gone to look for Barry, to try to talk some sense into him, and came home with two cracked ribs and a black eye. When Iris gasped and put her hand up to his face he had brushed it down and looking through her, past her, said, "I beat the shit out of the bastard!" That was when it finally came home to Iris what Barney's smile hid. And she began to treat his silences with a little more respect, knowing that he was wrestling down the anger that dogged him as if he were still living at the ranch under his father's thumb, he and his half-brother still eyeing each other across the dinner table.

She brought the pot of soup to the table and began to serve it. Barney finished washing and sat down at the table. Lannie pulled out her chair and sat down too. She lifted her soup spoon and dipped it into the creamy liquid. Bits of parsley floated on the top and small flowerets of broccoli broke the surface.

"I'm going to change the cultivator shovels this afternoon," Barney said. "Then I'm going to start seeding. If the weather holds, I'll be out as late as I can stay awake." He looked at Lannie. "What are you up to today?"

"Nothing much," Lannie said. Barney reached for a sandwich and lifted a corner to see what it was made of.

"Roast beef and lettuce," Iris said. How many times in the seventeen years they'd been married had she seen him do that? As many times as I've made soup and sandwiches for lunch, she thought.

When they were finished eating, Lannie excused herself and went back to her room. Iris and Barney could hear her footsteps in the upstairs hall and then the door to her room close. Barney shook his head.

"What the heck does she do up there all alone for hours at a time?"

"Reads," Iris said. "Thinks. Maybe she writes letters to her friends. I don't know."

"Funny girl. That goddamn Howard," he said. "But gosh she grew up to be a good kid. No drinking. No drugs." He turned to Iris. "Didn't she?" he said to her. "Got you to thank for that." Iris smiled at him. Sometimes Barney would touch her so deeply by something he said or did that she would remember with a sudden flash of feeling how much she loved him and appreciated his goodness and his devotion to her and Lannie.

"And you," she said, touching his hand, "a young girl needs a decent man to be an example to her, and that's what you are." Barney looked away, embarrassed. Iris leaned over and kissed his forehead.

"I love you," she said. The palms of her hands were suddenly moist. How can I do this? she asked herself. Already the moment was gone. Barney was frowning now, leaning back in his chair and placing his hands on his thighs.

"Wonder how Quinn's doing these days." They could no longer hear Lannie moving around above them. The inner kitchen door was open and through the screen door they could hear a meadowlark. Barney turned in his chair and looked out thoughtfully toward the dozen steel grain bins that stood in a neat double row along the backyard. The bins blazing in the sun. No matter what he says, Iris thought, he would have liked a son. I suppose with Fay and Barry separated so much of the time he thought he could be a father to Quinn.

Twice she and Barney had gone to get him when Barry was gone and Fay, unable to manage him any longer, turned to her brother for help. While he was staying with them, Barney had stopped curling, stopped having a drink in the bar after an R.M. meeting, stopped finding reasons to run into town to the cafe for coffee. He took Quinn out to the field with him after school, played catch and watched television with him. But both times Quinn had run away, back to his mother, to his shabby home, to the fighting, to the father who came and went at will. Funny how children seem to want their own home, the place where they were raised, no matter how awful it is, she thought.

After the last time Iris went to Quinn's room to call him for breakfast and found it empty, she had said, "It's no use, Barney. Let him go back to his mother if he wants to." Seeing the look on Barney's face, she had thought, we should have had children of our own, and she thought it again now.

"Your mother didn't say how he's doing?" Iris asked. Barney snorted without looking at her. The meadowlark called again.

"No," he said. "But I can guess." He turned back to her and put both arms on the table, cradling the coffee cup in his hands.

"It's too bad Barry won't take him rodeoing with him. Maybe that would help."

"Maybe," Iris said. They sat silently, immersed in their own thoughts. Iris smiled. "Remember the old Indian Ridge rodeo?" He smiled back at her.

"Yeah, I remember." He said it as if his mind were on something else, or as though he remembered something that he knew would be different from Iris's memory.

Rodeos were an aspect of local life which her family, along with many of the farm families, viewed with indifference. But one day when she was in grade twelve, Iris was walking down Main Street toward the cafe to meet some of her girlfriends when she saw Barney across the street.

He was leaning with one shoulder and hip against the brick wall of the bar, his thumbs hooked into his belt, one leg bent at the knee, the other straight from the hip. The sunlight flashed on his belt buckle just once and she turned her head and there he was, slowly pushing himself upright with a gesture that was both controlled and casual, unaware of anyone watching him, or even of what he had just done. But the movement had unexpectedly stirred Iris in a way she didn't recognize, she had faltered and slowed and then, her vision blurring, had begun to hurry, afraid to look at him again, frightened by what was happening. That slow, rolling movement of his, the unexpected width of his shoulders, the long flat torso, the jeans hanging low and neat over narrow hips, and the quick smile at whoever he had been talking to. She could hardly breathe.

At home in her room that night she had gone over the moment again and again. She wanted to see Barney, to talk to him, to put her hand on his arm. But he wasn't in school anymore, she didn't go to the bar, he rarely came to the dances in town. Rodeos. That was where she would find him. And the Indian Ridge rodeo was this coming Sunday, or the next.

She talked her parents into going. She could easily have found a boy who would take her, or have persuaded a carload of girls to go, but she wanted to see Barney. She wanted to look for him if she had to, she wanted to talk to him, to shake that smile of his and see it falter while interest crept into his eyes. She could imagine him dropping his hands from his waist while he watched her, then taking a step so that he was beside her, lifting one arm and laying it across her shoulders . . . she shivered as she lay in her bed.

So they had gone. Her mother packed a lunch of fried chicken and fresh rolls and fruit and they drove up into the hills over stone-paved roads that gradually became narrower and rougher. Her father shook his head.

"Could never farm this land," he said over and over again, shaking his head. "Look at the rock!" The stony road became a dirt trail. The closer they came to the rodeo grounds, the thicker the traffic became, until they were part of a slow-moving line of cars and half-tons that appeared and disappeared through the cloud of fine, gray-brown dust that boiled upward with every movement of horses or vehicles over it and then hung above them like a fog.

They drove through the gate, a wire with brightly coloured pennants flying from it, strung across the top of two high fenceposts. Ahead of them in the cradle of the surrounding wooded hills, sat makeshift rodeo grounds with unpainted weathered pens and worn corrals attached to either end of the arena. In the sunshine the rows of cars and trucks parked around the arena and on clear spaces up the hillsides danced with light.

Her father edged their car through the parked vehicles and the children and groups of cowboys standing together talking, and drove up on the hillside, parking the car so it faced the arena below.

When she got out of the car, Iris stood in the fine, silky prairie grass, still green from spring rains and flattened by its own delicate weight. It was dotted with bluebells, small wild pink roses, wild sunflowers, and tiny yellow and white daisies. Three children trotted by on ponies—a bay, a pinto, and a grey. The smallest rider couldn't have been much more than four years old. She was so small that her horse paid no attention to her, no matter how hard she hauled on the reins and yelled at him, and her huge straw hat with three feathers trailing down the back was almost bigger than she was. When they were past, Iris wandered down the hillside, saying hello to people she knew, seated on the hoods of their trucks or on blankets spread on the grass. The men wore clean white western shirts with designs sprinkled on them, and held bottles of beer in their thick-fingered, brown hands; the women were busy wiping the faces of little ones or changing diapers, or rummaging in the picnic box.

She crossed the track, her white sandals already grey with a coating of dust, and came up to the arena. All the ranching people in the district were there. They were sitting in family groups—children, women, grandfathers—on the grass around the arena fence, wearing their wide-brimmed stetsons for protection from the sun that poured down over them. Children already dirty from the dust thrown up by the horses in the arena dashed past her in pairs, their shirttails hanging out, their big straw hats glued firmly to their heads. The announcer, who was standing in a booth suspended above the pens of bucking horses and bulls, was describing the action to the crowd in an accent that sounded as though he had just arrived from Texas.

She paused and looked up and down the fence at the people. For a second the sound of the loudspeaker, the murmurs from the crowd, the thud of hooves receded. It was as though she were watching from somewhere else. Who were these people? Where had they come from? She had a sense of them as an isolated pocket, a stubborn throwback that wouldn't give way to the rest of the world trying to march over them, erase them as though there had never been a West, never been horses and cowboys and cattle sprinkling the southern plains. The sun beat down on the straw stetsons, little boys dressed identically to their fathers ran by, there were horses everywhere, the cattle in the pens bawled, a bronc in the chute under the announcer reared and reared again, his hooves striking the gate, splintering the wood, his eyes rolling back, his mane flashing and then he went down. The crowd roared at the rider in the centre of the arena.

"Bobby Brock on Thunder! . . . And that's a rank little horse! Whoooaaa! . . . and Bobby, he says, that's too much for me, I'm a-leavin'!"

Iris sat down on the grass in an empty space close to the fence. She picked up a discarded program from the grass and saw that Howard Christie (he used the Christie name although his own was something else) was entered in this event. She was pretty sure Barney would be in the chute helping his brother cinch up the rigging and holding the horse while Howard got on.

She studied the men dotted along the corrals inside the arena. After a while she picked out Howard. She recognized his black hair when he lifted his hat, brushed his hair down and then re-settled the hat more securely. He stepped off the corral and slid down into the chute onto the back of the bareback horse he'd drawn. When she knew she had found Howard, she was sure the man leaning down, holding onto the horse's rigging, was Barney. The two men holding the gate shut suddenly stepped back, the gate opened and Howard was out into the arena, the horse bucking and twisting, the dust churning up around him. Iris watched Barney. She stood up, brushed the grass off her skirt and started walking toward the back of the pens. Barney and Howard would go back there after Howard's ride. She forgot to wait and see if Howard made it to the whistle or listen for his score.

Behind the pens and outside the arena gate the barrel-racing girls were clustering on the racetrack, waiting for the men to set up the barrels. Iris said hi to a girl mounted on an apaloosa, she went to school with her, and skirted the horses that were jumpy and keyed-up with waiting. She passed gingerly behind the row of horses tied to the corrals. She had never had much to do with horses and they frightened her. She tried to keep her distance, but it was hard to do with the barrel-racers milling around and people riding past and the horses tied to stock trailers and fences. She was beginning to wish she had stayed on the grass by the arena fence. Suddenly one of the horses tied to the corral next to her jerked his head back, twisted, and his reins came untied. She backed up hurriedly.

"Whoa," a voice said. She looked around, embarrassed among the ranch kids and the cowboys.

"He's okay, he won't hurt you," the voice said, its owner moving past her to the horse's head. It was Barney, and Howard was standing beside her. The shoulder of Howard's blue-flowered shirt was thick with dust. A scrape on his cheek oozed blood.

"Hi," she said lamely, and then could think of nothing else to say. Barney grinned at her over his shoulder as he led the horse back to the fence. She tried to walk away casually.

She laughed. The meadowlark called again and Barney looked up from the table.

"What?" he asked.

"I was just thinking about the time I got Mom and Dad to take me to the Indian Ridge rodeo so I could try to get you to notice me." She laughed again. The sun coming through the screen door struck the back of his head and made his hair shine blonde. Already it was beginning to bleach, as it did every summer.

"Oh?" he said, smiling. "I didn't know that."

"I guess not," Iris said. "You didn't even notice me."

"I didn't know that's why you were there," he said. "But I did notice you. You had on a white sundress. You looked out of place."

He laughed. "Well, I guess . . ." He got up from the table, went to the door and picked up the heavy green overalls he had left lying on the floor. "You gonna bring supper out to me?"

"No," Iris said firmly. "I'll bring you out lunch about four-thirty, but I'm not bringing you supper. You need a break if you're going to work most of the night. That's how accidents happen. You get too tired."

Barney sighed and bent his head to hide his smile. Iris knew he would come in for supper grumbling, but she knew too that it pleased him when she defied him for his own good. He was used to men who never spared themselves or their women and never listened to their women.

"By the way," she said. "I'm going into town this afternoon. It's my day to clean Jake Springer's house for him." Barney was pulling on his coveralls. He stopped with one leg on and his foot in the opening of the other leg.

"Oh, yeah," he said. "Shouldn't we have him out to supper again?"

"I suppose," Iris said, trying to keep her voice neutral.

"I thought he enjoyed himself the last time he came," Barney said, pulling on the other leg. "Maybe after seeding."

The one time Barney had persuaded James to come home for lunch with him—it had been just after the curling bonspiel, when Iris had gone to James's house alone—they had talked about farming, about the moisture supply, the prospects for next season's crop. Iris had laughed.

"It's the dead of winter, you two," she said. "Why can't farmers take one thing at a time?"

"Farmers do," James said. "They don't have any choice."

Later, when Barney had fallen asleep on the couch and James was leaving to go home, Iris had walked him out to his truck. He stopped with the truck door open and looked at her. Iris could tell he wanted to speak to her, but didn't dare. They looked at each other and she saw in his blue eyes the look that must have been there since he was a child, impish and piercing, intelligent. The whole of his soul was in his eyes, everything that he was. The rest of his face faded away into inconsequence. His age meant nothing. Even the waves in his white hair might as well have been the black waves of his youth. Iris felt a weakness in her knees. It began between her legs, higher up, spread like softly lapping water upward to the pit of her stomach, and downward through the tender flesh of her inner thighs to her knees. She grasped the truck door with both hands.

"When will I see you again?" he murmured.

"Tomorrow, one o'clock," was all she could say, relinquishing her last scruple. He turned back to his truck, climbed laboriously in, and drove away. She walked slowly back to the house, not noticing where she put her feet. When she opened the porch door, she began to sing, softly, in a low soprano, not quite on tune. This was not sensible. It was not reasonable.

Barney was doing up the zipper now and reaching for his cap, which hung on a peg by the door. He brushed his thick, springy hair down with one hand and flipped his cap on with the other. Iris, watching him, was once again overcome with love for him. How decent he is. How hard he tries to be like my father—loyal, responsible, undemanding. She jumped up and went over to him, pulled his head down close to hers and kissed him. He patted her on the bottom, smiled, and then went out. She loved him now as much as when they were first married.

If you love him, she asked herself, why do you do what you do with James? She sat down at the table again, and put her face in her hands. But it was true, it really was, that loving James didn't stop her from loving Barney, or the other way around. It seemed to her that she loved James out of some other part of herself. She felt she was only beginning to learn about the largeness of the human heart.

Chapter Five

FOR A MOMENT BARNEY STOOD still, smelling the spring sunshine on the land, looking out across his fields, which disappeared into the horizon on three sides. His work was cut out for him: getting the machinery ready, seeding, summerfallowing. He still had enough of his upbringing in him to feel good at the prospect of work. He had a lot of acres to cover, several weeks of long, hard days if the weather held. He'd have to see about getting some help, maybe that McCormack kid.

He crossed the yard to the shop and pushed back the heavy steel door. The air inside was damp and chilly, and the screech of the door echoed in the cavernous interior. Two pigeons flew out, cooing frantically. Three of his tractors sat across the back of the shop, arranged in order of size from smallest to largest. He paused for a moment to admire them. He'd traded in almost every piece of machinery that had once been Iris's father's. He had done it slowly, deliberately. Jack had built the house he and Iris still lived in, but Barney had torn down the small wooden sheds and granaries and put in the steel grain bins. Maybe someday he'd be able to feel that the place was his, his alone and that he wasn't just looking after it for the Thomas family who might at any moment leap out of their graves and reclaim it.

He knew he shouldn't feel that way. Jack Thomas had been

relieved when Barney accepted his hesitant, tentatively-made offer. He'd been scared to death that Barney was going to steal his little girl from him and take her away, up into the hills, turn her into one of those impassive, wind-tanned, tough-talking women in boots and levis who came down into town every once in a while.

"I'll treat you like my own son," he said. "You live here, work with me, I'll let you buy the place bit by bit. It'll be yours and my girl's." And Barney had gone away wearing a sombre expression, saying he'd have to think about it.

Think about it! Hell! There was nothing to think about. Of course he was going to do it. His old man might never forgive him for it, but he couldn't help that. He wanted something to show for all his hard work. He wanted a little money in his pocket and the chance to sit at home during a blizzard instead of putting on his sheepskin and saddling his horse to go searching for cattle.

But he figured he better not be too eager. So he went about his business for a week or so, solemn, steady, while all the time inside him a buoyancy was growing and a huge sense of relief, of reprieve. It had been a good time. Iris, warm, innocently seductive, his. And the future looking white and hopeful for the first time in his life.

"I've had a crush on you since I was fourteen," she had said, the first time he asked her to go out. The sort of thing only a girl like Iris, who had always got whatever she wanted, could say. He didn't tell her, oh, I saw you, but I knew I couldn't have you, you were too good for the likes of me, although that was the truth of it. He'd laughed instead, as if he thought she was teasing him, although he could see by her eyes that she wasn't. God, he'd been proud to walk around town with her beside him. But inside he was thinking how he wouldn't mind farming her father's big place, working hard for a few weeks in the spring and fall, taking it easy all winter and getting paid well for his trouble. And Iris so goddamn pretty and loving.

He went to the workbench and got out his acetylene welder, his cutting tools and impact wrench. He had pulled the cultivator into the yard, using his biggest tractor, and now he set to work changing the cultivator shovels.

Funny Iris had never changed her mind about him. He'd invited her to come up to the place sometime and she mentioned that day. He said they'd be de-horning that day, assuming she knew all about de-horning and wouldn't want to come, so he didn't bother to tell her not to. He and Luke and Howard—it was Howard's last year on the place—were going to de-horn forty head of Luke's steers before they chased them out for the summer.

It was a bitter day, the wind howling, the sky dark, threatening rain or snow. When he saw her car drive into the yard and stop at the corrals, he climbed over and went straight to her, told her to go up to the house and help his mother get the meal ready.

"That's what I came for," she said. "To help your mother. With Fay in school it's only right that I help her." Even then she was always worrying about what was right. He was relieved that she hadn't wanted to stay down at the corrals.

He hated de-horning. If they were his cattle he would never do it, he kept saying to himself, never mind that they complained at the stockyards and docked you at the sale ring. Luke never minded hurting his cattle if he thought it was necessary. He'd do caesareans in the spring snow, branding, de-horning, none of that bothered him. But Barney had always found it hard. The first de-horning he could remember from childhood he escaped by hiding behind the barn. Now that he was a man, he did what he had to, and hid his feelings.

They did a few more steers and then he said he was going up to the house to get some water for the men. He found Iris drinking coffee with his mother at the shaky old oak table in the kitchen. Pots and kettles were steaming on the stove, pies sat on the counter and the air was warm and heavy with the smell of roasting beef.

Iris jumped up and hugged him. He had been embarrassed by her open displays of affection at first, but he was over that. He saw admiration in her eyes—for him—tall in his riding boots, black leather chaps with the fringes down the sides that he wore to protect his pants from the blood, his old torn riding jacket and his oldest, battered felt hat. Sure she'd fallen in love with the cowboy, but it was the man he had learned to be, by modelling himself after her father, that had kept her.

"Barney," she said suddenly, drawing back. "What's that on your jacket?"

"Blood," he said, surprised. She was looking up at him with a puzzled, shocked look and he said quickly, "Don't come down to the corrals today, eh? It's too cold. There aren't any women down there." Behind Iris, his mother watched them, her eyes alert, her face expressionless. But Iris had put on her red jacket and tied her blue and red scarf over her head and come out to the corrals anyway.

Barney was chasing the cattle up the chute and into the squeeze. He chased the steer forward using the cattle prod if he had to, quickly dropping the gate behind it, while at the head, one of the neighbours slammed the headgate around its neck. Wesley wanted that job but he wasn't fast enough and Luke would never let him. So Wesley usually wound up chasing one steer at a time forward from the pen behind Barney into the chute where Barney took over. If the animal that was trapped in the squeeze backed up instead of lunging forward when the headgate was opened, Barney would get splattered with the blood that shot from the two fresh red holes on the crown of the animal's head.

As soon as the steer was held by the neck in the headgate, Luke caught the nose pliers in the steer's nostrils. Then he pulled on the rope that went through the handle of the pliers. He leaned back, dug his heels in and pulled with all his strength till he had immobilized the steer's head against the side of the squeeze.

Then Howard took over. He was the biggest and claimed to be the strongest of the three. The de-horners were shaped like giant pliers but had razor-sharp cutting edges and even though they were a couple of feet long and heavy, he handled them as easily as Iris handled her manicure scissors. As soon as Luke had the animal's head still, Howard fastened the de-horners around the horn, down deep, taking a little hair and flesh too. He jammed the handles together, taking the horn off in one easy motion, part slice and part gouge, while the steer bellowed and roared and then a new note, a high-pitched squeal of pure anguish, pierced the heart of anybody listening. The steer staggered, its eyes rolled back in its head, but before it could recover, someone else, one of the neighbours, set a heated branding iron where the horn had been, where blood now shot in a ten-foot fountain from each side of its head. Smoke rose from the branding iron, the smell of burning flesh and fresh blood hung in the air. The animal, still mad with pain, in shock, his roaring blending with the roar of the propane fire, used to heat the branding iron, was let go into the next corral, where he ran shaking his head, staggering, bellowing.

That was what Iris had seen. He didn't know how long she'd been sitting on the corral across from him before he noticed her. There was an expression of such horror on her face that he knew she'd seen enough to get the full impact of what they were doing. He slammed the gate on the steer he was chasing in and hopped over the alley fence to her as fast as he could get there.

She was staring at the men's feet, where the ranch dogs were nosing among the bloody stubs of the horns, fighting over them. He climbed up beside her, deliberately blocking her view with his arm and shoulder.

"You'd better go up to the house," he said. "It's too cold for you here."

It was hard work up at the head. Luke and the Merrill brothers had taken off their jackets to work in their shirt sleeves. When the men came into the house for dinner, Iris's face had actually paled at the sight of Luke's shirt. For a moment Barney thought she was going to be sick. Luke's shirt was plastered to his chest and right arm, dyed a deep scarlet, soaked, sagging with blood. When he saw Iris's face,

Luke, smiling strangely, stepped back into the porch and took it off. His wife hurried to the bedroom and came back with a clean shirt. Nobody said a word. Barney was watching Iris to see if he had lost her. She was hurrying from the stove to the table, serving the big bowls of food, her face flushed—it might have been from the heat in the kitchen—but he thought she was refusing to look at him.

All through the meal the wind moaned around the old house, mingled with the wailing of the stunned, wounded cattle in the corrals. He began to see that he couldn't spend the rest of his life doing these things, day in and day out, in the cold and heat and the wind, working day after day with his close-mouthed, powerful, headstrong father.

Afterwards, Iris, crying, had said to him it wasn't the *look* of it, Barney. It wasn't the *look* of the blood, it was the *smell*. I couldn't stand the smell. It was true, they all came in smelling of blood. It sprayed up on their faces, covered their hands, dropped onto their boots. And suddenly he felt as revolted by it as she did.

It was after that Jack Thomas made his offer. Iris had had a hand in it, of course. And for the choice he made, his own father would never forgive him.

Barney straightened up, the last shovel in place, the afternoon almost gone. He looked across the fields again, gazing till the long, flat expanse met by endless sky calmed him. Then he climbed into the tractor, started it, and drove it out of the way so he could bring his drills out, fill the seed boxes and start seeding.

In the house, Iris had quickly stowed the dishes in the dishwasher and wiped the table. She knew there were crumbs on the floor, but they could wait till she got back. She hurried up the stairs to the bedroom, humming to herself. Which one? The light blue sweater and matching skirt? The slacks? No, not the slacks. Ahh, her new green shirtwaist with the dozen tiny buttons down the front. The fitted bodice showed off her small waist and nicely shaped breasts and she would tie her mauve paisley scarf at the neck. She dressed quickly, her movements economical, a lightness suffusing her body.

"I'm going now, Lannie," she called before she started down the stairs. Lannie opened the bathroom door.

"Okay," she said. Iris started downstairs. "Pretty dress," Lannie added, but Iris was almost at the bottom of the stairs and didn't hear her.

She backed her small car out of the garage, drove around the gravelled circle in front of the house, out of the yard and down the grid road.

Iris had lived on the farm all her life. It never occurred to her that she might live anywhere else. She had been away only the one year she went to college. A couple of years after she and Barney married, her father retired and he and her mother moved to town and she and Barney moved into the big house. After her father died, her mother lived alone in town until her health became so bad that she had to be moved to a nursing home in Swift Current. Usually Iris went once a week to see her. She thought guiltily that she had been neglecting her since this business with James began. Not that her mother would notice. She would sometimes wake from one of her dozes and say, "You here again? It Sunday already?" Other times she didn't recognize Iris.

Iris steered around the ruts. The graders would probably be out tomorrow. The land lay before her, stretching out toward the sky. She could see the elevators of all the villages ten miles or more away in each direction. It always made her feel like she was flying. To the north, across the valley where the town lay, there was still snow in the coulees on the high ground people called 'the bench.' Beside her in the ditches, as she bumped along, there was a hint of green underneath the taller yellow grass, which still stood from the year before. Gophers perching on the roadside, ears erect, paws held chest high, suddenly froze, dropped, and skittered across the road in front of her.

She turned onto the blacktop and began the last hilly stretch before the descent into town. The land here, too hilly to be farmed, was used for grazing. On her right, Forrester's Angus cattle, just turned out for the summer, stood like black wildflowers against the yellow hillside, their calves bounding up and down the grass around them. Watching the calves play, she couldn't help but wish that Barney would keep a few cattle. But he hadn't looked back since leaving the ranch. He was a farmer now.

As she descended toward the town, a hawk floated above the stony hillsides, wings outspread, lifting on an updraft, tilting, planing, circling serenely between the small white clouds and the steep coulee bottoms. Iris had lived all her life in this scene. She no longer even thought of it as home. It just was. It had entered her body and her heart. Part of her was soaring with the hawk above the landscape— the rock warming in the sun, the clear water that trickled through the gravel on the coulee bottom.

Iris thought of a dream she had before she was married. Her cousin Caroline had just had a baby, a pretty little girl—Thomas babies were always pretty—and sometimes Iris looked after the child. In the dream, the baby lay sleeping in her carriage, wrapped in blankets. Huge old trees surrounded the plot of grass where the carriage stood. An air of pulsing benevolence flowed from them. In the everyday world there was no green as vivid as the green of their leaves, the green of the grass which lay thick and luxurious beneath the trees and the carriage. The sky was intensely blue and fathomless, the air clear and pure, and yet textured. Everything was alive— grass, trees, sky, child—except the concrete sidewalk that lay dead and ugly beside the grass. Then Iris saw the meaning. The trees, the sky, the baby, were all one, parts of the same whole, equal in value. She hadn't been afraid, had felt only the benevolence, love.

Was it a vision? Yes, she thought, it must have been. What it meant she didn't know. She understood the message all right. She could hardly miss that. But what good was it to her? How should she apply it to her life? She didn't know.

When it was gone and the bone-deep knowledge fading, as though someone had given her a much-coveted gift and then taken it away, when it was gone, she had only questions left and the hope that another vision might come and tell her more. And now she was forty-two years old, think of that, forty-two years, almost half a century and she still didn't know what it meant. Sometimes when she was very upset it came back to her, when her two cousins were killed in a car accident on Christmas Day, for instance. And now she loved James and he loved her. And it was wrong, and yet, possibly, it wasn't wrong. She didn't know.

She drove through town to a side street by the river, where James lived. The house was dilapidated now, although it had once been a handsome place, set in one corner of a grassy lot. It was a single storey, rambling, old-fashioned house, much too big for James now that he was alone, but it would never enter his head to buy a smaller house, or one more convenient to the store and post office. It had been white with blue trim, but it needed paint now. A verandah, its sloping, shingled roof held up by turned, white-painted pillars, ran across the front and down one side. Aurora had had a big vegetable garden on the side that was now overgrown with two-foot-high weeds. High, wild groves of lilac bushes served as fences down both sides of the yard. Soon they would be blooming again, filling the yard and house with their scent.

Iris parked, got out of her car and walked down the cracked cement sidewalk to the front door with its set-in oval window. She knocked lightly and without waiting for an answer, turned the worn brass doorknob and went in. He was waiting by the door.

"You're here," he said. She could imagine his waiting in the dim, whispering interior. He put his arms around her and kissed her on the mouth. She kissed him back, leaning against him. "You're late," he said, kissing her forehead, her cheeks, the top of her head, her neck.

"I came as fast as I could," she answered. "Let's sit down." It tired James to stand for any length of time.

"Is the girl back?" he asked, his fingers brushing down the side of her face.

"Yes," Iris said. "She's home. I'll bring her to see you."

"I'd like that," he said. "I knew her father. Wasn't good for much."

"No," Iris said, still indignant after all the years that had passed. "I wonder if he's still alive."

"Let's not talk," James said. He reached behind her and snapped the lock on the front door.

"But my car's out front," Iris said.

"It doesn't matter," he said, guiding her toward the bedroom. "Nobody comes to visit anymore. Especially not in the afternoon." She could feel his trembling through the hand that rested between her shoulder blades. He had a way of touching her that was so light that she hardly felt it and yet was so expressive that through it, she understood his love, his passion. How could she not love him?

In the bedroom he sat down on the bed and looked up at her as she faced him, undoing the tiny buttons down the front of her dress. She could read the eagerness in his eyes, the fear. She bent over and kissed his forehead. He caught her by the upper arms and held her, kissing her face.

"I'm always afraid you'll get over this," he said. "I'm always afraid you'll see what you're doing and you won't come anymore." He released her. She continued calmly unbuttoning her dress. "I'm an old man," he said.

"This is no time to be sad," she replied gaily. She had taken off her bra and was stepping out of her panties.

He made love to her on the big double bed that had been his and his wife's. She did not feel guilty about this. He was so gentle, so tender with her. She hadn't known that a man could show such tenderness. But with James she also discovered what passion was. He had only to touch her and that painful, delicious ache would start between her legs and nothing would satisfy her but James and his gentle mouth and hands. She had never known anything like this. She would never be able to stop. She did not want to stop.

Afterwards, she dressed carefully, engrossed in the details of the buttons, the straightening of her pantyhose, the brushing down of her skirt, the exact fall of the scarf, while James watched her from the bed, his eyes soft with love. Then she put on fresh makeup and combed her hair in front of Aurora's mirror, above the silver-backed brush and comb Aurora's children had given her.

When she was satisfied, she turned to him, and, without speaking, he rose from the bed and sat down on the leather-bottomed chair beside it. She had been coming to see him for five months now, and they had developed a ritual of which this was a part. She began to make the bed. When she was close to him, he reached out and touched her as if to make sure that she was really there and that he could touch her if he chose to. It was at this point, while she smoothed the sheets and fluffed the pillows, that often she cried— for the perfidy of her behaviour and her helplessness to stop—her tears making dark leaves on the flowered cotton.

Today was no different than all the other times. She didn't know if James could tell that she was crying. She supposed he knew, because so often he knew what she was feeling before she was sure of it herself. It was as though his age had worn away the outer surfaces, leaving his emotions closer to the air and allowing him to feel at once what younger people could not. She supposed he said nothing because he was afraid that if he talked to her about their affair, she would have to think about it and then she would not come anymore. And anyway, once she was dressed and neat again and the bed was made, it was almost as though it never happened. Then she stopped crying and her usual cheerful self returned.

When the bedroom was tidy, she said, "Now for the kitchen," and turned toward it like a general leading the troops into battle. James followed her slowly into the kitchen. He could no longer move quickly.

She put a pot of coffee on to perk, while he sat in his easy chair in the corner. He lit a cigarette and leaned back, watching her, the smoke drifting slowly upward. She could feel his contentment at having her here in his kitchen. She filled the sink with hot water and began to wash the dishes. Over her shoulder she said, "I'm going to clean the windows today, and while I'm at it I'm going to shine up Aurora's picture. The frame is all tarnished."

"She gave me that picture before we were married," James said. "I always liked it. She was just like that."

"She was beautiful," Iris said. She wrung out the dishcloth and wiped the front of the cupboards. Then she turned to the fridge to wipe the door. She glanced at James and saw that he was sitting forward in his chair, with one hand shading his eyes, as if the light were too bright. He cried so easily, like a child. It was at moments like this, coming so soon after his age had not mattered, that she saw most clearly how very old he was.

She wiped her hands on the towel and put her hand on his shoulder. He lifted his face to look at her. In that position the loose skin of his face fell back and she saw the shape of his bones, the skeleton he would soon be, when his already spare flesh would melt away. He gripped her by both wrists.

"Oh, I loved that woman," he said.

"I know, I know," Iris whispered.

"And I love you, too," he said and pulled her toward him so that his face was against her breasts and his crying was muffled. After a moment he drew back. "Don't ever leave me," he said. "You're all I have left. If you leave me, I'll die." Iris's eyes began to fill with tears. How sorry she felt for him, for the emptiness of his life, his children gone, his wife dead.

"I'll never leave you," she said. Each time she said this to him she meant it, although when she was not with him, she despaired of being able to keep her promise. And yet it seemed to her that what he asked of her was not much and was easy to give. It hurt no one.

She decided at the start that she would never leave Barney. How could she when she loved him? She tried to be fair to both men. But deception was new to her and she found it uncomfortable and demeaning. How she wished she could go to Barney and tell him the whole thing and assure him that everything between them was unchanged, that her affair with James wouldn't last because he was old, and that it would not hurt Barney. But of course that was impossible. Besides, there was the startling, consuming desire she felt for James, which was wholly different from her feeling for Barney. She looked into James's face again. He was staring into space, one arm around her waist as she stood beside him, his head resting against her arm.

"What are you thinking about?" she asked him.

"About you," he said. "I wish you could stay." He didn't look at her. His voice had the same quality as when he first told her he loved her, as though he were struggling to speak through some immense pain.

"No, I can't stay," she said, moving back to the sink. "I can never stay. Be happy with what you have, James." She felt like crying again because she couldn't be everything to both James and Barney and she knew it was easy for her to say such a thing to James with Barney waiting for her at home. She had someone to sleep with at night, to eat breakfast with, to go places with. She didn't even know what loneliness was.

"When will I see you again?" he asked at the door as she was about to leave.

"Next week," she said. "Maybe sooner if things work out."

"Come as soon as you can," James said.

Lannie was strolling up the long avenue of pines toward the house, her hands in the pockets of her corduroys, her head forward and down, as Iris turned in at the farm. She did not look up until Iris's car was beside her and when she did, the look on her face was that of someone who has been disturbed from a dream: bewildered, pained. Iris stopped.

"Want a ride?" Lannie shook her head. Iris put the car in gear and drove slowly into the garage and got out. She waited till Lannie caught up with her.

"Hi, Barney been in?"

"No," Lannie said after a pause, as if she had to dredge up the word, having forgotten about speech. There was a husky note to her voice, and, after speaking, she pulled her hands out of her pockets, lifted her shoulders and shook her head, her face raised.

Iris's smile faded as she saw how pale Lannie looked.

"Are you feeling all right?" she asked. Lannie turned her head away from Iris, appeared to be watching the crows up in the row of pines that Iris's father had planted thirty years before.

"I'm fine," Lannie said. When she turned back to Iris, she seemed to be finally pulling herself out of her dream world.

"I guess I'd better get his lunch ready then," Iris said and went inside.

Lannie watched her, thinking how vivacious she was, how her eyes sparkled and her hair gleamed. It seemed to her that Iris looked prettier now than ever before. Some notion flitted through her head—the dress, the sparkle. She frowned, trying to catch it and then let it go.

Her period was due any day now. When she thought of it, sweat broke out between her breasts and on the back of her neck. Now that she was back on the farm, she remembered the impossibility of keeping it from Iris. When it got bad, just before she passed out, she always whimpered, could hear herself whimpering, the sound coming from somewhere else in the room, another person, not herself. She couldn't stop the whimpering any more than she could stop the pain. Anxiety drove her outside to pace, the wet palms of her hands thrust deep into her pockets. Sometimes if she allowed herself to think about it, she despaired of living out a life punctuated by this kind of suffering. Sometimes she thought she would be better off dead.

Chapter Six

IT WAS EARLY AFTERNOON. Lannie lay on her back on her bed, her legs spread loosely, one arm by her side, the palm turned up, the other arm bent, the wrist against her forehead. She had been lying this way for some time, staring at the light fixture without blinking. When it blurred, she shifted her eyes to the edge of the patch of sunlight that spread itself up one wall and spilled onto the ceiling.

Her period was five days late. That was two days longer than it had ever been off since Iris had taught her to count the days. She was trying to think about this, but her mind refused to hold onto the slippery thought; each time she tried to grasp it, it slithered away.

"I may be pregnant," she said out loud. The sound hardly made a ripple in the stillness of the room. She listened for its echo in her head. No, she said. Stop listening. Think. Pregnant. What does that mean?

Again she examined the patch of sunlight on the ceiling, the perimeter setting it off distinctly from the darker ceiling. But now, as she watched, she began to see the irregularities on the ceiling's surface, how actually there was no line, the exact boundary between light and dark was blurred and uncertain.

She jerked her thoughts back. Pregnant. What did it mean? Pregnant. Angela, her stomach bulging out in front of her so that her back swayed to support the burden. The spots of unnaturally high colour in each cheek. Iris would cry. What would Barney do? No, she said again. What does it mean to be pregnant?

She took her wrist down from her forehead and placed her palm flat on her abdomen, the fingers spread out. Suppose there is a child growing in there. Suppose. She could feel the warmth from her hand spreading across the surface of her stomach. She could not imagine the fetus as a living child, only as a small glowing red light buried inside the deeper reds and purples of her body.

Her mind wandered again and she turned her head so that the branches of the tall poplar outside the window were now in her view. She thought of Misty and a picture of Misty as a baby sleeping against someone's shoulder, probably their mother's, suddenly appeared before her. Her eyes so tightly shut that the sleep had a life of its own, her round flushed baby cheeks, the tiny, precisely shaped pink mouth, the little nose so small and delicate, bluish around the nostrils, her fine blonde hair pressed in damp curls against her neck and temples. The picture was so clear, so unexpected, that Lannie felt an inaudible thud in her chest, a pause when all her senses hesitated and the air turned crystalline and sharp.

She flung herself over onto her face.

"Oh, my God," she whispered. She began to cry, clutching the bedspread in each fist, her body contorting with her sobs. Misty, she had taken Misty for walks, pushing her carriage proudly up and down the sidewalk and sometimes her mother would set Misty in her arms and let her hold her, for just a minute. On cold mornings when Misty was older, Lannie had often wakened to find her sister snuggled beside her in her bed. But one day they took Misty away; she had been helpless to stop them, helpless to save Misty or her brother, or herself. There could not be a baby. There could not.

Finally her tears stopped. She sat up on the side of the bed, reached for a kleenex, blew her nose and wiped her eyes. It was always best to know the worst, she thought. It didn't matter how hard the knowledge might be. But for now all she could do was wait, examine her alternatives carefully and calmly so that, should the worst be true, she would be ready.

She stood at the window. Iris, wearing a floppy brown Panama hat and yellow slacks, was crouching down below in her garden. Lannie could hear her singing off-key in her light soft voice as she moved up and down the rows with her seed packets.

She had to do something. She would go to see Angela. There was always the hope that she might see something at Angela's that would help her know what to do if . . . Until she knew, (how long would that be?), she had to find ways to pass the days, or she would go crazy with the waiting and the thinking.

Iris would let her use her car, if it wasn't her day to clean for Jake Springer. Iris wouldn't miss that. She seemed to enjoy going there so much you'd almost think that something else drew her there or that . . . or that she doesn't really go there at all. Maybe she has a lover in town. Lannie laughed out loud at the absurdity of the idea. She remembered the green dress with the row of tiny buttons down the bodice, and then frowning, dropped the curtain and turned away from the window. She was glad she didn't have a curved, lush body like Iris's.

She felt better now that she had something definite in mind to do. She went downstairs and out to the garden. Iris heard her coming and stood up, smiling.

"Isn't it a wonderful day?" she said, lifting her head and examining the sky.

"Yes," Lannie said. She looked down at the carefully tamped rows Iris had planted. "Can I help?" Even to her own ears her voice sounded dubious.

"Not unless you want to," Iris said. "I love planting. I love the way the ground smells in the spring. I like the seeds. See?" She held a cluster of round pink-brown seeds cupped in her palm for Lannie to see. "Radishes," she said. "Can you imagine? Each one of these will grow into a round red radish that's white as snow inside and that will crunch when you bite into it. It's a miracle." She laughed and lifted her other hand in the too-large cotton glove, particles of earth clinging to it, to push back her hair with her wrist. "I sound like an idiot," she said, laughing.

Lannie scuffed the earth with the toe of her moccasin. It seemed to her that some thoughts were better left unsaid.

"Can I borrow your car?" she asked. "I'd like to visit Angela."

"Well, of course," Iris said, too eagerly. Lannie dropped her eyes. She felt the familiar downward plummeting: Iris's expectations that she couldn't meet, Iris's hopes for her. "The keys are in it." Iris said.

"Thanks," Lannie mumbled. Iris was stooping again, dropping the seeds one by one into the damp black earth. Now and then she picked up a lump of soil and crushed it slowly between her fingers. She began to sing again, almost tunelessly, her internal melody sifting outward, the words lost. Lannie, about to turn the corner of the house, watched her. The lift her decision had given her was dissipating in the face of Iris's contentment. How simple Iris's life was, how clean and uncomplicated, how good.

Iris was still in the garden when Lannie drove out of the yard. I must be practical, Lannie told herself. She straightened her back and gripped the steering wheel more firmly.

When she reached the long hill above the town, confusion took hold of her. The town lay below her, jumbled, greying, the roofs and streets speckled with a coat of spring green from the budding trees. On her left was the end of town where she had been born. The house was still there. A two-storey house, once yellow, with warped and torn screens on the verandah across the front and a door that still hung crookedly. If inadvertently she passed the house, she could sometimes feel the muscles in her shoulder jerk covertly with the memory of pulling and lifting that sagging door to open it. The grass was never cut anymore and in the winter there was always a path tramped over the snowbanks to the door. In such a small community she could not avoid knowing who lived there now, even if the toys and bicycles had not told her of the eight-child family. This was the poor part of town, where she rarely had reason to visit anymore. She looked away quickly.

At the end of the road she was now descending was the centre of town. The hardware store, the cafe, the drugstore, the grocery—narrow-fronted, neatly painted wooden buildings with moulded tin ceilings on the inside. Out back along by the alleys were the sagging stairs, an unpainted row of unidentifiable buildings, old tires lying in the tall grass or mud and clusters of rusted burning barrels leaning against each other. She hated the buildings for their ugliness. She didn't care about their history.

The few streets with new houses were off to the right. The new houses were mostly three-bedroom bungalows painted white or yellow with neat flowerbeds under the windows and gardens at the back. The bank manager and teachers and business people lived here. For the most part the real wealth of the community was out on the farms, not in town. Above the river and behind the town, the hills sat serenely, like a painted backdrop in a western movie.

She turned at the co-op toward the river and the old section. Angela and her husband had bought one of these small older houses because it was all they could afford and because it had a large treed and fenced yard.

"For the kids," Angela had told Lannie. Angela was not even pregnant at the time. Lannie stopped in front of a house that was freshly painted a dark green and trimmed with a shiny mint colour. It sat far back from the street and was surrounded by tall old poplars inside the white picket fence. The branches formed a canopy above the house and the massive grey trunks leaned protectively toward the little bungalow. The yard was littered with branches that were always crashing down in the wind. There was a gravelled driveway to one side of the lot ending at a sagging wooden shed, also painted green, that was no longer useable as a garage. Lannie pulled into the driveway, parked and climbed out.

The front door opened and Angela came out to stand on the sloping cement step. Lannie saw her blonde hair pulled back in a ponytail and her round belly in its blue and white checked cotton shift. A small blonde head peered around from behind Angela's legs and stared at Lannie as she came toward them. Lannie suddenly felt dizzy. For a second her vision blurred and then cleared. Angela was waving.

"Lannie," she called, and started heavily down the step and across the damp yellow lawn toward her. "Oh, it's good to see you!" She hugged Lannie. The little girl beside her peered up at Lannie suspiciously, the fingers of one hand in her mouth, the other clinging to her mother's skirt. "Emma, take your fingers out of your mouth," Angela said to her, bending to pick her up. "Say hello to your Aunt Lannie," she coaxed.

"Hi, Angela," Lannie said, as though Emma were not there. Realizing this, she said, "She's grown." She looked at Emma. The child stared back at her.

"You haven't seen her since she was six months old," Angela said. They were walking toward the house. "You never come to visit."

"I mean to come," Lannie said.

"Oh, I know how it is. When you get home, there's relatives, and Iris and Barney don't see much of you either, so they kind of hog you." She laughed, holding the door open for Lannie to enter in front of her. It was dark inside and smelled faintly of washday. Lannie was reminded again of her home. "Anyway, I'm really glad you came," Angela said. She kicked a yellow plastic clothesbasket full of diapers out of the way with one foot and walked into the living room. Lannie sat down on the couch.

"I'll just put Emma to bed," Angela said. "Time for your nap, honey." She had picked up the child and set her astride one hip. Emma had a bruise on one knee and another on her shin. There was a scab on the side of her nose. Angela left the room and Lannie could hear her in the kitchen and then further back in the house a door shut, Emma wailed twice and then was silent, and the fridge door opened and shut.

Lannie looked around the small room. It was furnished with a worn brown chesterfield and chair, probably hand-me-downs, an old-fashioned light wood coffee table with outward-slanting legs, several red and yellow plastic stacking chairs and a rocking chair. In the middle of the floor a small brown rug with unfinished edges was littered with toys. She is satisfied with so little, Lannie thought. She wondered why she had come. This was what she tried to avoid, too much intimacy, nothing to say, their worlds too far apart. And Angela always seeing through her.

Angela came back in, carrying a plastic tray with two glasses of lemonade and a plate of cookies on it. She pushed a plastic horse on wheels out of her way with one foot and set the tray on the table in front of them. Then, sighing, she sat down beside Lannie and picked up one of the glasses.

"Whew!" she said. "I'm getting so heavy that I get tired just dragging myself around from one place to another." Lannie smiled, for some reason she was embarrassed, she picked up her glass, casting around for something to say.

"How's Orland?" she asked finally. Angela closed her eyes as though resting for a moment, or praying.

"He's okay," Angela said. "He's a foreman now. He'd like to have his own company." She looked around the living room and toward the kitchen, as though the house explained his ambitions.

"What does he think about the new baby?" Lannie asked, curious suddenly, remembering Orland in school, big, muscled, poor in his classes, often in trouble for smoking or skipping school, looking over the heads of the other kids as if he didn't notice them or knew he didn't belong in school with them. Angela looked surprised.

"He wasn't surprised," she said. "I mean, we said we were going to have four kids, and this is only number two." She gestured toward her stomach. She is a true mother, Lannie thought.

She remembered Angela standing beside her during recess and all noon hour the day she came back to school after her mother's death, while the other kids walked around her, left her out of their games, made too much room for her in the lines, as if losing your mother was a disease they might catch.

Angela had held her hand, its warmth was comforting, she could still feel it. She had let Angela lead her around the school grounds, Angela not talking to her, just holding her hand when she was so alone and frightened.

"What about you?" Angela asked. "How are you making out?" Lannie blinked and fiddled with her glass, chasing the dripping moisture back up its side with her thumbs. I have found out that there is no end of things to know? No end of troubles? That life is ugly? That people can't be trusted?

"I may be pregnant," she said, and set her glass down. She hunched forward, looking down at the tray with the dish of cookies on it, and listened to what she had just said. I may be pregnant. I may be pregnant. She felt dizzy again. Angela sighed.

"I guess you're too attractive to stay a virgin," she said finally. Lannie laughed, a strangled sound, and put the tips of her fingers against her eyes. "How late are you?" Angela asked.

"Five days," Lannie said. She placed her hands on her thighs and leaned back again.

"That's nothing," Angela said. Lannie shrugged.

"For me it is." She could feel Angela watching her, could feel Angela's sympathy flowing toward her. She stiffened as though to deflect it. Angela set her glass down.

"What will you do if . . .?" she asked, carefully, waiting. Lannie shrugged again, leaning forward and pushing the little red napkin around. "You should get married," Angela said. Her voice was all matter-of-fact as if they were discussing new shingles for the house. "I like it," she said. "It feels good to have your own house, your own family." Lannie didn't answer. "The father , , " Angela began.

"It could be more than one person's," Lannie said.

"I doubt that," Angela said. She laughed.

"I mean . . ." Lannie began.

"I know what you mean, I'm surprised at you, Lannie. You were always so, so . . . I mean, when we were kids you never had much to do with boys. I always thought you didn't care about them, or none of them were good enough for you, or something."

"I'm surprised, too," Lannie said, thinking about the first time with Tim. Just that once, she had wanted, hoped, to be loved by a man. A flash of memory, her father leaning over her, passed by her eyes and she stood quickly and walked to the window. She wiped her eyes with the back of her hand and stared at the lilac bushes under the window. "They should be flowering soon," she said.

"If he's a decent guy, marry him," Angela said, as though the matter were settled. Lannie turned abruptly.

"Angela, promise me you won't tell Iris. I should never have told you. Maybe I'm not even pregnant, maybe it's just a false alarm." Angela had disarmed her again, and she felt both annoyance and relief. Her breath coming quickly, feeling her eyes widen, she looked at Angela.

"Of course I won't tell anybody." She made as though to get up but finding this too difficult, sat back instead. "Don't you want to get married?" Lannie didn't answer. "From the time I was a little kid that's all I ever wanted. A husband and babies of my own." Angela sighed again and looked down at her stomach.

"You're barely twenty," Lannie said.

"So?" There was no rancour in Angela's voice. "What do you think life is for? What do you think is a good thing to do with it? Do you think an anchorwoman on TV or some movie star or that lady prime minister are better people than I am? Do you think they're doing something better?"

"I don't know," Lannie said finally. She sat down in the rocking chair in the corner of the living room. She pulled a rag doll out from under her, setting it absently on her lap, beginning to rock slowly, the doll hanging loosely across her knees. She couldn't imagine being married to Tim. Tim was only a boy. She needed a man, someone like her father. And what if the baby had curly black hair? She shuddered and covered her face with her hands.

"Oh, Christ, Lannie," Angela said. "It's only a baby. It isn't cancer." In the silence that followed, Lannie could hear Angela breathing as though she had to struggle against the child she was carrying for each breath. "Anyway," she added, "it's probably a false alarm."

Lannie took her hands down from her face. "Tell me about your boyfriend," Angela asked, as though Lannie had not explained that there was more than one man. She was sitting on an angle in the corner of the couch, her dress smoothed over her belly, her hands clasped protectively over it. Lannie forced herself to look away.

"He's tall," Lannie said. She could see his uncombed blonde curls, the soft, child-like curve of his cheek, she could feel the touch of his hand on her back, his breath on her face. "I can't," she said. She stood and picked up a cookie, then sat back down in the rocking chair. She sat looking at the cookie, then took a bite. She forced herself to swallow.

When she got up to leave, Angela said, "Now don't you disappear again. I want to know what's happening. I know you. You'll just swallow it all by yourself. Now you listen to me. You can depend on me, Lannie." Tears were threatening Lannie again and she put her head down so that her hair swung forward and hid her face.

"All right," she said. Her hand was on the doorknob, her back to Angela. She could smell the faint odour of detergent and damp clothes again. Suddenly she turned. "Thanks," she said, "for not having a fit."

"Iris wouldn't have a fit either," Angela said. From somewhere near the back of the house Emma began to whimper, then to wail.

"A baby's well worth the trouble," Angela said. "This is not such a bad life." Lannie nodded without speaking and opened the door, blinking at the sudden light.

As she walked across the grass, her shoes getting wet in the melting frost, she was thinking, she doesn't see that I'm not like her. She doesn't see that I don't have the love to give that she has.

A baby seemed repulsive to her, fat and damp, smelly, clinging to her, demanding things from her she didn't have to give. She climbed into Iris's car and drove away.

When she reached the drugstore, she parked and got out of the car. She was just about at the door when the woman who had met the deaf children at the bus came out and stood back, holding the door open. One by one the six deaf children came out onto the street. The first one, a sturdy little six or seven-year-old boy with a runny nose and a big blue bruise on one cheek, stopped just through the door. The child coming behind him, his thick glasses sitting crookedly on his face, reached out and tugged hard on the shoulder of the first boy who turned, while the second one began to sign, making a high wailing noise at the same time. The woman reached down and touched the second child's shoulder. The boy looked up at her. She made rapid movements with her hands and the two boys moved away from the door. The remaining four children, each holding a candy bar, followed. They all seemed to be bruised or cut somewhere. Why, that's how they communicate, Lannie thought, by thump and shove, because they can't convey their thoughts rapidly enough by signing.

The first boy wandered past, his candy bar in his mouth, his eyes moving idly over her face. She wanted to slap him, the way the chocolate was smeared on his mouth. Her tears were coming again. She turned her head forcefully, it was as though other hands had done it, to pull her eyes from his. She pushed past the children into the pharmacy and stopped in front of the shelves of shampoo bottles, not seeing them, her heart thumping in her ears.

A few minutes later, when she came out, cradling a bag of shampoo and toothpaste in her arm, they were gone.

Lannie wasn't really looking at the countryside on the way home, but she couldn't ignore, just as she turned into the farmyard, a twenty-foot patch of bright yellow buffalo beans along the curve of the ditch. As she turned down the row of pines, a flock of red-winged blackbirds scattered upward out of them, the scarlet patches on their wings flashing in the sun.

Lannie parked the car in the garage and went into the house. As she passed the kitchen, she noticed Iris sitting at the table, leaning forward, her forehead resting in one hand, her bent elbow resting on an open magazine. Lannie could hear the shaky intake of her breath, followed by the quick, damp expulsion. Iris was crying. Lannie didn't think she had ever seen Iris cry. For a second she was so shocked she was paralyzed, but then, collecting herself, she hurried up the stairs, placing her feet heavily on the treads so Iris would hear her and know she wasn't alone. When she was near the top, Iris called, "Is that you, Lannie?" Her voice sounded husky, but the intonation was normal.

"Yes," Lannie called back. "Thanks for the car."

In her room she sat down on the side of her bed, feeling weak in the knees. Something was wrong. Iris crying? What could have happened? She's had a fight with Barney, but no, Iris and Barney never fought seriously. Maybe she was crying over a story in her magazine, but no, Lannie thought, not like that.

So, Iris cries, she thought. Everybody cries it seems. Is there no life without tears? If anyone had a life with nothing to cry about, surely it was Iris. Maybe her life is empty, maybe she has moments when she wonders why she's alive. Lannie stared at the Renoir print on the opposite wall, at the sun-dazzled woman melting into her surroundings.

"I don't know what life is for," she said out loud. "I don't know."

Five more days passed. Lannie counted them over and over again. Ten days. Each morning when she woke she lay still on her back, and tried to feel something. She listened to her body for sighings or whisperings from another presence, she searched her breasts for tenderness and waited breathlessly for the first twinge of nausea.

On the tenth morning she thought she felt a kind of stuffiness deep in the pit of her stomach, not queasiness or nausea, not the usual menstrual heaviness, just a feeling of something being there, as though a hollow had been filled. There was a presence. She sat up and threw her legs over the side of the bed. She would find a doctor today. She stood up and put on her dressing gown. Her fingers trembled on the fastenings. Her mind raced.

The doctor in Chinook was out of the question. Everyone in town would know in the space of an hour that she had been in for a pregnancy test. In Swift Current the chances of running into someone she knew were too high. She would cross the border and go to the nearest town of any size in Montana. She might see someone she knew there, but it wouldn't be in a doctor's office (you had to pay cash to American doctors), and since people often went to Milk River for a day's holiday, she wouldn't have to explain why she was there. She would borrow Iris's car again.

She didn't realize she knew anything about pregnancy and childbirth, but during this waiting, bits and pieces of information she didn't know she knew surfaced. Scraps of conversation overheard as a child, whisperings among the girls at school and at college and from her endless reading. So she knew she had to bring a urine specimen.

She bathed carefully, nervously, and then dressed in a pale blue linen skirt, a white cotton blouse, and sandals. She carefully placed the jar of urine in her small macrame bag. When she went into the kitchen, Iris looked up from a cookbook and smiled at her.

"Can I borrow your car for the day?" she asked, before Iris could even say good morning. "I want to spend the day . . . driving around . . . looking at things." She realized too late that she hadn't thought to invent a suitable lie. Her reason sounded lame even to her. "You know," she added, twisting the cords of the purse in her hands. Iris hesitated almost imperceptibly.

"Of course, dear," she said. "It has a full tank." Lannie thought, it's probably her day to clean for Jake. She must be going in more than once a week.

"Oh," she said. "Do you need it?" She hated to relinquish it even if Iris did need it. Now that she had made up her mind she couldn't stand waiting any longer.

"I'll use the half-ton," Iris said. "Barney's off getting some repairs on the four-wheel drive so he won't need it. Or I could take the Chrysler too."

"You're sure," Lannie said, edging toward the door.

"Positive," Iris said. "Will you be home for supper?"

"Oh, probably," Lannie answered. It was a parody of casualness, though she tried to make her answer seem natural. "I just had an urge to drive off into the country somewhere and . . . look at things," she finished vaguely, lifting one hand to fuss with the ends of her long hair.

Iris watched her leave, saw her speed around the driveway, spraying gravel into the trees. She frowned and dropped the curtain. What was bothering her? Lannie had stood in the kitchen with two high spots of colour in her cheeks, her eyes glittering, holding her handbag against her stomach nervously with tense, white hands. Lannie always behaved a little unnaturally, but not in this way. Still, Iris thought, it was the first time she had looked other than depressed since she had come home.

For the first time in all their years together Iris felt like forcing Lannie into talk. Things were getting worse with Lannie, not better, and unless Lannie started acting more normally soon, she would have to take some drastic step. Iris realized helplessly that she didn't know what such a step might be.

Today was the day she spent with James. Now that Lannie was gone and Barney wouldn't be back for lunch, she could go in as early as she chose. She went to the phone on the counter by the back door and dialled James's number, waited nervously for him to answer, hearing her own breathing too loudly in the little space created by her body, the cupboards and the back door.

"Hello," he said, in a neutral voice, even though aside from his children who called long distance once in a while, she was the only person who ever phoned him.

"I'll be in early today," she said, breaking into an involuntary smile at the sound of his voice.

"I'll be waiting," he replied. She held the receiver against her ear, close to her mouth, saying nothing, listening, and then she hung up.

For the first hour Lannie drove through farmland—long, bare stretches laid out in a rolling curve that met the sky miles away. Then small pastures of native grass appeared, interspersed among smaller grain fields. Gradually the balance between grazing land and farmland was reversed. Short patches of broken land were flanked now by long stretches of pale native grass. Here and there herds of cattle grazed peacefully. Now a sea of hills, the muted blue-green of early spring, lay beside her on each side of the road and ahead of her around the curves, as far as she could see. This landscape was calming, and she slowed down without even noticing.

When she came around the stretch of hills known as Old Man on His Back, where the land lay spread out far below to the west, a long rolling lake of green unbroken by rectangular swaths of plowed land, the idea struck her. She could keep going west over the plains, across the mountains, all the way to the sea, leaving all this behind.

Then she rebuked herself, told herself that this trip was merely a formality, something that had to be done, something that the logic of things required of her. She knew she was pregnant. She could not be certain who the father was. She had slept with both Armand and Tim in one week (she would not think about the bars), she had failed to take the pill, she did not know when.

She could see it was an act of defiance, but how else could she find release? So she had gone downtown, rushing, her feet clacking on the bridge, angling across the park in the dusk, slowing in the downtown streets, till she reached the bars and the nightclubs. She picked up men who moved slowly, gracefully, big men with handsome, blank faces, and no words. At such times she could not bear words.

But afterwards, she would have only a few days of respite, sometimes not even that much, there was always guilt, more guilt adding itself onto what was already there. The torment would begin again. She would feel herself sliding, sinking into the quicksand while she clawed at the bank trying to save herself. A repeated, desperate tactic, she would take her birth control pills out of her purse and drop them into the garbage under the sink. Once, determined to stop herself from what she knew was compulsive behaviour, she had walked out onto the bridge high above the green river that flowed smoothly beneath her, and leaning over the wide concrete railing, she dropped the pack of pills and watched them fall till she lost sight of them far below. They didn't even make a splash. She imagined her own body falling, falling . . . but then she turned away and went back to her apartment. But this act did not save her. The craving didn't go away. Before long, she went out and refilled her prescription. She knew that too soon, losing count or not caring, she would go to bed with Armand, or find herself succumbing to Tim, or wander into another bar.

And now she was pregnant. Armand, Tim, some stranger. When she saw the baby, she would know. But there could not be a baby. She gripped the steering wheel desperately and ground her teeth.

She remembered coming to Milk River once with Iris and Barney, and passing a medical clinic on the main street. Now as she drove down the main street of the hot, dusty town she waited for it to appear. When it did, she parked nearby, got out of the car, and locked it. She had rehearsed this so many times this morning that for a moment she almost forgot why she was doing it. Holding her bag tightly, she pushed open the glass door and went inside. She crossed the tiled floor to the building directory on the opposite wall and began to read it as though perhaps she had an errand to run to one of the offices, or was looking for a dentist. Nobody waiting for the elevators beside her, or sitting on the lobby couches behind her, paid any attention to her. She studied the names under General Practitioners. There were only four. Dr. Keith Holmes. She liked the name. It sounded like a television doctor's name, someone kind and middle-aged and fatherly. She would try him.

She moved over to the elevators and waited. Beside her a gray-haired man sat skewed in a wheelchair, his misshapen fingers fluttering over the plaid blanket that covered his knees. Lannie felt her muscles tighten as the elevator rose. She felt short of breath and had to clench her jaw to keep her teeth from chattering.

Dr. Holmes's office was directly opposite the elevators. She crossed the white tiled floor in two long steps and pushed his door open quickly, stepping into the waiting room on a surge of cool air. All around the room heads lifted to stare at her. She stopped in mid-step, her hand on the doorknob. Every chair was taken. A teenaged boy lounged sullenly against the wall, reading a comic book. Two children sat on the floor playing with plastic blocks, their small backs barely out of reach of the feet of the other patients. A nurse, who was writing rapidly at a desk behind a glass wall on the far side of the room, looked up irritably when Lannie opened the door. Lannie looked across the room at her, she could not imagine how she could get past the people, how she could speak aloud in this room full of strangers, the nurse was pursing her lips with irritation and tapping her pencil, and then, trembling, dizzy, Lannie turned around, pulled the door open again and stepped back out into the hall. The door shut with a sigh and a click.

She held her purse in both hands, chest high, and looked to the right and then to the left. She saw a red exit sign at the end of the hall. She hurried toward it, pushed open the fire door and started to run down the stairs, the quick tapping noise made by her sandals echoing in the stairwell. She wanted to run to the car, get in and drive away. She wanted to see the trail of yellow dust billowing up behind Iris's small red car.

Dropping from the fourth floor to the third, from the third to the second, slowing, Lannie realized she could not give up. She could not go home till this was done. She was calmer when she reached the main floor and when she stood in front of the directory this time, her face flushed, she had already thought to look under 'Obstetricians and Gynecologists.'

"Dr. Harold Levitt." A homely name. She was done with fantasies of kindly television doctors. She would try Harold Levitt. She took the stairs this time, two at a time to the second floor, her hands perspiring, her breath coming quickly. Outside his door she stopped and stood still for a moment with her eyes closed. Then she opened them, tucked her blouse in more securely, and opened the door.

Two women, huge in the last stages of pregnancy, sat on opposite sides of the waiting room. The walls were dark green, the furniture rattan, she could hear the murmur of a male voice coming from somewhere down the hall past the receptionist's empty desk. A long, sheer, white curtain lifted on the breeze from an open window and then floated back in pleats. A door opened and she could clearly hear the voice say, "So call him, tell him I'll be late." A slim, blonde woman in a red skirt and red and white striped blouse came out. She held a notepad and pencil in one hand.

"Mrs. Jackson," she called. One of the women heaved herself to her feet and walked with a rolling gait like a sailor's to the door the receptionist held open. The receptionist closed it, walked into the waiting room, and sat down at her desk. She smiled at Lannie, a neat, professional, curious smile.

"May I help you?" Behind them, the other woman turned a page of her magazine and sighed loudly.

"I . . . could I see the doctor?" Lannie asked. The woman lowered her eyes to check the appointment book open before her. Lannie could see a faint blackening near the roots of her hair along the part line. "He has an opening at three-thirty," she said. "Have you seen Dr. Levitt before?"

"No," Lannie said, hoping this didn't mean she would be turned away. The woman glanced down Lannie's body before looking back to the papers on her desk. The curtain again lifted and then suddenly collapsed.

"Fill this out," she said. "And we will require payment before you see the doctor, of course." She tapped a spot on the long sheet she was handing to Lannie. Lannie took the paper and sat down in one of the rattan chairs with the yellow-flowered cushions.

Address: Havre, Montana, she wrote. It was a town a few miles down the road. Next-of-kin: She wrote her father's name. When she was finished, she took the form back to the desk and handed it and the fee to the receptionist. Barney's money again.

"Reason for the visit?" the receptionist asked, a new note in her voice, careful not to look at Lannie. The question surprised Lannie. She had not thought there could be any other reason for her to be standing there. In her confusion she said, "I may be pregnant," in a strained, unnatural voice. The woman wrote something. She lifted her head, smiling without warmth, and said, "Three-thirty, then."

It was three o'clock. Lannie went back to her chair and sat down. There was no point in leaving and then coming back. She clasped her hands on her lap and stared straight ahead, trying to calm herself. The other woman in the room looked up from her magazine and glanced at her. Lannie realized that it must look strange to be sitting staring straight ahead, so she picked up a magazine from the table beside her and began to turn the pages. Mrs. Jackson came out of the inner office. Lannie turned the pages noisily. Her hands were cold. The receptionist called, "Mrs. Barton." The remaining woman, fat, middle-aged, tired and bored-looking, pushed herself to her feet and went into the inner office. Lannie abandoned the pretense of reading and sat very still. After a moment the receptionist said, "Come with me, please." Lannie followed her to a room beyond the one the others had entered. She opened the door and stood back so that Lannie could pass. Lannie was taller than she was. She read the name card on her lapel—"Mrs. Cathy Blanchard."

In the centre of the room was an examination table, wrapped in white paper, the stirrups on each side collapsed. Lannie's vision became very acute, suddenly there was pressure in her head, she thought she might faint. Mrs. Blanchard said, "Put that on," and pointed to a folded gown lying on a counter. "Then lie down. The doctor will be with you in a minute." She had stopped meeting Lannie's eyes, stopped looking at her. She went out.

Lannie obeyed, fumbling with the buttons of her blouse, her body sticky with sweat. When she was naked, she put on the gown and looped the ties at the back. Then she climbed onto the stretcher and lay down.

Suddenly the door opened and a short, stout, balding man of about fifty hurried in. Behind him, a nurse wearing her striped cap on the back of her head, the pins on her chest glittering, closed the door.

"Alma," the doctor said, ignoring Lannie, "where are those new gloves?" His starched lab coat crackled when he moved. The fringe of hair around his bald spot was black. His cheeks were ruddy. He would soon need a shave. He looked at Lannie with dark, piercing eyes.

"So you think you may be pregnant, young lady," he said. "That's not good, not good." He stood against the table and leaned on his fists which were planted beside Lannie, one at her shoulder, one at her hip. She knew then with a helpless dread that she should have lied about having a husband. Alma silently adjusted the light that hung above Lannie's knees and then set out a tray of gleaming instruments at Lannie's feet.

"We'll see," he said. Alma adjusted the stirrups and with chilly hands helped Lannie set her feet in them. She had begun to sweat now. It was trickling down the sides of her face and into her ears. "I can't do a thing until you're more relaxed." He stood back as he said this, seemingly eager to wash his hands of the whole business.

"Take deep breaths," Alma said pleasantly. She moved behind the doctor till she stood by Lannie's head. "Breathe slowly," she said. "In and out, in and out." Lannie obeyed, the sound of her breathing the only noise in the room.

Alma went back to stand at Lannie's knees. The doctor planted himself between her ankles and drew on the filmy plastic gloves. When his hand was inside her, Lannie began to cry. The tears ran down the sides of her face, mingling with the sweat. They trickled into her hair. Alma and the doctor seemed not to notice.

"Mmmm," he said. He withdrew his hand. "I can feel something," he said. "Did you bring a specimen?"

"My purse," Lannie whispered. Alma handed her purse to her and Lannie took out the bottle and handed it back to Alma.

"Sit up," the doctor said, looking at her disapprovingly. She could see that she was not supposed to cry. "We'll send it over to the lab," he said. "We should have the results by late tomorrow or the next day." Alma left the room, carrying the sample as casually as she might have carried a chart or a thermometer. Dr. Levitt lifted his stethoscope and came toward Lannie. "But it's just a formality. You're pregnant all right." He began to listen to her heart. She sat very still. He took her blood pressure. "We'll have to do some blood tests."

"No, Lannie said. "No, it's all right. I . . . I just wanted to know if I'm pregnant." She had stopped crying and was looking at the doctor. Suddenly he yanked the stethoscope from his neck. "I look after mothers and babies," he said. "I'll have nothing to do with abortions." His voice was sharp, clear. "I don't kill babies," he said. "Ladies come here, mothers, I help them. I've got no time for people who feel sorry for themselves." He turned his back on her and fiddled with the blood pressure set. Lannie could not imagine how she would ever escape. "I'll have nothing to do with abortions," he said again. Then abruptly, he left the room and shut the door behind him.

For a moment Lannie couldn't move. Her insides were frozen, her limbs paralyzed. Then she realized that she could leave, that she could escape and never come again, never see this doctor again.

She jumped off the table and dressed as quickly as she could with shaking hands, not bothering with the top button of her blouse or bothering to pull shut the drawstring of her purse. She hurried past the doctor's open door. He called to her, but she kept going. She slipped past the receptionist, who was saying, "Call us late tomorrow or the next day."

Afterwards she couldn't remember how she found her car or how she left the town. She could remember how the air had felt when she stepped outside, she could hear the sound of tires on gravel, she remembered stopping for a red light. And now she was driving down a gravel road several miles from town. It was only four o'clock. She would be home by six.

Her cheeks still burned with the horror of the examination, with the unaccountable words the doctor had spoken to her. I'm pregnant, she thought for the thousandth time. She stepped harder on the gas. Once she had to slow down for some cattle being herded across the road by three half-tons. She crossed the border without trouble and began driving east toward the farm through the ranch land that in the morning light had looked soft and meadow-like and now, in the longer light of late afternoon, had a surreal quality.

The wind was up and the small red car was chased down the road by dust devils. To the north a huge purple cloud hung low in the sky and fat drops of rain flattened themselves noisily against the windshield. As she drove, Lannie's mind began to slow down, her breathing became more measured.

She was going to have a baby. She had to think. No. There was nothing to think about. She could not have a baby. An abortion. He had said he would not do an abortion. But she had not asked him. Had not even dreamt of such a thing. She had only thought about being pregnant, had put all her energy into anxiety about the possibility. She had erected a wall between herself and any thoughts about what she should do. The doctor's words had caught her when she was vulnerable, unguarded. He had broken a gaping hole in the wall and she could not patch it. She was pregnant and now she would have to do something. Get married. Have an abortion. Or . . . or? For a second the view through the windshield darkened as the cloud hid the sun. Misty's face came between her and the road. No. No. She could not even think about an abortion, the knives, the scraping at her flesh, the doctors touching her in such a way.

And then a kind of silence settled over her, as though she were riding in a sound-proof vehicle, as though she were an actress in a silent movie. The long orange rays of the sun, glimmering now and then through the breaks in the heavy cloud reached out across the land, and touching the car, made it ring with light.

At last she reached the farm. She parked the car in the garage and went into the house. Barney and Iris were sitting at the table eating supper. Lannie sat down at her place.

"What's the matter?" Iris asked at once. Her fork was poised at her mouth. She lowered it carefully, without taking her eyes off Lannie. Barney looked up, glancing first at Iris, then following her eyes to Lannie.

"Where were you?" he asked. Lannie looked from her plate to Iris's dark eyes alive with concern. She looked at Barney, still chewing, his jaw moving slowly, his cheeks ruddy, the top button of his blue denim work shirt open. The two of them seemed hardly real. Their concern did not touch her, could not disturb the calm in which she moved.

"West," she said. Then, "Nothing's the matter." She looked at her plate again. "I drove fast," she remarked.

Iris sighed and glanced at Barney. He was stirring the casserole on his plate, apparently thinking.

"At least you beat the rain," he said, without looking at Lannie. They all turned to look out the window. It had grown dark in the room. Iris reached up and put on the lamp that hung above the table. Long, glittering silver trails slipped soundlessly down the window glass.

"Yes," Lannie said.

"Here." Iris pushed the casserole toward Lannie. Lannie looked at it and then looked questioningly at Iris.

"Oh," she said and gave a little start. Her voice was lighter, higher-pitched even than usual and had a false brightness. The rain hissed around the house. Lannie served herself some food.

"Not hungry?" Iris said, when Lannie made no move to touch the food on her plate.

"It's good," Barney said, watching her again.

"No," Lannie said slowly, as if she had been considering whether to eat or not. She lifted her hand and touched her hair in a meaningless gesture. "I . . . ate," she said, although she had not eaten since the day before. "Excuse me." She stood, hesitated as though she had something more to say, and then without speaking, left the room.

That damn kid, Barney thought. What the hell has she been up to? Was Howard's bad blood finally showing up in her? He'd been afraid of that for years. His mother married Howard's father when she was sixteen and pregnant and then he ran off and left her with a three-year-old boy. Eventually she had married Luke and had three more children, none of them at all like Howard. Howard's hair was black, he was tall and heavy-boned, had a violent temper and was as stubborn as a goddamn mule. Sometimes Barney thought he could see Howard's stubbornness in Lannie. Sometimes he wished she had never come to live with them, so he could forget who he was, forget about his father and Howard, the fistfight they had had, blood oozing from Howard's lip, his swollen eyes, torn shirt and the dirt all over his back. Howard had got up from the ground, turned away from Luke, who was doubled over against the corral, blood dripping from his nose onto the ground, shot that accusing look at Barney, and walked away. And never came back to the ranch. Never made it up to Luke, the man who raised him. Instead, he'd gone to town, got a job as a mechanic, married Dorothy, got her pregnant three times and after she died, left his kids for other people to raise.

"I'll be back," he'd said. Barney had looked into his eyes and seen only the wildness in them, the eagerness to be off, to be free, hardly stopping to kiss his little girl, not looking back. Then he strode out of the kitchen, leaving the kid standing by Iris, looking like she'd just been run over by a truck. I hope the bastard is dead, he thought. He moved his hand and almost knocked over his water glass.

Iris set down her fork. They looked into one another's eyes and he felt the rage easing in him. He lowered his eyes and willed himself to be calm. Leave it up to Iris, he told himself. Let Iris handle it. It's women's business.

Lannie shut her door behind her and stood waiting for the sense of peace that usually came when the latch clicked shut behind her. It did not come and she waited. Her legs began to ache. She sat down on the side of the bed. After a while her back began to ache. She stared at the white wicker chair in the opposite corner of the room. Iris had bought it for her when she was fourteen. It's very pretty, she thought, echoing the words she had said to Iris years before when she had come up to her room after school and found it sitting there, Iris standing in the doorway smiling hopefully.

She could feel the pain in her back spreading upward to one shoulder blade. Before she had willed it she found herself walking to the chair and sitting in it. She could feel the pattern of the wicker pressing into her back. The pattern seemed to detach itself from the chair until it was a sensation that floated free of her body and seemed to exist beside her. She contemplated this not unpleasant sensation.

The room grew darker. The shadows spread slowly along the floor and up the walls till everything—furniture, clothing, pictures—vanished in the blooming darkness. Presently she heard Iris and Barney coming up the stairs, passing her door, heard water running, the toilet flushing, more footsteps, Iris's murmur, Barney's answer. Then, silence.

She stood, marvelling at how light her body was. It seemed to float upward from the chair. She began to undress, dropping each piece of clothing. They fell slowly to the floor. Moonlight shone in the window and bathed her body in its glow. My body is silver, she thought with surprise. She lay down on the bed. The cold sheets burned her body. She welcomed the cold, could feel herself melting into the bed.

Chapter Seven

"IT'S NOT EASY TO LOVE TWO MEN," Iris said. "It's funny, you'd think it would be easy. I mean, I do it, I can't help it, but it seems that . . . love takes . . . concentration or something. And if I concentrate on you, then it's hard to concentrate on Barney. And when I'm with Barney, I can't be with him all the way, if I've been concentrating on you . . ." James traced his finger over each of her eyebrows. There was always a faint tremor in his hands.

"Your eyebrows are black," he murmured. "So are your eyelashes." Iris smiled and closed her eyes. Barney never noticed such things and his touch was different. "Don't talk about Barney," he said. He was running his hands over her hair and touching her face with the tips of his fingers as if he were blind. He kissed her. "Don't talk about him," he said again, and buried his face against her neck. His breathing was loud in her ear.

"But James," Iris protested, turning her head toward him so that he had to lift his. "He's my husband. I mean, we can't just pretend I'm not married."

"Why not?" he said. His voice was husky. "When you're with me, you're mine." He put his hands on her breasts. "If I could only have you all the time."

"Look at the time, James," Iris said. "I have to get dressed. I should be home in an hour."

"Not yet," he whispered. He was aroused again. Iris was always astonished by this.

"You're like a boy," she said, laughing, running her hand down his shoulder. The skin was smooth under her hand. It had a papery feel.

"It's you," he replied into the hollow of her neck. Iris put her arms around him again, feeling, as her hands passed around him, the thinness of the flesh covering his ribs. Tenderness flowed through her and she raised her body to meet his. He was so close to death. Every time she touched him she was reminded of how little flesh stood between him and the white bones of his death. His passion for her both thrilled and frightened her. She had come to accept that his nature allowed him to love totally, that he was a man of passion, and always had been. There was nothing she could do about it. And not for the first time, she worried about how this might end.

When she was making the bed, she turned to James and said, "James, how long do you think this can go on?" He lowered the hand that held a cigarette, she could see how it trembled, his lips parted, there was fear in his eyes.

"Are you leaving me?" he said finally, his voice sounding parched, like someone who has had a high fever for a long time. His eyes glistened. She dropped the sheet she was straightening and went to him, leaning over to kiss his forehead.

"No, no," she said. "Sometimes I think I could never leave you. I . . ."

"Because if you do, it will kill me," he said. There were tears running down his cheeks now. She wiped them away. He grasped her arms. "You're all I have," he said. "Don't leave me." Iris allowed herself to be pulled onto his knee. She began kissing him.

"I'm not leaving you," she whispered. "I'm not leaving you. It's just that I worry sometimes. What if Barney finds out? And even if he doesn't, it isn't right, James. You know it isn't right." She pulled back to look at him.

"No," he said heavily, dropping his arms, "it isn't right." He looked at her again. "But I don't care," he said. "I don't care if it's right or wrong. You're all I want."

Iris kissed him with renewed tenderness. The certainty was growing in her that if James's death did not end their affair, somehow or other it would have to end anyway. She couldn't bring herself to think that she would have to end it. She hoped that something, some fluke of nature would happen that she was not responsible for, that would force them apart. But then, she wondered, who would ever touch her again the way James did? Who would ever love her again as if she were the most precious woman in the universe? She kissed him quickly and stood up, turning away so that he wouldn't see that she was crying.

Barney was washing his hands in the half-bath by the back door when she came in.

"You're late," he said, over his shoulder.

"I had to stop for groceries." Iris could feel herself flushing. She set the two bags she was carrying on the table and went back out again. Barney followed her.

"Here," he said, and took the heaviest bags. She picked up the one that was left and shut the car door. "How's he getting along?" he asked.

"Who?" Iris said. "Oh, Jake." She closed the kitchen door behind them and began to put the groceries away. "Oh, he's sort of sad," she said. She turned back to the table and began to pick out the items that went in the fridge. Barney had pulled out his chair and was leaning back in it, his long legs crossed at the ankles. "There's not much I can do for him." Her hands, unpacking the cans of fruit and vegetables, slowed for a second.

"Still," Barney said, "it's better for him to have a friend, somebody he's always known, cleaning for him instead of somebody he hires. And he's used to a clean place. Aurora was a good housekeeper."

"How do you know that?" Iris asked, pausing with the fridge door open.

"My old man used to take me to their place sometimes. Jake kept his cattle on land next to ours in the summer."

"Oh," Iris said. She saw Aurora washing dishes in the sink where she now washed them while James sat in his easy chair and smoked and watched her.

"They're coming on Sunday," Barney said.

"What?" Iris asked. She turned toward him. "I was rattling the bags, I didn't hear."

"I said mom and the old man are coming for supper on Sunday." He looked at her with that uncertain look that always appeared in his eyes when his family was mentioned. Poor Barney, Iris thought.

"Don't worry," she said. "I'll take care of it. And Lannie's here."

"Yeah," he said. "I had to ask them. It's been a long time. And I thought I'd rather have them here than go there." He turned toward the table and put his elbows on it, brushing his face with his hands. "I think," he said. Iris laughed and went over to where he sat. She put her arms around him from behind and kissed the back of his neck. It was plump and full and tanned dark red. She ran her fingers through his hair, where it curled down his neck, and admired the blonde gleam.

"Are they bringing Wesley?" she asked

"What the hell else are they going to do with him?" Barney said.

"I'll have to think of something for him to do. He likes to help me," Iris said.

"Maybe I should get a load of gravel in. He could spread it on the driveway," Barney said. "That'll keep him busy most of the after-noon."

They could hear Lannie moving around upstairs. "That kid," Barney said. He turned to Iris. "I don't like the way she's been look-ing lately. Do you think she might be sick?" Iris blushed. She could feel her heart speeding up. Selfish, she thought. How could I be so selfish. I stopped even thinking about her this afternoon. And thought again, this has to stop. This can't go on.

"I don't know," she said. "I'll pay more attention," she was reassuring herself as much as Barney. "I'll try and get her to talk to me." I don't suppose it will do much good though, she thought. Lannie was coming down the stairs. They could hear her feet brushing the carpet. "Maybe it's only her period." Barney looked at his boots. "God," Iris said, banging a pot on the counter. "I wish we could get that straightened out." Lannie came into the kitchen. She looked at both of them as if they were strangers or as though she were waking from a dream. She glanced around the room.

"Did you lose a book?" Iris asked.

"What?" Lannie said. How pale she is, Iris thought. How thin. Has she lost weight since she's been home?

"A book? No," Lannie said. She sat down and then stood up again. "No, I came to help." She walked to the counter by the sink. "I'll peel the vegetables," she said. Behind them Barney said, "Talk to her, Iris." He walked out of the room and in a moment they could hear the murmur of the television set in the living room. Iris handed Lannie a paring knife.

"Barney's worried about you," she said. "He wonders if you're sick. Are you all right dear?" Iris stopped working and looked up at Lannie. "You're awfully pale."

"I'm okay," Lannie said. She began to scrape the carrots.

"You're not eating enough," Iris said. She was peeling potatoes— slicing the long pink curlicues of skin onto a paper towel. The silence in the big, bright room grew. Lannie scraped the carrots awkwardly, their orange staining her fingers. "And you don't get out enough." She turned to Lannie. "I know," she said. "Next time I go to clean for Jake, you come with me. I want you to meet him. He likes to have visitors, you know. He hasn't much left in his life." She began to run water into a pot. "That reminds me. Your grandparents are coming on Sunday."

"All right," Lannie said. She continued to scrape carrots, her knife making a whispering sound. In the front room Barney had turned the sound louder and they could almost make out what the voices were saying. Iris tried to think of another approach.

"Are you sure you're feeling all right?" she asked. "Now that Barney's finished seeding we could go to the city, find another specialist."

"No," Lannie said quickly, her knife hesitating for a second above the carrot she was scraping. Iris was silent.

"At least think about it," she said. "Lannie, we love you. We can't stand to see you hurting." She could feel tears springing to her eyes. She longed to put her arms around Lannie to comfort her, but Lannie would never allow that. Had never allowed it. "Why do you think you have to suffer alone?" she said finally, her voice high with tension. Lannie, if anything, paled more.

"I'm not suffering," she said in her clear thin voice. Iris could practically see the words formed in quicksilver in the air between them. Neither of them spoke again. Iris vowed to watch her more closely, to spend more time with her, to think of excuses to get Lannie to come with her, maybe have more people in to visit. She sighed. She would try, but she supposed that Lannie would, as usual, work out whatever was bothering her by herself and she and Barney would never even know what it was.

"I'm going to Angela's for supper tomorrow," Lannie said. Well, Iris thought, that's more like it.

"Good!" she said. "You can take my car." She was thinking, Angela is such a good influence, and she could not help feeling hope returning.

Lannie did not want to go to supper with Angela and Orland in their tiny, stuffy house. She did not want to see their marriage, or be forced to view the mother, father, family thing, or Angela's pregnancy. It was all too intimate, too suffocating. The very air in the house smelled of the things she didn't want to think about; the way it was arranged made her look at things she didn't want to see. And Angela would ask questions. The very shape of Angela's body would wring answers from Lannie she didn't want to give, and then she would have to talk about what was happening to her. But she couldn't say no to Angela, knew it was no use even to try.

She set out grimly. She might have been going to town to buy groceries or run errands or have her hair done, had she been a woman who did that sort of thing. She pulled up to Angela's house and sat for a minute before getting out of the car. Orland's truck was parked in the driveway—a battered old brown Ford, with nicks and scrapes in the paint. The box was loaded with tools and other equipment. A long, paint-stained ladder with a red flag fluttering from the end hung out over the bumper. There was a roll of barbed wire in the back among the cans of paint and nameless hunks of iron. Lannie wondered what he would be doing with barbed wire. Were they buying land?

She opened the car door and climbed out, slamming the door behind her, and started for the house just as Orland opened the front door. Lannie looked at the figure standing there in his grey worksocks that she knew would have red and white stripes around the top. His dark green workshirt had paint splattered over it and the sleeves were rolled up over his elbows, exposing his thick, muscled forearms and the black hair that grew on them. His jeans were faded and patched. When he pushed the outer door open further for her, Lannie saw his shirt stretch tight over the muscles of his upper arm and the fringe of black hair in the opening of his shirt collar created a stir in her that caught her by surprise.

Inside the dim hall, with Emma toddling toward them, she saw that Orland lent the house a substance that had been lacking when she was there before. He grinned at her.

"I'm glad you came," he said. And she wondered why, remembering him at school, never even looking at her.

"Orland," she said, shyly. He had been a boy at their wedding and now he was a man, like her father, he even looked like him, and she couldn't think of anything to say. In the small entryway she could smell him, caught herself leaning forward slightly to inhale his full scent, but he was turning away.

"She's in the kitchen. I'm watching Emma."

"I'll just . . ." Lannie mumbled and slipped past him to go into the kitchen.

Angela was moving between the cupboards and the table, stopping on her way past the stove to stir something, supporting her back with the other hand. Her cheeks were red and she looked tired and flustered and dazed. Impulsively Lannie stepped close to Angela and kissed her cheek. Angela's eyes cleared and she looked at Lannie with surprise and then recognition. Lannie backed away and turned her head.

"Just look at me," Angela said, gesturing around the kitchen at the half-set table, the crusted spot on the stove where a pot had boiled over and the place not been wiped, at the bright plastic horse lying on its side between the stove and the table, and the pile of folded diapers half of which had fallen off the chair they had been placed on and were lying in disarray on the none-too-clean, shabby floor.

"I'll do that," Lannie said. She took the spoon from Angela and continued stirring the gravy. Angela looked around helplessly and then sat down at the table, inhaling the steamy air deeply and then breathing out with a long, sighing exhalation.

"When are you due?" Lannie asked. She set the spoon down for a moment and moved the red and yellow horse into a corner, then returned to the stove and continued stirring.

"Tomorrow, today," Angela said. "Oh, I expect I'll be late," she added, rubbing her forehead with both hands.

"I shouldn't have come," Lannie said. "I didn't realize."

"Don't be silly," Angela said. She was coming back to herself now. Again Lannie set the spoon down and this time gathered the diapers, setting them more securely back on the chair. She tried to quell the trembling in her hands but the diapers were so soft, they smelled of babies. "Have you any idea how long the last week is? I need you to take my mind off the waiting." Lannie went back to the gravy.

They could hear Orland and Emma in the living room. He was teasing her and the television news was punctuated by Emma's giggles. Angela smiled, listening. "I hope this one's a boy," she said. "But if it isn't, we'll just keep trying."

Lannie moved the spoon around and around. Had she stirred the gravy for her mother? She couldn't remember, but the smell, the motion, evoked some memory that had no picture, no words, only pain and longing. Her body ached, she could hardly stand. Her father had black hair. He had been tall, too. She, Lannie, was just like her mother. Everyone said so.

The room was too hot. The smell of beef roasting in the oven was too strong. She stirred the gravy round and around. It gleamed its rich brown surface swirling slowly round and round. She could hear Orland laughing in the living room and Emma squealing. Emma's small delicate face was turning into Misty's. She stirred the gravy. Around and around.

"You're pregnant, aren't you?" Angela said from the table where she was sitting very still now, alert, her eyes sharp. She stood awkwardly and went to Lannie, put her arm around Lannie's shoulders. "That's enough," she said, and took the spoon out of Lannie's hand. "Sit down," she said. Lannie obeyed. Angela faced her.

"We'll talk about it after supper. Orland's going out to finish a job. I'll put Emma to bed." She began to put the vegetables into bowls, leaving Lannie alone at the table, where she sat motionless. Angela poured the gravy into the gravy boat, then took the roast out of the oven, releasing a wave of hot air, and began to carve it.

"I'm calling Orland now," Angela said. Lannie tried to smile. Orland came in carrying Emma on his shoulders. He bent and set his yellow-haired daughter into her highchair, and in his mass of black hair and the protective bending motion, he became for a moment, her father. He went around to the end of the table, pulled out his chair and sat down. He smiled at Lannie when he saw her watching him, became himself again.

"When are you getting married, Lannie?" he asked, as though she were fifty and not merely a couple of years older. Lannie didn't answer. Angela had begun to feed Emma. "Just imagine," Orland said, still teasing, "you could be like Angela here, swollen out like a balloon." Angela swatted him.

"Be quiet, Orland," she said. "Nobody wants to look like this." She wiped Emma's mouth with the corner of her apron. Lannie thought suddenly, Tim would marry me. She tried to imagine him sitting in Orland's place, but she could only picture him the way she had last seen him—tall and rumpled, his features blurred with misery. She couldn't remember what he looked like exactly. But she knew he was only a child and she needed a man for a husband. Someone like her father. No, she did not want a husband. She looked at Orland, who was eating now with the concentration of someone who has nothing else on his mind. Although she did not even know him, she wanted to bury her face in the black curls at his neck, to feel his thick dark arms close around her. She glanced at Angela. Angela wasn't eating.

"I haven't much of an appetite right now," Angela said. "It's a good thing, or I'd be big as a house."

"You are anyway," Orland said. They smiled at each other without speaking. They like each other, Lannie thought, and it was an unexpected perception with a keen edge. She knew her mother and father had not. She could remember, not words, but the air, how cold and frightening it had been sometimes, how cold she had been standing beside the bed in which for some reason her mother was lying, looking up at her husband, and how her father had suddenly taken Lannie's hand and pulled her away. She could not remember anything but the pull of his hand and the bleakness in her mother's eyes. And the time her father had wrestled, yes, wrestled with her mother and her mother was crying and then he had gone out and slammed the door and her mother had crumpled into a chair, her light-coloured cotton dress folding and the pattern of flowers on the stomach vanishing as her mother bent over, got smaller.

"Eat, Lannie," Angela said. "Lord, I can't stand to see you so thin. Now eat that." Lannie glanced at her. "Eat," Angela repeated. Lannie put some vegetables on her fork and lifted it to her mouth.

"Are you trying to starve yourself?" Orland asked. "I like a woman with some meat on her bones," he said, looking at Angela. Maybe marriage wouldn't be so bad, Lannie thought. Why am I so afraid of it?

After Orland had gone and Emma was in bed, Angela and Lannie sat on the couch in the living room. The television was on but Angela had turned the sound off.

"So, you're pregnant," Angela said. "Have you told your boyfriend?"

"No," Lannie said.

"It's his baby too," Angela said. "He's got a right."

"I don't love him," Lannie said.

"I know you," Angela said. "You haven't even tried."

"Tried?" Lannie wanted to laugh, but no, that was how Angela did things. Everything had to make sense to her, good clear, common sense. Lannie thought, nothing makes sense to me, nothing.

"It may not be his baby," she said. Would Armand be any better than Tim? She shuddered.

"Oh, Lannie," Angela said. "Once a baby is born, who cares? Everybody finds resemblances whether they're there or not. What colour is his hair?"

"Blonde," Lannie said. Too tight curls, he never gets it cut, it sticks out all over, and she was overcome for a moment with a bittersweet longing to be like other girls, getting married, proudly wearing a tiny, bright diamond on her finger.

"Your father had black hair, didn't he?" Angela said. "And yours is sort or red, so you're covered, no matter what."

"I don't want a baby," Lannie said.

"Every woman wants a baby," Angela said. "She doesn't always know it, that's all." She folded her hands over her stomach. The refrigerator clicked on in the kitchen, its vibrating hum reaching them clearly in the quiet house.

"I'm afraid," Lannie said.

"So am I," Angela replied. "But that's the way it is." She looked reflectively across the room, her eyes distant, for a moment lost in the experience ahead of her. She turned to Lannie. "What is it you're really afraid of?" Lannie was startled. How did Angela know things about her she didn't know herself?

"I don't know," she said. "Angela, I can't have a baby. I am . . . alone. I . . . I can't make it real. I can't be a . . . mother. It is not . . . possible." She was looking at Angela and Angela was looking back. Then it was Angela who looked away.

"Maybe you should have an abortion then," she said, looking at the floor. "It's a terrible thing, but I suppose," she sighed, "sometimes it may be for the best." She slid her hands over her abdomen. "Maybe it's what you'll have to do." She smiled at Lannie. She looked very tired and suddenly much older. "They say it's not so bad. Sometimes you can go home the same day. You could go to Calgary." There were tears in her eyes.

"I can't do that either," Lannie said. She put her face in her hands. "I can't." Angela stirred.

"Why not?" she asked in a gentler voice.

"Because . . . I can't let them touch me," Lannie said. "Not like that." There was a silence.

"Then call him," Angela said. "Call him." For a long time neither of them spoke. The room was warm, but Lannie's hands felt like lumps of ice on her lap. She shivered. Angela looked so worn. She hoped Orland would be home soon to look after her.

She looked around the cluttered room, the plastic basket full of Emma's toys sitting under the window, the pile of Emma's clothes on one of the stacking chairs by the door, the papers and magazines on the coffee table, the TV flashing silent pictures, Angela leaning back on the sofa, her eyes closed. Lannie stood. This was not the life for her. She was born for silence, empty rooms, no voices except the one in her head.

"Good night," she murmured. Angela did not seem to hear. Still she leaned back, eyes closed, hands folded over her abdomen, listening to the secret inner song of her body. Lannie let herself out quietly.

"Did you talk to her?" Barney asked. He and Iris were lying in their bed when they heard the car drive up and the sound of Lannie opening the front door and shutting it, her muffled footsteps on the stairs. Barney's left arm was under Iris's head. He turned toward her and put his other hand on her stomach.

"I tried," she said. "She wouldn't talk." Barney rubbed his hand lightly across her breasts. "I'll keep an eye on her, that's all I can do."

"I don't know, Iris, sometimes I think we should have had kids," he said. Iris held her breath.

"I don't miss them," she said, her voice sounding wistful in the darkness. "Anyway," she said more loudly, "it's too late now." She tried to contain the guilt that was making her uneasy again. But it had been a mutual decision. Barney hadn't wanted a family till he was more secure financially, and then, when Iris was thirty-two, Lannie had come along and they had put off babies till she was settled in and now she was forty-two and it was too late.

"I wish my goddamn family weren't coming," he said. He moved his hand downward. Iris turned on her side facing him.

"It won't be so bad, Barney," she said. "I'll get the food on the table right away. They always leave after they eat." She lifted her hand and rested it on the side of his neck, feeling the firmness of his flesh under her palm. She ran her fingers upward into his thick wavy hair. "I hope you never lose your beautiful hair," she said. His arm was around her now sliding down over her hips. He pulled her nightdress up and she raised her hips to help him. She thought, not unhappily, but with some surprise, it is always like this. We don't even talk anymore. Every time, the same.

"You've got a nice fat bottom," he said. She laughed.

"Don't say fat," she said. "Do you ever want other women?"

"Mmmm," he grunted. "Sure."

"You don't!" Iris said, surprised.

"Sure I do," he said. "But I don't think about it. I just like the way they look. All men do," he added. Iris did not believe him.

"Oh," she said. His body pressed against hers. She had opened her legs. It always surprised her that after making love to James she and Barney could have sex and Barney wouldn't notice it. Afterwards, he lay on his back. She leaned on one elbow and kissed him.

"I love you, Barney," she said solemnly.

"Smart girl," he said, and she laughed.

"I hope the old man doesn't get started again," he said.

"Mmmm," Iris said. They listened to the door to Lannie's room close for the second time. "I think maybe she'll let you buy her a car now," she remarked.

"You think so?" Barney asked. "Good. Make sure I don't forget to find out about Fay, eh? Maybe you could talk to mom." He yawned.

"I will," Iris answered, almost asleep.

Lannie lay in bed. She did not know what to do. Every avenue seemed closed to her. She could not forget what Angela had said about the father having a right to know, but it didn't move her. It made intellectual sense, she knew, but from the gut it made no sense at all. What did he have to do with it? With the child? The child was always the woman's burden, her life. But she had no life to give. And anyway, who was the father?

Suppose she arbitrarily picked Tim to be the father? Would he guess? Probably. Would he care? Some, she supposed, but he would have her and that was what he wanted. What he thought he wanted. He was so foolish.

Perhaps if she just put one foot in front of the other, just phoned him, and then let things fall as they might. Just dialled the number. She was not, after all, the first girl to get pregnant without a husband. There had to be a way, there had to be. But every way she looked, they were all impossible, all things she could not do.

She tossed restlessly. She began to think about Barney's parents, her grandparents, and her Uncle Wesley, no, her step-uncle Wesley. Such strange people. How did Uncle Barney ever come out of that family? Did he make himself the way he was now? Was it an act of will? If Barney could make himself a new personality, a new life, could she do the same?

Iris checked the roast one more time. It would be ready by six. Barney was brooding in the living room. Lannie had gone to her room to change clothes. Iris wiped her hands nervously on her apron. It was not so hard for her, Luke gave her a sort of grudging admiration, Mary Ann was actually rather sweet and she could deal with Wesley. But for Barney it was all very painful. He and his father always got into a fight even though Barney always vowed he wouldn't say a word no matter what his father said. Iris stood in the doorway of the living room and watched Barney's back. He was looking out the window, the old anger growing in him in spite of his efforts to stifle it. His father could never say, I was wrong, son, you made a good life for yourself. His father would never see him as anything but a son who had betrayed him.

He saw them drive up in the half-ton, the stockracks still on the back from some trip to the vet or moving horses. He felt a stirring of homesickness. He heard Iris call Lannie and then Lannie coming down the stairs. He pulled his shoulders back, then dropped them, forced a smile onto his face and went to open the front door.

Lannie and Iris stood on the steps flanking him. Their presence made him feel stronger. He put his arm around Iris's shoulder and she leaned pliantly against him for a second. On his other side Lannie stood erect, the sun striking sparks of red in her hair.

He looked for the old man, and when he saw him climbing out of the truck, a nervous seething started in his stomach, but while cursing it inwardly, he managed to widen his smile. He glanced at his mother and his older brother, Wesley, who were climbing out of the side of the truck nearest them.

"At least they could have made him put on pants," he muttered to Iris. Wesley was wearing bib overalls. Then his father was in front of him and he stepped forward to shake his hand. The old man's grip was still powerful, his muscles like coiled springs. For what? Barney asked himself. So he can work himself to death and think he's better than other people for it.

"Putting on some lard there, son," his father said.

"You're still looking great, dad," Barney said. "Ma." He bent to kiss her and then shook Wesley's hand. Wesley was taller than Barney, but gaunt, and his face was deeply lined and a dark red colour. He wore thick glasses with dark brown frames. His hair, turning grey at the temples, was the same colour as Barney's. It was receding from his forehead in a deep v. His clean cotton shirt was buttoned tightly up to his throat although he was not wearing a tie. Barney's mother gave Wesley a little push and the group on the steps went into the house.

"How's the calf crop?" Barney asked. They were all sitting in the pretty, grey and blue living room and Luke looked irritated and out of place.

"Good," Luke said. "Lost a few in the last blizzard. Couldn't find 'em all in the bush." Wesley stood up and began to move around the room, touching the marble bookends on the shelves along one wall, the brass horse on the TV, the crystal vase holding the daffodils Iris had bought at the co-op the day before and placed on the polished teak table by the sofa.

"Sit down," Luke said.

"I've got some work for him to do," Barney put in quickly.

"Good," Luke said. There was an uncomfortable silence while Barney said, "Come on, Wes," and led him outside. Barney was glad to escape, if only for a minute. Wesley walked beside him, matching his stride to Barney's.

"Watcha got?" Wesley asked.

"Shovelling gravel," Barney said.

"Good," Wesley said, imitating his father. Jesus Christ, Barney thought. They should have sent him away to school so that he could have learned to do something besides work all the goddamn time. He gave Wesley a shovel, showed him what to do, stood back and watched him for a moment, and then, stifling his guilt, turned back to the house. He would have to be sure to come out in another half hour to make sure that Wesley rested. If he didn't, Wesley would work till he dropped.

In the summer heat, if their mother did not keep checking on Wesley, he would be found unconscious in the sun by the woodpile or in the doorway of the barn, still clutching a pitchfork of manure. Luke was always angry when this happened, full of self-rebuke and despair, but a perverse part of himself kept him from checking on Wesley as closely as he needed. Some part of himself probably wanted Wesley to die.

The one thing about his father Barney could understand was that guilt. Barney had gone off and left his father with only Wesley on the ranch, and Barney knew his father would never forgive him for it. He could not forgive himself, no matter how hard he tried, how wide he smiled, how much help he gave to his sister Fay.

When Barney went back into the living room, Luke was seated uncomfortably in a hard-backed chair, his long legs in their tight western pants crossed at the knee, his shiny riding boots catching the light from the window.

"Feel like a drink, dad?" Barney asked.

"Could do," his dad said. Lannie, without being asked, went to the sideboard and poured two glasses of rye and added mix. When she came back from the kitchen with ice, which she added to the drinks, Mary Ann and Iris were talking.

"How's your garden?" Iris asked.

"Coming along," Mary Ann said. "I think we've had the last frost." Lannie handed the two men their drinks. Luke took his without looking at Lannie. She was the daughter of his wife's son by her first marriage, the daughter of the boy he had raised who had turned on him, and he had never been able to forgive her for that. In the face of his silent hostility, Lannie always turned passive and humble. Barney hated him for that, too.

"That a new television?" Luke asked.

"Yes," Barney said. "The old one wouldn't stop flipping. Picture was fuzzy," He waited, knowing Luke couldn't let it pass. The two women watched nervously.

"Looks expensive," Luke said.

"Everything's expensive these days," Iris put in quickly. Barney smiled inwardly.

"You always did spend money like it was water," Luke said, looking away as if someone else had spoken, not him. Barney's stomach started to churn again.

"Oh, I can afford it," he said, smiling. Serves the bastard right, Barney thought. Luke didn't speak. Iris stood. Lannie was leaning on one arm in the blue velvet chair by the window, looking out at the scenery, muted by the sheer white curtains. She did not appear to be listening.

"I have to check the dinner," Iris said. Mary Ann followed her into the kitchen.

"Now, what can I do?" she said.

"Everything's pretty well done," Iris said. "We'll have to set the table, though. You're looking well, Mary Ann."

"I'm fine," Mary Ann said. "How's Barney?"

"He's fine," Iris said. "He never changes. Always cheerful, hard-working."

"He's a good boy," Mary Ann said. "I just wish . . ."

"I know," Iris said. "I know." They smiled briefly, wryly at each other. Iris moved to the fridge.

"How's Wesley doing?" she asked. "He doesn't look any different."

"He's slowing down some," Mary Ann said, pulling out a chair and sitting down heavily. "Follows me around more."

"Fay and the kids okay?" She looked at Mary Ann when she asked this. The light glinted off her mother-in-law's glasses.

"Barry's out of work again."

"Maybe Barney should go see her again, do you think?" Iris asked.

Mary Ann sighed. Her shiny dark red dress made a slithering sound on the chair when she moved. She placed her plump, wrinkled hands on her thighs in an almost masculine gesture.

"I hate to ask him," she said. "Don't tell Luke, promise you won't . . ."

"Never," Iris said.

"I know you won't," Mary Ann said. "You know how Luke is about taking anything from Barney, but Fay's having a hard time of it, and she won't come home." Iris looked at Mary Ann's feet and ankles. They looked swollen, her small feet bulged out of her black patent pumps. "Well, I can't blame her for that," Mary Ann said, sighing. Iris wondered if she was thinking back to the long-ago time when her first husband had beaten her and left her. "But we ain't got much to spare in the way of cash. You know how it is." She sighed again. "So . . ." Iris wanted to tell her to take her shoes off, to rest her feet, but she said only, "I'll tell Barney. He wants to help if he can."

She and Mary Ann began to set the dining room table, carrying the dishes from the cabinet to the table. Iris set the silver and the china on the table without paying attention to it, carelessly. But Mary Ann lifted a plate and ran her fingers around the flower design on the rim and touched the silverware reverently. She put out a thumb and finger and made the crystal water pitcher ring and then smiled.

"I love this stuff," she said. "It's so pretty." She was like a child with it.

"It is beautiful, isn't it," Iris said, pausing to look at it. "I don't see it anymore." Mary Ann reached across the table, the fat jiggling her plump arm, and set the water pitcher near the centre of the table. It caught the light and sparkled and threw a rainbow on the wall.

"You're lucky," she said to Iris without looking at her. Iris was suddenly ashamed. To have so much. It was true. She did not deserve it, and she wondered for the first time, why she should be the one to have everything, why her life should be so easy, and Mary Ann's so hard.

Lannie had come in from the living room.

"Sorry, I didn't come sooner," she said. "I was daydreaming." Mary Ann turned to her.

"How's my pretty little granddaughter?" she asked, catching Lannie to hug her. Lannie allowed it passively.

"Not so pretty," she said, embarrassed.

"Not so little, either," Iris said. They all laughed, Lannie turning away flustered, looking for something to do.

They put the food on the table and called the men. When everyone was seated, Barney said, "We'll have to buy some more beef from you soon, dad. You thinking of butchering?"

"As soon as you come out and give me a hand," Luke said. Wesley sawed at his meat.

"Let me help you, Wesley," Iris said.

"Let him do it himself," Luke said. "He's older than everybody here except his mother and me. Let him cut his own meat." Mary Ann said, "He sure likes the snowmobile you give him."

"It goes fast," Wesley said. "Got lotsuh power." His voice was deep and uncontrolled.

"Eat your supper," Luke said. "At least he's good for something. Checks the cows on it. I don't know what will happen to him when we're gone."

"I've told you and told you, dad, that Iris and I will take care of him," Barney said, putting his knife and fork down in exasperation and then quickly picking them up again.

"Have some more salad, Luke," Iris said. "I made the kind you like. It has apples in it."

"Do you have any colts this spring?" Lannie asked. Everyone looked at her. It always surprised everyone when Lannie spoke.

"One," Luke said. He didn't look at her.

"It's a sorrel," Mary Ann put in quickly. "White feet." She smiled at her granddaughter.

"How's Blackjack?" Barney asked, buttering a slice of bread.

"He wintered all right," Luke said. "Getting old though. I don't know why you don't bring him here, if you're so worried about him."

"You know I haven't got any pasture, dad," Barney said.

"Plowed up every goddamn inch old Thomas hadn't already plowed up."

Lannie had stopped listening. As soon as they left she would call Tim. At least that would be something. She had to do something. She had been sick this morning, nothing serious, she hadn't thrown up, but it was the first real sign that she was really pregnant. With a real baby. That's when she decided to call Tim, when she realized she was really carrying a child. Whenever she thought this her hands turned clammy and everything in her field of vision shifted and then righted itself again. Angela had said it wasn't cancer, but she wanted to say, it might as well be. Iris went to get the dessert.

"You stay here and talk to Barney," she said to Mary Ann. "Lannie and I will clear the plates. Barney doesn't see enough of you."

"Well, mom," they heard Barney saying as they went into the kitchen, "how's the garden this year?"

They were gone by eight-thirty. Barney, Iris and Lannie sat in the living room like a crew of shipwrecked sailors. Iris laughed.

"Look at us," she said. Barney tried to smile.

"They're as glad to get away as we are to have them go," Barney said.

"Wesley and your mother like to come here," Iris said. "And you know what I think? I think Luke's proud of you, but he'll never admit it."

"You think so?" Barney asked. And then, "Ah, who the hell cares." But he wouldn't meet Iris's eyes.

"He's still mad you left the place, but he's proud that you're so successful," she said. "He could never tell you that though."

"Christ," Barney said. "I couldn't make a living there. It would never support two families. Your father'd never have let me marry you if you'd had to go live there. We woulda starved."

"Well," said Iris. "It would have been hard." Barney yawned and stretched and turned on the television.

Lannie had been sitting quietly in one of the blue easy chairs, her eyes on the two of them but distant. Now she stood and went into the kitchen. Iris called, "I'm going to see Jake tomorrow. Will you come?"

"Yes," Lannie called back. She shut the kitchen door. Barney and Iris looked at each other. She was going to phone somebody.

When she heard Tim say hello on the other end of the line, for a second Lannie couldn't speak. Then she said, "Tim?"

"Yes," he said. Then, "Lannie, is that you?"

"I wonder," Lannie said. "I wonder if, would you like to come and visit me?" She held her breath, coiling the phone cord around her hand.

"Sure," Tim said. "Is everything okay?" She couldn't hear him very well. His voice sounded faint and far away. She could hear laughter coming from the television in the front room. She closed her eyes.

"I'd like it if you could come for a visit," she said. Again she held her breath. Tim said, "I can't come till the end of the week. I'm working the evening shift till then. Is that all right?"

"Yes," Lannie said, breathing now. "Will you drive?"

"Yeah," Tim said. "I'll borrow my dad's car. Are you all right?"

"Yes," she said. "I'm fine. I can't hear you very well."

"I'll phone you on Thursday before I leave, okay?" he asked.

"Yes," she said. "Bye."

"Lannie?" he said, but she was already hanging up.

Chapter Eight

"I'D LIKE YOU TO COME along today, Lannie," Iris said. "Jake is looking forward to seeing you." Her last words were cut off by the roar of the tractor as Barney brought it into the yard. Lannie was standing at the stove stirring the soup. She didn't lift her head, but mumbled something which Iris took to be assent; she couldn't hear the words.

It was getting harder and harder to elicit any response from Lannie. Drifting around the house and yard with that sleepwalker look on her face, she seemed to have retreated so far that Iris doubted if she could bring herself back even if she wanted to. For the first time Iris thought with absolute seriousness that she would have to get help for Lannie. But she couldn't imagine where to get it, and the problem wrinkled her forehead and made her turn back to the grilled sandwiches she was making without seeing them. A minister? A priest? Even though Lannie was not a Catholic? A doctor? No, not a doctor, she'd had enough experience with doctors and they'd never helped. A psychiatrist. Ah, that was it, but how did one go about seeing a psychiatrist? And would Lannie go? But in her state, Iris thought, she'd do anything. She just wouldn't be there.

The sandwiches were beginning to burn and she hadn't noticed, even though she was standing in front of them. She took them out of the toaster-oven, burning her fingers and pulling them back quickly. I'll have to talk to Barney. This made her nervous. There was something there, she didn't know what, but she was no longer sure what Barney would say. The roar outside swooped down an octave and stopped. The silence was so sudden, so complete, that it stunned her. She felt off-balance and the dialogue in her head ceased.

The screen door opened and Barney came in, letting it bang behind him. He washed his hands quickly in the bathroom and entered the kitchen. Lannie had begun to serve the soup and he leaned toward her as if to kiss her but changing his mind, settled for a squeeze around her shoulders.

"What kind of soup?" he asked her, stepping back and putting his hands uncertainly against his back pockets. She didn't answer. Iris said, "Vegetable." While she brought the sandwiches to the table, Lannie ladled soup into three bowls.

"What's up?" Barney asked, looking from Iris to Lannie and back again. He pulled out his chair and sat down.

"Nothing special," Iris said, trying to sound cheerful. "Lannie and I are going to Jake's this afternoon." They ate in silence, Iris and Barney exchanging glances across the table past Lannie. Barney's expression was puzzled and pained. Iris smiled and gave a quick nod at him to let him know that she understood his concern and would talk to him later.

When Lannie finished her bowl of soup, (a single ladleful and she didn't touch the sandwiches), she left the kitchen without speaking. Barney leaned toward Iris.

"What is it?" he asked. She put her hand on his arm, filled with tenderness for him, for his concern and his helplessness to deal with what she knew he thought of as a female problem.

"I better talk to you about it tonight," she said. "There's nothing new, but I think we have to do something." He leaned back, looked at her for a moment and then turned his head to look out the back door at the grain bins and the warm spring sunlight striking them.

"All right," he said finally. He stood slowly. "If it takes money . . ."

"I know," Iris said, and would have kissed him, but he had turned and was walking away, out the back door to his tractor and his fields.

Iris sat at the table. She had awaited this afternoon with James with eagerness, as she waited for each meeting with him, and she regretted losing it. She would not even be able to kiss him with Lannie present. He would understand about Lannie. Still . . . desire for him swept over her and she dropped her head in her hands and gave in to it. When she thought she heard a noise upstairs, she straightened briskly and began to gather the dishes and put them in the dishwasher.

As she slid each plate into the rack she tried to remember what it had been like before James. It had been peaceful, it seemed to her, very calm. Now she felt the pressure of James's need every hour of every day and sometimes, especially now with Lannie in trouble, she found it oppressive. She wished, in a second's revelation, that she did not have him to worry about, that his children would come and take him away, or that he would lose interest in her. She did not think, 'or that he would die,' but the thought flashed through her mind before she could stop it and she knew it was there now and would not go away. She was horrified. She had never thought of death before except as something terrible that happened to people, and she was ashamed of having thought such a thing about anybody, much less about James, who loved her.

And when he died, who could take his place? "No one will ever love you the way I do," he had said, and it was true. She wondered how much time he had left. His health was not good. He was often tired, his hands shook, he slept badly, and he said he lived only for her. How long would his body support such a life? Iris leaned against the counter and allowed tears to take hold of her. How had her easy, reasoned life come to this?

When she and Lannie were ready, Iris backed her car out of the garage, and with Lannie sitting silently beside her, set out down the gravel driveway, past the pines, down the road to town.

"How are you feeling?" she asked. She could not think of a devious way to extract a clue from Lannie. She wanted something she could thrust through Lannie's barriers, that would reveal even a glimpse of the concealed centre of the girl.

"Fine," Lannie said. She was looking out the window at the crops, which were now a thin green carpet across the fields. Iris tried to think of something else to say.

"You should have one of your friends down from the city for a week or so," she said. "Or maybe you should go up to the park for a week. Rent a cabin." Lannie didn't answer, but she smiled at Iris and then looked away again. Iris was encouraged.

"Are you in love?" she said suddenly, so surprised that the car swerved on the gravel and she had to put both hands on the steering wheel to steady it.

"In love?" Lannie repeated. She blinked several times, rapidly, then turned away again. "No," she said.

"Would you like to go to Vancouver with me?" Maybe Lannie needed to get away, maybe that would help. But then, she thought, how will James get along without me? And my garden, what will happen to my garden if I'm not there to look after it? And then, angry with herself, she said, "Please think about it. We could buy some clothes, go to some nightclubs, have a good time." The idea was beginning to appeal to her.

"No," Lannie said.

"I just thought . . ." Iris said. They drove another mile in silence before Lannie said, as though she had been practicing this sentence for some time, "I'd rather not talk about it." She was facing straight ahead now, her head held high, her back straight, her neck rigid. Again Iris saw the fragile little girl she had wanted so much to love and the old urge to sweep her into her arms almost overcame her. It was quickly followed by a sinking feeling of defeat and she almost cried again.

"Of course," she said, swallowing the lump in her throat. She patted Lannie's thigh.

They were driving through town when Lannie spoke again. Again it sounded as though she had been trying for some time to force the words out and they came finally in a rush.

"I've invited a friend for the weekend." Iris was pleased, and then did not trust this. What could it mean? But surely it was a good sign.

"That's lovely," she said. She wanted to ask, is he your boyfriend? Is it a girl? But she didn't dare.

"A friend," Lannie said again, nasally this time, her head still turned away as though she were hiding tears. "Tim," she said. But Lannie never cried.

Iris parked in front of James's house and went ahead up the path. The door opened before she could knock and James stood there, the sunlight slanting across his body, his shabby workpants, his wrinkled shirt, his slippers. He blinked and stepped back out of the light. He had been smiling but when he saw Lannie standing behind Iris his expression underwent a subtle change and then closed.

"Hello, James," Iris said evenly. "I've brought Lannie."

"Come in," he said, and Lannie thought, James? She heard, through the fog she moved in, the gentleness of his voice. Surely old men were garrulous, crusty and indifferent. He gestured toward the couch with his hand in a courtly manner. When the women were seated side by side, he sat down in a worn leather armchair and lit a cigarette.

"Home from school?" he said to Lannie after drawing on the cigarette.

"Yes," Lannie said. She sat upright, a watchful expression on her face, looking at him in quick glances, which she hurriedly withdrew. He studied her through the film of smoke that drifted between them.

"You look like your mother," he said. "She was a pretty girl." Lannie pressed her hands together, then slid the fingers of one between the fingers of the other and folded them carefully.

"She was," Iris agreed. Lannie was silent. Her mother leaned toward the camera, her arm around her husband's waist, a thin figure, her short hair drooping over one eye, her mouth curved in a smile, her eyes pained and desperate. Lannie's father towered over her, dominating the picture with his unruly black hair, his black energy.

"I was ten when she died," Lannie said suddenly. "I believe it was meningitis." She was not looking at either of them. She spoke as if she were referring to some fictional character or a distant relative she had never known. Jake watched her. Then he drew slowly on his cigarette and looked away.

"Knew your father too," he said.

"Everybody knew him," Iris said quietly. "Let's talk about something else."

"You come to help Iris?" he asked. His voice was soft. He gazed at her. She could not see his eyes through the screen of smoke, but she imagined he could see her clearly.

"Yes," Lannie said. Iris and James's eyes met. Iris rose slowly, her dress rustling by Lannie's arm, the faint scent of violets reaching Lannie and then fading.

"Let's get to work," she said. Lannie rose too and looked uncertainly around the dim, crowded room. It seemed to her that she had moved backward in time to some forgotten place, the dusty, dying plants, the greying lace doilies, the sunlight slanting mutely through the dust motes.

"I'll start in the bedroom," Iris said. "You vacuum in here." She smiled at James who sat leaning back in his chair, looking up at the two of them, waiting. "It's in the closet in the back hall," she said to Lannie, pointing, Lannie moved in the direction Iris showed her. "Come and talk to me while I make the bed, James," Iris said. He rose carefully. In the bedroom he sank into the chair at the foot of the bed.

They listened to Lannie pulling the vacuum cleaner into the kitchen and then the living room.

"How are you feeling?" Iris asked, pulling back the bedcovers. In the living room the vacuum cleaner began to roar and suck. Iris dropped the covers and went to James and kissed him. He reached up and put his arms around her and pulled her to him. She stroked the side of his face and his hair and then buried her face in his neck. He ran his hand over her breasts and then her hips. "I had to bring her," she whispered into his ear.

"I know, I know," he said. "I'm glad you did." They kissed and Iris went back to making the bed.

"Have you been sleeping?" she asked loudly.

"With the pills," he said. When she passed around the foot of the bed, he brushed his hand down her hip and leg and she smiled again.

Without switching off the vacuum, Lannie had gone to the bedroom to ask Iris if she should move the furniture out from the walls and she had seen his hands on Iris's breasts and Iris's closed eyes and flushed cheeks, her acquiescence. Now she was pushing the vacuum cleaner back and forth on the living room carpet. She closed her eyes. Her father's face appeared. Through the dim, steady pain that now stayed with her all the time, she was like a patient with an incurable disease, she felt a thudding in her chest. It must be my heart, she thought. She pushed the vacuum cleaner back and forth and listened to it roar over the rug.

The child she was carrying would be born or it would not be born, and if it was born, it was only to die. It had no significance, it had nothing to do with her. And now she knew with appalling clarity what she had been waiting for all these years, and now she knew that her father would not return.

Iris and Jake were talking in the kitchen. She did not know how she could hear them over the noise of the vacuum cleaner but Iris's voice struck her, note by note, like a tuning fork.

She had finished the living room and pulled the vacuum cleaner into the bedroom. She expected something from this room and she stood still in the doorway and studied it as if she were looking at a picture in a gallery. The wide bed with the dark headboard and foot-board was neatly made. Not a wrinkle marred the surface of the yel-low quilt. Beside it on the scarred table with the spool legs, was an ashtray, a small lamp with a paper shade tilted crookedly, several bot-tles of pills, and a half-full glass of water. A woman's silver-backed dresser set gleamed darkly in the half-light. The closet door was open and Lannie could see shirts and suits hanging in the dim interior. This is what is left of a marriage, she thought. Of two lives, only this.

She began to vacuum the rug. By the bed and in front of the dresser, its pattern had vanished with wear. When she was finished she straightened the crooked shade and picked up the glass of water, knocking over one of the pill bottles, noticing the size of the capsules inside, and then righting it. She took the water glass into the kitchen.

James was sitting in a rocking chair in the corner. The room was hazy with cigarette smoke. Iris had tied on an apron and was wiping the front of the fridge.

"Finished?" she asked, smiling at Lannie as if the world was the same as always, around the village roasts still being placed in ovens to cook, women still shaking rugs out the front door in the sun-shine, hanging out sweet-smelling wash and children still skipping home from school. Lannie nodded. "I put some coffee on," Iris said. Jake said, "Sit down." He indicated a chair at the table. Lannie sat down. From behind the veil of smoke James continued to study her. At the sink Iris clattered the dishes. The coffee began to perk.

"I think I'd better go see Fay," Barney said. Iris turned to face him. He lay on his back, his arms under his head, looking up at the ceil-ing, which appeared to have come closer to them in the moonlight.

"I suppose so," Iris said. She put her arm across his chest. He low-ered one arm and taking her hand in his, began to play absently with her fingers.

"For all I know, Barry might not even be there. He might have left again to look for work in Calgary or someplace."

"Or just left," Iris said.

"Yeah," Barney said. "Summerfallow's done. I guess I'll go tomorrow."

"You want me to come?" Iris asked. Barney turned his head quickly. He sounded surprised, although Iris couldn't see his face in the darkness.

"Of course," he said.

"I was thinking about Lannie," she apologized. She had been thinking about James too, but as soon as she said Lannie's name she knew she should not go. "It's time we got help for her," she said.

"What kind of help?" Barney asked. The fingers that held her hand stopped moving.

"I think a psychiatrist," she said.

"A psychiatrist," Barney said, the word sounding strange when he said it. For a long time he didn't speak. Then he said it again, "A psychiatrist." This time he sounded pained.

"I don't know what else to do," Iris said softly.

"But if she's having this friend come at the end of the week, she can't be that bad," Barney argued.

"I can't figure it out," Iris said. "Why would she invite him when she's so unhappy? Do you think she might be trying to cheer herself up? Or maybe they had a fight and she wants to make up?"

"It could be something that simple," he said. "Well, look," he turned toward her. "Let's wait for this friend of hers to come. Then, if she's still acting funny next week, you do whatever you think is best."

Iris lay beside him in the darkness. It would be such a relief to leave it for now and yet something urged her not to wait, uneasiness pricked at her. But the practical problem of finding a psychiatrist (Were there any in Swift Current? Could you just phone and make an appointment with one?) in the end forced her to accept Barney's suggestion. She thought of James, imagining his mute sadness at her absence, and she sighed. Barney squeezed her hand. "She's probably all right," he said. "It's probably nothing."

In the morning he phoned Fay in Swift Current.

"She says he's away right now," Barney said to Iris, coming back slowly from the phone to the breakfast table where Iris sat. "I told her we were coming up for the day and just thought we'd drop in. She wants us to stay overnight." Iris reached out and put her hand on Barney's arm.

"I'll tell Lannie we'll be gone overnight," she said.

"I don't think she'll notice," Barney said.

When he had gone out to check the car and fill the tank with gas, Iris went to the bottom of the stairs and listened. Hearing nothing, she went to the phone and dialled James's number. "Hi," she said, and waited for a moment, trying to think what to tell him.

"Hello," he said. There was another pause. Iris could hear him breathing. It was a heavy, shallow sound as though he had been running.

"Will you be in today?" he said finally, reluctantly.

"Today I have to go with Barney to visit his sister in Swift Current." She might just as well say it, she thought. He didn't say anything for a second. "The one who married that Campbell good-for-nothing?" Iris laughed.

"I'm afraid so," she said.

"So you won't be in." Through the simplicity of the remark, Iris heard the despair.

"No," she said, more gently. "But I'll be thinking about you."

"Maybe tomorrow?" he asked. He could not keep the plaintive note out of his voice. Iris felt a touch of irritation.

"I'm afraid not. I don't expect we'll be back till evening." There was another pause. "I'm really sorry," she said, suddenly allowing his pain to touch her.

"I'll miss you," he said. It might be that he was trying not to cry. Iris wanted to hang up the phone. She wanted to say, it's only two days, you'll survive, and at the same time she felt such pity for him that she could feel her own tears starting.

"I have to go, James," she said. "I'll phone you as soon as I get back." She hung up quickly. She leaned against the counter, her eyes closed. She could picture him setting down the phone clumsily, slowly, then turning away from it in the dim, silent house, to sit and smoke and stare into space waiting for her. What did he see, she wondered? Her hands were trembling, and suddenly she was angry with him, with herself. How long can this go on, she asked herself? But she was not ready to face this question. She had things to do. She pushed herself away from the counter and went with firm steps toward the stairs.

Sometime later she met Lannie in the hall as she came from tidying the bathroom. She said, "Lannie, while we're gone I'd like you to go visit James Springer for me. Will you do that?" Lannie stopped. She had been going from her bedroom to the bathroom. She was wearing a long, pale blue nightgown without a dressing gown or slippers. Her hair wasn't brushed and it stood out in a fine tangled mesh around her head. In the light from the bedroom windows, the long slim outline of her body was visible through the gown. Her face was in shadow. Iris moved to one side to see her face better. She was startled to see how pale Lannie was. "Are you sick?" she asked.

"All right," Lannie said, responding only to the first question. There was some quality to her voice that made Iris stop re-folding the damp cloth she was holding.

"Are you okay?" she asked, more sharply this time.

"Yes," Lannie said.

"Because I don't have to go," she said. Already she was making up her mind to stay behind.

"I'm fine," Lannie said. She went silently into the bathroom.

"I'll stay," Iris said. "I won't go. Barney won't mind." Lannie came out of the bathroom again.

"I want you to go," she said. "Please go. I don't want you to stay behind." Iris hesitated. She felt sure she should stay, and yet it was only overnight and Lannie would be upset if she stayed and so would Barney.

"All right," she said, finally, skeptically.

On the road to Swift Current Barney and Iris sat side by side in the big Chrysler without speaking. Iris was thinking how complicated life turns out to be. How little we can really do for one another. James, for instance. I try to help him by being what he wants me to be and I become his prisoner. And in the end, he will die anyway. I've been trying to stave off his death. That's what I've been doing, and what's the use of that? He'll die anyway. And one person can't change another person's fate.

And here we are one more time on our way to help Fay. And in the end what good will it do? The kids are already lost, the boys anyway. It'll take more than money to change their lives, and what they need, we can't give. It's too late anyway. She thought of Fay's destroyed prettiness, of the half-empty bottle of rye that could always be found now in the kitchen of whatever shabby little house she and the kids, for the time being, called home.

Lannie, she hoped, would be a different story. For her at least she hoped they could do something. At least they would try. But even as she thought this, she struggled against hopelessness. Whatever will become of her, she asked herself. Whatever will become of us all?

Lannie was going to see Jake Springer. There was something she had to do there. She couldn't say exactly what it was, but she fastened onto the intention and held it in her mind so she would not forget where she was going.

She turned Iris's car down the long hill. The air resting on her face, her neck, her bare arms and hands holding the steering wheel felt strange and while part of her mind was fixed on where she was going, the other part was evaluating the sensation. It seemed that she was not attached to the body that was feeling the sensation of the air. They were her hands on the steering wheel, her feet on the pedals, she knew that, but she didn't feel the connection, didn't feel responsible for them. Each time she turned the steering wheel and the car turned she was surprised. When she was about to turn at the Co-op she was surprised to find the car stopped at the stop sign. The car seemed to find Jake's house by itself. It stopped, she got out, and walked up the sidewalk. It seemed to her that her body met no resistance from gravity, that she was weightless. Perhaps no one can see me, she thought.

She knocked on the door, waited, then it opened slowly and Jake stood there. He seemed more stooped than the last time she had seen him and there was a heaviness about his movements that had not been there before. She walked past him without speaking, glancing once into his face, seeing the emptiness in his eyes, the flatness where before there had been a riveting blue centre. She knew with the satisfied feeling of having solved a problem that her own eyes were the same. She stood in the centre of the room. He came past her and sat down in his armchair. She wondered why it was that when he moved he did not disturb the air. Because he's dying, she answered herself from a part of her, newly exposed, that knew such things. It occurred to her that such knowledge was forbidden, was not natural. She could feel the certainty of his impending death in all she had seen since he had opened the door. It washed over her and then vanished.

"Sit down," he said, and Lannie sat down.

"Iris sent me," Lannie said. He grunted.

"Did she." There were tears gathering in his eyes. He stared across the room rather than at her. After a moment he lit a cigarette and looked at her. "How are you?" he asked. He threw the book of matches onto the coffee table near her.

"Fine," she said. She was sitting very still with her hands clasped on her lap. Jake studied her.

"You don't have to be too bright to see that you're not fine," he said. "What's on your mind?" Lannie blinked.

"I came to visit," she said. He snorted.

"Young girl like you," he said. "Boyfriend trouble?" Lannie didn't answer. "I suppose it's none of my business," he said. "But you're driving Iris crazy. She wants to help you, and she don't know how." He seemed to be waiting for her to speak, but she did not. Finally, she said, "How old are you?"

"Seventy-four," he answered.

"Are you afraid to die?" she asked. If Jake was surprised, he didn't show it.

"Yes," he said. "But sometimes I think I want to."

"Why?" she asked, so quickly that even she was surprised. He looked away again.

"It gets lonely," he said finally. The room was still. Lannie could feel a vibration in the air that worked itself past her skin into her chest and set her heart to vibrating.

"You have a family, don't you?" she asked.

"Three kids living," he said. "All gone away. They're busy."

"I know your wife died," Lannie said, almost to herself. She looked at her hands. She lifted her head. "Isn't that enough?" she asked. "I mean you had them, and now you're old." She waited for him to speak. He was searching her face now, his eyes suddenly blue again.

"You never get over needing somebody," he said. His voice was gentle. "Oh, I loved my wife," he said, as though she had questioned him. "And I'll never stop missing her, but . . ."

"But you have Iris," Lannie said. He looked away again.

"You know about that," he said. "Iris tell you?" He was motionless.

"No," Lannie said. Neither of them spoke. "I have no family," Lannie said, "so I suppose you could say that I'm lonely too." She looked around the room with the bewilderment of someone waking abruptly from a sound sleep. "But I don't feel lonely," she said. "I feel alone."

"Same thing," he said. He leaned forward to flick the ashes off his cigarette.

"No," she replied. "I belong to no one. No one belongs to me. I am alone. It is not the same thing."

"Then what do you think loneliness is?" he asked. She stared at him.

"Thinking you should have somebody, I guess," she said. "Or expecting to have somebody." Their eyes met.

"You won't make trouble for Iris," he said.

"Trouble?"

"It's all right," Jake said, in the gentle voice he had used earlier. "You have a family," he said suddenly. "How can you say you don't? What about Iris and Barney? They love you. They've looked after you for years now. I don't know what they'd do without you." Lannie's expression didn't change.

"They are not my mother and father," she said. "I don't belong to them. They don't belong to me."

"You have a brother and a sister," he said.

"They were stolen from me," she replied as if she were commenting on the warmth of the day or the quality of the birds' songs. Jake didn't reply. He was staring at her now as if he were seeing her clearly for the first time.

"I suppose they were," he said. "Why don't you go to see them?" Lannie blinked again, several times.

"They might as well be dead," she said, in the same conversational tone. "We all might as well be dead." She was sitting upright on the sofa looking either at her hands or straight ahead. Jake searched for something to say.

"Would you like some tea?" he asked. Lannie turned her head toward him and seemed to relax.

"Yes, please," she said. Jake pulled himself to a standing position. When he was upright, he asked, "Why don't you cry?"

"Cry?" she said.

"You'd feel a lot better if you cried, or screamed, or something," he said. "Or got into a fight." He laughed. "I always used to get drunk and get into a fight when I felt bad. Come home all beat up. I'd feel better then, or else I'd feel so terrible I'd forget to feel miserable for a while." He laughed again. Lannie looked politely up at him. It occurred to him that she wasn't listening. There was something so strange and distant about her expression, about her voice, that he realized in a rush that whatever was the matter was deadly serious. "I'll make the tea," he said. He went into the kitchen, trying to think. He put the kettle on, hearing Lannie moving in the other room, got two mugs down from the cupboard, and put two teabags into a small teapot. Then he went back to the living room.

Lannie was sitting now on the end of the couch nearest the door to the hall where the bedrooms were. He thought he could see her trembling.

"Listen, girl," he said, sitting down heavily. "There's never a day goes by that I don't ache for your aunt. I love her," he said, "but look at me. I'm old. I'm ugly. I'm not good for anything anymore. Can't work. Can't fight. Can't steal a woman I want. I'd be better off dead. What have you got the matter that's so awful? What the hell could it be, compared to somebody like me?" He sounded angry although he was not. Suddenly he stared at her, his mouth part way open, alert, his eyes flashing blue at her. "You're pregnant," he said. "I never thought of that," he said, when she didn't speak. "Neither did Iris or Barney. You just don't seem the type." Lannie turned to him and he was struck by the way her yellow-brown eyes seemed flat and shiny, without awareness or emotion.

"I have to go now," she said, as though he had not spoken. She stood up slowly, gracefully. He tried to think of something to say. She was walking to the door now, slim, erect, seeming not to move at all.

"I want to talk to you about your father," he said. It was the only thing he could think of that might stop her.

"Good-bye," she said, and then she was gone. He watched her get into Iris's car and drive away. He could hear the kettle boiling in the kitchen. He went there, supporting himself with one hand on each piece of furniture as he passed it. He made himself a cup of tea and sat down to drink it.

He would have to tell Iris as soon as she got back. Maybe Iris could do something with her once she knew what was the matter. Iris. He put his head in both hands and, with his eyes closed, imagined her, the delicacy of her skin under his fingers, her black eyelashes lying against her cheeks, her smile, the plump curve of her breasts, and for a moment, hope left him.

When the familiar silhouette of the farm, dark against the mauve and pink sunset, came into sight, Iris relaxed into the car seat. She hadn't felt relaxed since leaving home. The sorrow that lay just beneath the thin skin of James's civility at all times kept alternating in her mind with what she was beginning to see now as Lannie's struggle with despair.

In their two days away, something had happened to Iris. It was as though the veil of optimism and faith through which she had always viewed life was lifted. Now with sadness she was seeing a world she had not noticed before. It was a world in which things did not happen for the best, a world where people really felt what happened to them, where they suffered and struggled and died, sometimes too soon, and did not come back again. She was quiet now, the active, uneasy impulse to do something about James, about Lannie, transformed into a stream of feeling flowing through her, deep inside, an ache that she knew would not leave her. So she was glad when once again she saw the farm sitting quietly in the trees in the dusk and smelled the scent of the long, dark row of pines. There was still home.

She got out of the car without speaking. Barney seemed lost in his own reverie. She didn't think, as she once would have, he is only tired from driving. She knew he suffered for his sister and for her children. They walked side by side into the house, their arms brushing against each other now and then and both were glad for the touch of the other.

When Lannie didn't answer her call, Iris went straight upstairs and knocked on Lannie's closed door.

"We're back, dear," she said. "Come and say hello." She waited for the sound of Lannie's voice. When it came, it was muffled, distant.

"I think I'm getting the flu." She didn't open the door. Iris leaned against it, putting her forehead against the wood.

"Do you want me to call the doctor?" she asked.

"No," Lannie said. "I took some aspirin."

"Well," Iris said, moving back from the closed door, "call me if you need me." She didn't try to open the door, thinking that the door between them had been closed for so long that perhaps the faint, muffled voice on the other side was only a product of her imagination, that there was no longer a person called Lannie in the room. In the morning, she thought, I'll know what to do in the morning.

When morning came she did feel more confident, less hopeless. After breakfast Barney kissed her and said he thought he'd go into town, do some banking, pay some bills, and she'd nodded mutely, understanding his need to lose himself in something concrete and manageable.

"This will all pass," she said to him and he nodded and shrugged his shoulders before turning to leave.

She poured herself another cup of coffee and sat alone at the breakfast table, sipping it, wondering how Lannie felt this morning. The phone rang.

A male voice, young, hesitant, spoke. "Is Lannie around?" For a moment Iris didn't react. Suddenly she straightened and held the phone tighter. These days nobody but Angela phoned Lannie.

"I'm sorry," Iris said, "she's still sleeping. Can I help you?" Should I wake her, she wondered? Maybe I should.

"This is Tim Quenell," he said, his voice seemed more assured now. "She invited me down today. I'm getting ready to leave, but I don't know how to find the farm." Iris had forgotten all about this. She was smiling into the phone.

"Oh, Tim," she said, pleasure lifting her voice. "This is her Aunt Iris speaking. How nice that you're coming." She explained to him how to find the farm from the town. He said that if all went well, he expected to arrive in the early afternoon.

When she had finished talking to him, Iris tried to think what she could do to show him how pleased she was about his visit. The house was tidy, there was nothing to do there. She looked around the shining kitchen. I'll cook a roast, she thought. She went down to the deepfreeze in the basement and chose one. On the way up the stairs she thought, a pie, boys always like pie.

She was sprinkling water into the pie dough when the phone rang again. She looked at the clock in surprise. It was only 8:15. She and Barney had gone to bed early and risen early. Shaking flour off her hands she picked up the phone gingerly with one finger and her thumb.

"Iris?" a woman said. Iris couldn't place the voice.

She raised her shoulder to hold the phone and tried to wipe some of the flour off onto a paper towel.

"Yes," she said.

"It's me, Angie."

"Angela," Iris said, forgetting the flour and grasping the phone. "How are you? You're due soon, aren't you?"

"That's why I'm phoning," Angela said. "I'm on my way to the hospital. The pains are about twenty minutes apart."

"Oh, my goodness!" Iris said. "Are you alone? Is Orland there? Is somebody looking after Emma?" Angela laughed.

"I'm fine, Iris. Orland's here and my mother has Emma." Iris waited, puzzled.

"It's this," Angela said. "I . . . it's just that I'm worried about Lannie. I thought I should talk to you." There was another silence.

Iris was about to speak when Angela rushed in over Iris's indrawn breath. "I've been so worried. All night. As soon as I thought I was going into labour I started thinking about her and I can't get her out of my mind. I had to phone you before I left. I had to." She paused again. "Iris, do you know what's wrong with Lannie?"

"No," Iris said. She held her breath.

"I don't like being the one to tell you," Angela said, her voice firm and steady now, "but I think I have to. I don't think Lannie will. I don't have any time to spare, Iris, so I'll just tell you." Iris waited. "Lannie is expecting a baby." Angela stopped, then said, "I'm sorry." Iris was so astonished she couldn't speak. She was holding the phone so tightly her fingers hurt. She changed hands. With one foot she hooked a chair, pulled it toward her and sat down.

"Thank God you told me," she said.

"I have to go now," Angela said. She sounded breathless. "I'll . . ." Iris interrupted.

"Of course, Angela, you go," she said. "Hurry now and thank you for telling me. Thank you so much. Good luck," she called, but Angela had already hung up.

Iris set the phone down. There was flour on it and she tried to brush it off. Of all the things she thought might be the matter with Lannie, it had never occurred to her that she might be pregnant. She could hardly believe it. Then to her surprise, she thought, that's all it is. It's only pregnancy. A baby. How wonderful. But it wouldn't be wonderful for Lannie. Lannie wouldn't want a baby. Tim Quenell! He must be the father. And that was why . . . She jumped up. Then she couldn't think what she should do. Poor girl, she thought, the poor kid. She started for the stairs, but stopped. Maybe I should tell Barney first, she thought, before I talk to Lannie. No, she decided, she couldn't predict Barney's reaction. Better to talk it over with Lannie first, find out what Lannie planned to do, and then they could go together to Barney. She started up the stairs. I must remember to phone the hospital about Angela, she thought.

Outside Lannie's door she hesitated, her hand in the air, and then knocked briskly. There was no answer. She knocked again. Still no reply. Goodness, she's sleeping soundly, Iris thought and pushed open the door cautiously.

"Lannie," she called softly, stepping inside the room. In the second it took her eyes to adjust to the light she saw that Lannie was lying on her back, her arms extended by her sides. The room was very stuffy. On the bed table there was a glass with water in it and an open vial of pills. Pills? Iris was surprised. She didn't say she'd been to the doctor.

"Lannie," she said again. She advanced into the room, her eyes on the pill bottle. She was aware that Lannie had still not moved. She pulled up the blind, and in one flash saw that Lannie was as still as death, that she was white, as white as the sheets she lay on, that the pill bottle was almost empty.

"My God," Iris cried. "My God!" Downstairs a door slammed. She stood, her hands by the sides of her face, staring down at Lannie.

"Iris," Barney called. Suddenly Iris moved.

"Barney!" she screamed. "Barney! Barney!" She began to cry, tears pouring down her cheeks. Barney came pounding up the stairs and into the room.

Instantly he saw Lannie. He was at her bedside in two strides, brushing past Iris, bending over Lannie, feeling her face, trying to find a pulse.

"Call the hospital," he said to Iris. "Quick, call the hospital!" Iris came to life. She ran down the stairs to the kitchen and picked up the phone to dial it, then realized she didn't know the hospital number. Behind her she could hear Barney coming heavily and slowly down the stairs. She tried to find the right page in the phone book but her hands were shaking so violently that she could barely turn the pages.

"Never mind," Barney said. "Open the door for me." She looked behind her. Barney held Lannie in his arms. Her long hair trailed down his leg, her white throat arched upward toward him. She's dead,

Iris thought. She's dead. She opened the kitchen door. "Come on," he said to her in a rough voice and she followed him. Barney knows she is dead. She opened the car door for him, and he lay Lannie down on the back seat. Lannie's arm rolled off her abdomen where he had placed it and trailed along the floor of the car. Iris climbed mutely in beside Lannie and made room for herself along Lannie's legs. She pulled Lannie's nightgown down and smoothed it carefully.

Barney was already in the driver's seat and was backing the car out. From the side Iris could see how pale he was. His movements were measured and deliberate. This was the way he looked the last time Quinn ran away, the way he looked when he came back from his fight with Barry. No, she thought, he looks different. He will look like this when he is dying. She lifted Lannie's long white arm and set it carefully across Lannie's chest. Then she reached for her other arm. She brought it out from under Lannie's body, rocking with the movement of the car as it sped along the road. There was something . . . her arms did not feel . . . dead. Suddenly there was a welling up of hope in her and she tried to find a pulse. She kept losing her balance, perched as she was on the edge of the seat with Barney swerving on the ruts, pushing the car as hard as he dared. She concentrated. Yes, there it was, a slight flutter, a delicate pulsation, irregular. Yes, she felt it again. It was there.

"Barney," she said. "Barney, she's alive." Barney turned his head and opened his mouth, but didn't speak. He looked back to the road and stepped on the gas harder so that the car fish-tailed on the gravel and he had to bring it back by gripping the steering wheel with both hands.

"Lannie," Iris called frantically. "Lannie, wake up! Lannie!" She tried to pull Lannie to a sitting position, calling to her all the time, briskly patting her face. "Lannie! Lannie!" Lannie kept falling back, her head falling lifelessly first this way and then that, the long reddish hair looking like a wig someone had jammed onto her pale body.

"We're there!" Barney called. He jammed on the brakes and Iris let go of Lannie and fell forward off the seat, banging her head against the front seat. Barney was out and had the door open and was trying to pull Lannie out before Iris could get up. "Run and get some help! Run!" he said.

Iris clambered out past Lannie's head and ran into the hospital.

"Help," she called to the first nurse she saw. It was Nancy Gagnon. She had gone to school with Nancy. "It's Lannie," she called to her. The nurse was running toward her. "She's taken pills," Iris said. Her voice cracked. They ran outside, the nurse ahead, Barney had Lannie out of the car now and Nancy held the doors for him, running ahead, Iris hurrying behind them.

"Call the doctor!" Nancy shouted to an aide and the doctor, his lab coat billowing out behind him, came running from a room at the far end of the hall.

They had her on a stretcher now and were pushing it into the examining room. "Pills," Nancy said to the doctor.

"What did she take?" he asked, his stethoscope out. Iris suddenly thought, I should have brought the pills. Barney reached into his pocket.

"This," he said, handing the doctor the bottle. Dr. Williams took it and read it silently, his lips tight. The nurse was slapping Lannie now, and calling her name loudly.

"When?" the doctor asked. Barney looked at Iris. Lannie made a sound, a faint moan. They all turned to her.

"I don't know," Iris said. The doctor handed the bottle back to Barney and ignoring them, went to Lannie's side. She was pulling her head away from them now and another nurse was running for instruments and machines in one corner of the room. Iris took the bottle from Barney. "Jake Springer" it said. Dizziness struck her. She began to totter as the floor slanted up one way and then down and up again.

"Take Iris out," Dr. Williams said to Barney over his shoulder. "I'll let you know as soon as I can." Nancy held the door open for them. She gave Iris a sympathetic pat on the back before she hurried back to the stretcher and the door swung shut, blocking the view.

Barney had his arms around her and was guiding her to a chair in the waiting room. There was no one else there. Iris was grateful for that.

"They were Jake's pills." she said. "His sleeping pills." She was crying now.

Barney dropped into the chair beside her. "Why?" he asked. "Why would she do that?" He covered his face with his hands. "If she dies . . ." he said. Then Iris remembered that he didn't know that Lannie was pregnant. Not now, she thought. I mustn't tell him now.

Chapter Nine

LANNIE EXTRACTED THE PILLS from the pocket of her skirt. She held up the small, gleaming vial to examine the capsules inside: long, shiny red, pushed in at angles to each other. There had been no time to pick and choose among the bottles on the night table, her only concern that there might not be enough. Hers would not be what psychologists called, in voices tinged with contempt, 'a cry for help.' She could not bear the ignominy of that. It was a full bottle, it was a barbiturate. She would take them all. She did not mean to fail.

She set the bottle on the stand by her bed and looked at it. Looking at it calmed her. She did not tremble as long as she concentrated on the bottle. She felt very heavy, very still. But breathing hurt. She took in pain with each breath. Pain entered her eyes with the light, moved like a wide, relentless river through her organs. She could see it, blue-black, oppressive.

She had given up fighting the pain. There was no use pretending it wasn't there or that she could make it go away. It had been a battle and she had lost. Her opponent was too strong for her. She was defeated. There could be no life for her because the pain had beaten her and she could not endure it.

She did not begin taking the pills immediately. She imagined herself swallowing them, imagined how they would feel in her throat.

She could see that she would have to be careful, swallow them one
at a time, end by end, because they were so large. She did not begin
at once. There was no reason to hurry. This was a sacred time, a
sacred act. It was necessary to give the ceremony its due in dignity
and ritual.

First she undressed slowly, undoing the buttons of her blouse
with care, hanging it and her skirt in the closet with the white louvered doors. She looked out her window at the poplar whose
branches touched the outer wall at the head of her bed for years,
when the wind blew, had lulled her to sleep with their soft scraping.
She looked beyond and below to Iris's garden, the green rows opu-
lent in the harsh sun, and then out past the garden to the carpet of
young, blue-green wheat that reached to the horizon, the mysterious, silent sky. She pulled down the blind slowly, using both hands.
Then she turned away, put on a long, pale nightgown and lay down
on her bed in the now dim and still room. The bed murmured softly
while she settled herself, then held her. She could feel the thick tufts
of chenille under her palms. She closed her eyes. She would think
about her mother, then about her father, then her brother, and her
sister, one by one. She would think about Barney. She would think
about Iris. Then she would think about Armand, about Tim,
about the nameless lovers and their bodies, their voices, their hidden eyes. She would think about the baby. She would not flinch
from any of it.

Later she slept. When Iris and Barney came home she answered
Iris. She was surprised how easy it was. She did not smile or move.
Soon it would be time. She was almost ready. She drifted off to sleep
again.

When she woke she could hear Barney coming down the hall.
Morning. Early. She sat on the side of the bed, pain sweeping
through her body, making her feel faint. She steadied herself and sat
motionless. She would accept the pain now. It would be her com-
panion. She would embrace it.

Dr. Williams was speaking to Iris. They were sitting in a small, white-painted office off the hospital's only nursing station. The desk Dr. Williams was sitting at had a sheet of glass over the top. The desk was clean except for a small blue notepad he had taken out of his pocket. It looked as though the doctor rarely sat there. They had closed the door behind them but Iris could hear the nurse and an aide chattering on the other side. As if nothing had happened, Iris thought angrily. Again she saw in a flash Lannie lying on the bed.

"Pardon?" she said to Dr. Williams. He smiled perfunctorily.

"I say, we must arrange for her to see a psychiatrist. I don't think I can release her until we do." Iris nodded. When Barney started to cry she had gone out. Barney was not a man to cry. He expressed all his emotions through anger. How much he must love Lannie, she thought. She frowned and touched the fingers of one hand to her throat.

"I was going to do that next week," Iris said. "I should have done it sooner, but I didn't know what was wrong or what to do. I just didn't realize." The doctor nodded sympathetically and cleared his throat.

"Do you have any idea why she might have done this at this time?" he asked. Iris found herself studying him, noticing how handsome he was, how smooth-skinned and calm. There was no sign in the neat part in his straight, light-brown hair, or the cool blue of his eyes, that he felt the import of the matter before them. He's too young, she thought. I wonder if he has handled a suicide attempt before. "That is, was there any specific incident involved? A fight with her boyfriend, perhaps?" He smiled encouragingly at her and she saw how white and straight his teeth were, gleaming in his tanned face. She hesitated, but she would have to tell him.

"She's pregnant," Iris said. She made a helpless gesture and then let her hands fall. Dr. Williams looked startled and began to rise, and then, changing his mind, sat down again.

"I see," he said. He picked up his pen and rolled it between his smooth, tapering brown hands. "A few weeks? You should have told me at once."

"I don't know," Iris said. "I guess so. She's only been home six weeks or so."

"From college?"

"Yes."

"She was refused an abortion, perhaps?"

"I don't know," Iris said again. "I just found out, but . . . I guess she couldn't decide what to do about it, I mean . . ." The doctor lowered his eyes from hers.

"Of course," he murmured. "Well, there hasn't been any sign. She hasn't lost it." Iris was thinking, now maybe she'll talk. Now she'll have to talk to me. Again she saw through the crack between the door and its frame, Barney crying by Lannie's bed and she frowned without realizing it. The doctor was studying her with his neat blue eyes.

"I just found out," Iris said. "She didn't tell me." The poor girl, she thought, the poor little girl. "I didn't have a chance to tell Barney," she explained, "and before anything is decided, I want to tell him." The doctor made a doodle on the pad in front of him. "The baby," Iris said, "will it be . . . damaged?" She held her breath. Flooding over her was the realization of what a baby meant. Suddenly she longed for it, longed to hold its warm weight in her arms, to touch her face against its silky skin, to inhale its sweet smell. There had been an ache there, an absence she hadn't even known about and suddenly it had revealed itself. For a second she was stunned.

"I can't be sure, of course," Dr. Williams said carefully. "But that she didn't abort spontaneously is a good sign." Iris's fingers were tangling with the lace collar of her blouse. She wasn't listening to him.

Lannie opened her eyes. And knew instantly that she had failed. The smell. A hospital. She closed her eyes, thinking of nothing, sinking again into blackness. There was a sound, an insistent sound; it stood out over the humming, rose above the blackness, pulling her up with it. Her eyes opened. The light hurt. She moved her head to one side. A quarter of an inch. It felt like a very long way. The room spun. She felt something cold touching her upper lip, her cheek. There was a tube in her nose.

Someone was leaning against the wall. A man. Barney. His back was to her, he was leaning on his arm. He was crying. That was the noise. He bent one knee and drew in his breath in a long, painful rasp and pushed his other fist against the wall. She closed her eyes.

When she opened them he was sitting beside her. Someone was holding her hand. Barney. He held it too tightly. She moved it. Their eyes met. His were swollen and red.

"Lannie," he said. "Lannie." She watched tears fill his eyes and spill over. He bent and kissed her face, her hair.

Suddenly Lannie realized that he was crying about her. About her. What does this mean, she thought, and the room began to pitch again. This wasn't what she wanted. To be awake through her own funeral. But I am alive, she reminded herself. That she had tried so hard, as hard as one could, to die, and still lived. She was filled with awe. It rose in her like a cloud.

"Uncle Barney?" she whispered. She lifted her hand and he took it in his again. She could feel how warm it was and how big. It enclosed hers. She wanted to tell him that she knew who he was now. He was her uncle who had raised her and who loved her. She tried to speak, but felt as if she might faint. The edges of her vision blackened and then cleared.

"I didn't know you loved me," she whispered.

"What?" he said.

"I didn't know," she took a breath, "you loved me." His face showed his astonishment, he didn't say anything. She could see hurt creeping into his eyes.

"Is that why?" he asked. "Because you didn't think we loved you?" His voice was louder. Lannie couldn't look at him.

"No," she said. She took a long, quavering breath.

"Why?" He had never talked to her, not since she had begun to grow. He didn't trust himself with her. "Why?" he asked again. She began to cry. Weakness overtook her, she could not even lift her hand. She thought how he would hate her when he knew.

"I'm pregnant," she said. He didn't move, didn't speak. The colour left his face, he closed his eyes. Now he had some of the pain too. She had planted it in him, she could imagine it growing inside him, a small, purple bruise.

Iris and Dr. Williams were finished their consultation. He held the door open for her as she walked through. The nurses in the nursing station stopped talking as Iris went past them, but she wasn't paying any attention to them. She was concentrating on the squares of sunlight lying at regular intervals down the long, tiled floor of the hallway. The television was on in the sunroom, a faint electronic murmur from far away. There was an unaccountable constriction in her chest.

"We can talk more tomorrow," Dr. Williams said, and looked at his watch. Iris remembered hearing that his wife had left him. She wondered why. He walked briskly away from her and disappeared into one of the rooms down the hall, shutting the door behind him.

For a moment Iris felt lost. She pushed her hair back from her face and turned toward Lannie's room. Hearing footsteps behind her, she turned around. A young man, very tall, with uncombed, curly, blonde hair, wearing jeans and workboots and a green plaid jacket, was coming down the hall toward her, looking directly at her as though he knew who she was and wanted to speak to her. Suddenly she remembered.

"Tim?"

"Yeah," he said, stopping just in front of her. "Tim Quenell. You're Lannie's aunt?"

"Yes," she said. "How did you know?"

"She has your picture in her apartment," he said. His expression was worried, intense and searching. What a mess he is, she thought, all rumpled and unironed, unbuttoned and untied. She wanted to straighten his collar and smooth his jacket, to lend him her comb.

"But how did you know to come here?" she asked.

"I was hungry," he said. "I thought I'd eat at the cafe before I went out to your place. I overheard it there." He shrugged his shoulders indicating that he understood the pain this might cost Iris, but couldn't help it. Iris sighed and shook her head. What could you expect.

"That's a small town for you," she said. He ran one hand through his hair and then put both hands on his hips, his lips compressed with concern.

"Is she all right?" he asked.

"She'll be all right," Iris said. She remembered the baby and added, "I guess," without looking at him.

"Can I see her?" he asked. So this is the father, Iris thought. "I want to talk to her," he said. "May I see her?"

"I'll have to see," Iris said. "You can't see her unless the doctor says it's all right." She turned to the nursing station behind them, where Mrs. Gagnon was pretending to fill in charts, listening to them. "Nancy?" Iris said.

"Yes," Nancy said in a brisk nurse's voice.

"May Lannie have another visitor?"

"Not yet," Nancy replied. "Only family for now."

"He's come from Saskatoon," Iris said. Out of the corner of her eye, she could see Barney coming out of Lannie's room a few doors down the hall.

"He'll have to wait until tomorrow," Nancy said. Iris turned toward Barney, who was near them now. Intending to introduce him to Tim, she stepped into his path. His face was pale under his tan, his mouth was set and thin. He hadn't even seen her and Tim until she stepped in front of him.

"Barney?" she said. He stepped around her, glancing up at Tim.

He wavered for a second, almost stopped. His expression changed and for a second Iris thought he was going to hit Tim and then he controlled himself, strode past them and out of the hospital, letting the glass door swing and swing behind him.

Iris stood, baffled, glanced at Tim, who also looked puzzled. Suddenly Iris understood. Barney knew Lannie was pregnant. Either he had figured it out or Lannie had told him, which meant she was awake, Iris thought, although at the same time she was thinking, oh, no. And then that thought pushed all others out of her mind. Barney knew and he was hurt and angry. He was very angry. She hadn't expected this. She started for Lannie's room again and then remembered Tim.

"Tomorrow?" she asked. He looked terribly disappointed. He closed and opened his eyelids and tears caught in his thick white lashes. Seeing this, Iris was brought back to him, to his presence, his place in this. "You'll stay with us tonight," she said. "I won't go back till visiting hours are over, but if you can find the way, just drive out and make yourself comfortable."

"No," he said at once, firmly. "I'll wait here. Even if I can't see her." She patted his arm, but could think of nothing more to say. The look on Barney's face, his tears, came between her and Tim and she was distracted.

"I'll just . . ." she murmured, turning from him. When she reached the door of Lannie's room, she paused before pushing it open.

Lannie was lying quietly, her arms by her sides, apparently asleep. The IV bottle dripped a colourless fluid down a tube into a needle in her arm. There was a little colour in her cheeks now.

"Lannie?" Iris said softly, but the slender body lay still, the chest rising and falling with slow regularity. The measured drip, the slow rise and fall, the room was calm. Iris stepped backward out of the room and pulled the door shut noiselessly. It would have to wait. It would all have to wait. She looked at her watch. Three o'clock. She was surprised to find so much time had passed, and now she realized that she was hungry, that she wanted to get out of the hospital and breathe fresh air.

At the nursing station she stopped to say to Nancy, who was getting ready to go off shift, "I'm going out for a sandwich. I should be back in a half hour or so."

"Fine," Nancy said. "I'll tell Mrs. Sawatsky where you are so she can call you if Lannie wants you."

"She's asleep," Iris said.

"She'll be sleepy for a day or two," Nancy replied. They nodded at each other. Iris paused at the waiting room, intending to take Tim with her. He was sitting with his long legs stretched out in front of him, his body slouched, his eyes closed. How young he is, she thought. How could he ever take care of a wife and baby? With his wide shoulders and narrow hips, he seemed strung out on a large, bony frame. She could see that he was not yet fully grown, that he would fill out more in the next few years as he became a man. And yet, despite his size, there was something tender about him, about his flesh, about the bones of his wrists, and his keen eyes. Then she remembered Barney and hurried outside, turning toward the parking lot, searching with her eyes for their car. It was gone. She turned back thoughtfully and started walking downtown.

Twice she passed someone on the way to the cafe, smiled politely, and kept going. She was determined not to give anybody the opportunity to question her about Lannie, would do her best not to reveal anything. Let them wonder. She would wrest as much privacy for Lannie as she could. With every step she was aware of the town's eyes on her and she wished Barney were with her.

It was a lovely spring day, the air warm but not yet hot. The lilacs had come into bloom, it seemed overnight, and the air was laden with their scent. Savouring the sweetness, she almost forgot Lannie, was almost able to put Barney's flight, his rage, out of her mind. She supposed he had gone home. He had nowhere else to go without abandoning everything and she knew Barney that well. He would never give up. Thank God he wasn't given to drinking when things went wrong, like Luke, like Howard.

Hank Osborne was coming out of the cafe as she was about to enter it. He held the door open for her and said, "You doing okay, Iris?" She was about to dodge under his arm, but paused, remembering and seeing again that he still held a great affection for her, that there was a wistfulness about him in her presence.

"I'm fine, Hank," she said, almost crying.

"She okay?" he asked. His head was bent toward her and she could smell the coffee on his breath. It dried her tears and she thought, why is it that some people can never be anything but distasteful to certain other people? And regretting again that long-ago intimacy with him, she thought, are we never allowed to forget our past mistakes?

"Yes," Iris said. "Thanks." She hurried past him and past the quickly averted faces of the dozen or so people sitting in the booths or at the counter.

She sat down in a booth. The waitress came quickly, maybe she understood that Iris would not want to wait. It was the same thin, dark woman who waited on Barney the night Lannie came home on the bus. Iris ordered a tuna sandwich and coffee. People passed her booth, coming or going, and said hello, their voices and faces solemn. She was struck by the hypocrisy. They want to know everything, she thought. They want her to die, so they'll have something to talk about. They . . . and she stopped, shocked at her own thoughts. The Harknesses, who had just passed her, were decent people, friends of her parents, they had had their share of troubles. The waitress set her sandwich in front of her. Iris pulled it closer to her and saw that her hand had begun to tremble. Milt Harkness had left one booth between them and was sliding into the next one, his leather jacket squeaking against the vinyl booth. Somebody laughed quietly at the counter and voices murmured in undertones behind her. Milt hadn't changed in thirty years, since she could remember, he still wore ranchers' clothes even though he hadn't had a horse or a cow for the last fifteen years, always courteous, especially to women, a little shy, an old-fashioned man. How could she think such things about him? Well, she thought, maybe it didn't apply to him, but not everybody is kind. Not everybody in this town is decent.

She ate her sandwich carefully, bite by bite, tasting none of it. She should have stayed at the hospital, where nobody hid things, where everything was out in the open and you could call a spade a spade. She had to hide a smile at that thought, what a shocking thing to say, she said to herself. Again dismayed by her wayward thoughts, she said, my God, what's happening to me? And replied to herself, it's because I can't quite get hold of this awful thing that's happened. I can't get used to it. Oh, where is Barney when I need him? She took a deep breath and tried to calm herself.

When she was finished, she paid for her lunch and left without looking at anyone. The cafe had been quiet while she was in it and as the door closed behind her and she was out on the sidewalk, she could imagine the level of the voices rising. She hurried back to the hospital, noticing that their car was still not in the parking lot.

She pushed open the glass door into the hospital. James. She had better call James and let him know where she was. The phone was in the waiting room, between the entrance and the nursing station. She would have to be careful.

Tim was awake now and standing at the window, but he didn't turn when she came in.

"Tim," she said. He jumped. "I'm back." He smiled at her and sat down on one of the dark green vinyl couches. They were too low for him and his knees bent up at an awkward angle. She put a dime in the pay phone and dialled James's number.

"Iris?" he said. His voice was full of relief. "I have to talk to you about that girl. Where have you been?" He spoke quickly, which he never did, so she knew he was agitated.

"I'm calling from the hospital, James," she said. "From the waiting room," she added pointedly. He was silent, absorbing this.

"Why are you there?" he asked. His voice was flat, cautious.

"Lannie, Lannie isn't . . . well," Iris said. "I'm here with her." Again he was silent, thinking. She wished Tim would go for a walk. She wanted to talk to James. She had to talk to him.

"She . . . she took my pills," he said. "I tried to phone you today when I realized what must have happened, that they hadn't just rolled under the bed or something."

"She's going to be fine," Iris said.

"My God," he said softly. Neither spoke. Then he said, "You know . . . what the trouble is?" Iris glanced at Tim. He doesn't know, she thought. Tim doesn't know.

"Yes," she said. "I know." Tim sighed heavily and threw the magazine back on the pile. He sat forward, his elbows on his knees, his fingers outspread and thrust into the tangled curls of his hair. She noticed how long his fingers were, his short, clean nails.

"Can I come and see her?" James asked.

"Tomorrow," she said. His voice softened.

"Are you all right, sweetheart?" he asked. For a moment she forgot Tim was there.

"Yes," she whispered. "I'm fine, I'm okay. You come tomorrow. I'll be here."

"Good," he said.

"Good-bye."

"Good-bye." They hung up together. Iris turned to Tim.

"Why don't you go for a walk," she suggested. "I'm going to stay with her till visiting hours are over at eight. Then we'll go back to the farm."

"I might," he cleared his throat. "I might do that." Iris smiled at him and started down the hall.

Barney could hear the glass door swinging behind him. He didn't care, let it bang, let it bang. His hand was on the car door before he realized he was there. In one move he swung the door open, got in and pulled it shut. His other hand was already turning the key. He was out of the parking lot and turning down the street, carelessly, recklessly, when he realized the car was headed for home. He concentrated on the feel of the steering wheel, on avoiding the ruts, on the sound of the motor, was it missing on one cylinder? Lannie . . . hadn't he just changed the oil? How could she have . . . the car swerved. He righted it and then slowed down because he remembered the feel of the drive into town with her in the back seat dead, dead he had thought, and he fell against the steering wheel and the car almost stopped before he sat straight again and put his foot back on the accelerator. His gut hurt. God it hurt. He straightened his back and blew out air. That didn't help. He rubbed his chest roughly, then put his hand back on the steering wheel. Jesus Christ, he thought, hanging onto the steering wheel, would he never get home? Lannie . . . the look in her eyes as they'd met his when she'd told him. He turned into the lane leading to the house.

He pulled up in front of the garage, shut off the motor, and then hit the wheel once, hard, with his fist, and put his hand across his chest and then lowered it. Nothing would stop the anger. He opened the car door and got out.

The house—big, painted dark brown with white trim, the blinds upstairs pulled. He didn't want to go into its dusky emptiness. There was no help there.

He began to walk, past his shop, past the row of grain bins. The crop grew in a curving line around the yard, behind the buildings and the line of pines down the driveway and the poplar bluffs at the borders. It was a smooth mat of green now, rising to meet the horizon on all sides. He felt drawn toward its green richness. For some reason it made him think of her, of Lannie. She was pregnant.

Lannie . . . pregnant. Some goddamn kid—he could see them—he could . . . he tried to shut that picture out of his mind, and the other one too, the shining whiteness of her skin, the silky red-gold of her hair, her small pink-tipped breasts. He forced his eyes to take in the crop, willed himself to think, looks good this year, seeded to just the right depth, it was blurring and he wondered why, and then he felt the tears running down his cheeks.

He wiped his eyes. Did all fathers feel this way about their daughters? Was it normal? He didn't know. He hadn't really thought of himself as a father before. But this, this . . . thing that had happened to her made him realize that he was a father. Her father. He saw her naked beauty again and shifted his feet nervously. This wasn't right, he had no right to think these things, but God, she was so beautiful, so beautiful. There was no one worthy of her, no one. He put his hands over his face and cried.

Lannie was asleep, Iris keeping vigil at her side. Her closed eyelids reminded Iris of fine china, white, blue-tinged and fragile. The freckles across the smooth, delicate skin of her nose were so faded they were barely noticeable anymore. The fragility of the girl touched Iris again as it had years before when Lannie stood in her kitchen, thin, pale, and withdrawn. How Iris had wanted to smother Lannie in her arms that morning, but she had been rebuffed, almost frightened by the impenetrability of Lannie's frozen grief and pride, and so had held back.

Now she knew she'd made a mistake. She should have caught Lannie in her arms, held her, rocked her, not stopped till Lannie had warmed and relaxed, cried, slept. She would never be able to forgive herself for her stupidity. Never. From that morning on Lannie never unbent. Why? Out of pride, fear of rebuff, or loss, or confusion about where her loyalties should lie? She thought children needed a measured, dependable life, that they needed good clothes, rooms of their own, nourishing meals, and affection. She thought that was all they needed and she had given Lannie that, she was sure she had. But she had been wrong. Children needed something more, at least Lannie did, and she didn't know what it was and worse, she hadn't even tried to find out. She had failed Lannie, she was responsible for this, and she felt the full weight of her guilt.

Lannie's eyelids fluttered, opened, her amber-coloured eyes were clear now.

"Iris," she whispered. Iris bent her head close to her. "Do you know that Iris is the goddess of the rainbow?" Iris drew back. "I always wanted to tell you that," she said. Her eyes were already closing. She was asleep again.

Iris was so touched and shamed by this that she began to cry. Then she stopped herself. No more tears, she thought. Tears are useless. They are selfish, because they're comforting and distracting. I must keep my mind on what I've done.

At eight o'clock, when the bell sounded to end visiting hours, (and Barney still had not come), she rose from the chair by Lannie's bed and went out of the room. As the door closed behind her, a wave of relief and exhaustion swept over her and she leaned against the smooth, white wall in the hallway and closed her eyes. Other visitors began to come from the other rooms and stood chatting in the hall. She straightened abruptly, and walked with firm steps past the nursing station.

Tim was leaning against a window frame, examining the fingers of one hand. He looked bored. When he saw her he pushed himself away from the window and looked at her expectantly.

"She's asleep," Iris said. "Let's go." Together, Tim holding the door open for her, they left the hospital.

"Does she know I'm here?" he asked.

"I'll tell her tomorrow," Iris said. He mustn't know about the baby. She wouldn't tell him.

"Over here," he said, pointing to the car. It was an old, dark green station wagon. "My father's," he explained, and this made Iris like him better.

They didn't talk on the way to the farm except for Iris telling him when to turn. She was very tired and Tim seemed to know this and kept quiet because of it. She was surprised to find such perceptivity in one so young.

She didn't know how Barney would react to having Tim under their roof now that he knew who Tim was. She didn't know how to cope with what she had seen on Barney's face. She hoped only that he was home and not somewhere else, because at least then she could talk to him. She leaned her head back against the headrest and closed her eyes.

Their car was in the driveway. So Barney was at home, he was not completely out of control. They pulled up in the gravel circle behind the Chrysler. Tim shut the motor off but made no move to get out of the car. Iris opened her door and as she got out, Tim opened his too and climbed out. He leaned on the car and looked around.

It was a calm evening, warm, sweet-smelling, barely twilight. The red-winged blackbirds were calling to each other in their high-pitched trill and a magpie flew straight as an arrow past them into the poplars. Tim straightened and followed Iris into the house. Barney's jacket was lying on the couch in the living room, but he was nowhere in sight.

"I went back to the cafe for supper," Tim said, before she could speak. "If you don't mind, I'd just like to go to bed. I'm wiped." Iris noticed then how tired he was, that what she had thought was boredom was, in fact, exhaustion. *So he is feeling the shock and strain.* Iris was glad of this for Lannie's sake. She led him upstairs to the guest bedroom next door to Lannie's room. He tossed his leather satchel onto the floor and sat down on the side of the bed. He put his head in his hands.

"I love her," he said, his voice muffled from behind his hands. "I really love her." He was crying. Iris was touched. She tried to think what to say to comfort him.

"Tomorrow," she said finally. "You'll see her tomorrow." He nodded without taking his hands away, and then made a gesture with one hand that said, never mind, it's okay, never mind. She went out quietly and closed the door behind her.

The door to Lannie's room stood open. That looked strange, because it had always been closed, closed for so many years. She wondered if they had left it open in the morning or if Barney had been in there since. She thought about closing it and then did not do it. Barney was in their room, sitting in the wine velvet, wing-backed chair in the corner. She didn't think she had ever seen him sit in it before. Usually he came in, pulled off his clothes, showered, and threw himself into bed.

When she entered, he looked up at her, his face puffy, his eyes dark and rimmed with red, and then he looked away again.

Iris walked across the dim room to him, her feet silent on the thick, pearl-gray carpet. She kissed his forehead without speaking. He didn't move or look at her. She went into their bathroom, undressed, washed and brushed her teeth. It wasn't even nine o'clock but she was so tired the only thing she wanted was to go to bed.

When she came out of the bathroom Barney had still not moved. She stood naked in front of the dresser and found a clean nightgown—it was pale turquoise with lace across the breasts and down the skirt—and put it on. Barney watched her from the chair. When she was leaning against her plumped-up pillows in bed, the blankets folded down below her breasts, he stood up slowly, undressed, and got into bed beside her.

She turned to him, running her hands over his body, kissing him. She wanted to comfort him. She could think of no other way.

"I can't," he said.

"Don't be angry with her, dear," Iris said.

"I'm not angry with her," Barney said. It was true. He wasn't angry with Lannie. Not with Lannie. He was angry, but he didn't know with whom. He turned to Iris and buried his face in her shoulder. Iris held him. Betrayed, he thought. That was it. He pulled away from Iris. He felt betrayed. But then he was confused again, because Lannie wasn't his, not that way. She was his daughter.

"Iris," he said. "I feel so . . . what I feel is so . . . wrong." Iris was holding him and kissing his face.

"It's all right, darling," she said. "It's all right. It's just that it was such a shock." She was running her fingers in and out of his thick hair, allowing it to curl around her fingers and then sliding free. "Tomorrow it will make more sense. You'll feel more like yourself after a good night's sleep." Barney was weeping again, but silently. He knew now that he could not tell Iris, that she wouldn't understand. He tried to stop his tears. Iris was thinking, he'll get over it. She tightened her arms around him. Already he's getting over it. But, she thought, will things ever be the same again?

Chapter Ten

IRIS WOKE, SEEING THE RUSH to the hospital, Lannie's clammy, bluish-tinged skin, the nurse slapping her, her head flopping back her hair dancing around her face and shoulders. She sat up, threw back the covers and was about to leap out of bed to . . . to do what? She sat still. Raising both hands, she pushed her hair back from her face. Her head felt heavy, thick, a dull ache was starting behind her forehead. The bed beside her was empty. Where was Barney?

When she stood up and reached for the kimono, draped over the chair by the bed, an unexpected soreness in her thighs made her wince and she remembered being wakened in the night by Barney holding her by the shoulders, shoving her legs apart, pressing his mouth over hers, pinning her with his body. When it was over, he had thrown himself aside, one arm over his face, and she had lain beside him, stunned. Almost at once he had turned back to her and run his fingers slowly, with infinite tenderness, through her tangled hair and held her against him, caressing her skin with his fingertips and kissing her face, her throat, until lulled, she had gone to sleep again. Now there was only the soreness in her thighs to remind her it had not been a dream. She pulled on the dressing gown and stepped into her slippers, which were tucked under the bed and half-hidden beneath the tumbled coverlet. She stretched one arm up, the wide sleeve of the gown falling back, and lifted her hair out from inside the collar, then touched her temples briefly with her fingertips.

First she would call the hospital and see how Lannie was this morning. She could smell coffee as soon as she opened the bedroom door. It was no wonder Barney couldn't sleep. The wonder was that she had. She went down the hall, her small silver slippers making a brushing sound on the carpet, remembering Tim when she saw the closed guest room door.

She went down the stairs to the kitchen. Barney was at the kitchen table, wearing a grey and beige plaid shirt, the sleeves rolled up above the elbow showing his heavy forearms, his arms bent to hold a coffee cup, knotting the muscle of his upper arm so that the shirt stretched and distorted the pattern of the plaid. His head was bent forward, his hair glistened blonde in the morning sun, his neck was red from the wind, his face pale under his year-round tan. She couldn't see his expression.

She touched his shoulder lightly, without speaking, when she passed him to go to the phone. She could feel him watching her as she looked up the hospital number and dialled it. Barney put his arms out on the table. The bleached hairs on his forearms glinted.

"It's Iris," Iris said into the phone. Her voice was too soft to disturb the quiet in the room. The coffee pot on the stove ticked now and then, and the early morning sun lit up the room with its clear light. "How is Lannie this morning?" She could hear a clatter on the other end of the line, breakfast trays maybe, or an aide gathering an armful of charts to mark in the morning temperatures.

"She had a comfortable night," Nancy replied. "She's fine this morning. The doctor has been to see her."

"Can we come in an hour or so to visit her?"

"I think the doctor would allow it," Nancy said. "But there's no need. She's still drowsy and I expect she'll sleep most of the morning."

"I see." Iris was silent for a moment. "Will you tell her good morning if she wakes, and we'll be in this afternoon?"

"Of course, Iris," Nancy said. "Now don't worry. She's going to be fine." Iris set the phone down carefully. She went to her usual place across from Barney and sat down.

"She's fine," she said. Barney raised his eyes from his coffee cup to meet hers and then looked down again.

"I have to talk to you, Barney," Iris said. This time Barney shot a rapid glance at her and then dropped his eyes quickly. Iris wanted to let the silence go on and on in the kitchen. She wanted to sit forever in her silver and pink kimono and watch the threads catch the light and sparkle, to listen to the meadowlark calling out in the yard, and not move and not think. She put her head in one hand, her elbow on the table, the sleeve of the gown slipping back again so that her soft white forearm was bared, and toyed with her coffee cup with the other hand, then pushed it away.

"I didn't know Lannie was pregnant," she said. Barney picked up his spoon and began to stir his coffee. "Angie phoned," she put her arm down, "and I was on my way to talk to her. That's when I found her." She put her hand on Barney's, the one that was still stirring, and he stopped. "That's why I didn't tell you, Barney. I didn't know." He didn't look at her and she took her hand away and waited. When he didn't speak or give any sign that he was going to, she said, "Tim must be the father. But I'm sure he doesn't know." She waited again. "He loves her, Barney. He told me so last night and I believe him."

"He bloody well better," Barney said, turning his head so that he was looking into the sunshine out the back door.

"But listen, Barney, I have to talk to her today and I'm not sure . . ." She began again. "No, I feel sure I know the best thing to do, but I need to know what you think." Barney kept his head stubbornly turned away from her. "I'm going to have to convince her to have an abortion." There seemed now to be a tremor in the air between them, and Iris could feel her heart begin to flutter in her throat. She swallowed and it stopped. Barney had gone pale again. She held her breath, frightened by the look on his face.

"An abortion?" he said, slowly, not speaking to her.

"It's the best thing," she said, leaning toward him, trying to make him help her. "She isn't married, she's not . . . settled in her mind. And . . . the baby might be retarded or something, from the pills, I mean." Barney didn't speak and her voice trailed off. The coffee gave a little hiccup from the stove. Barney's gold wedding ring shone. She couldn't take her eyes off it. For a terrible moment, she was not sure she was right. She almost threw herself against him, her arms raised and head bent. You decide, she wanted to say. You decide.

"Yeah," he said. "I guess you're right." He rubbed his forehead with the side of one hand. "It's better the boy doesn't know so he can't pressure her." He paused. Angrily, in a bitter voice, he said, "Better that she just get rid of it." Iris drew back, placing her hands on the edge of the table, her mouth opening. She felt as though he had slapped her.

"I don't think abortion is right," she said. "But the world isn't perfect, it's a mess, and what's the poor girl to do?" Her voice was blurring, she could hear it herself. She couldn't see Barney clearly for her tears. "I'd love a baby," she said, crossing her arms across her chest. "I'd love it," she said, tears streaming now. "I'd look after it. I'd . . ." Barney had put his hand over hers and with the other she found a crumpled tissue in the pocket of her kimono. She wiped her eyes. When she had control of herself, she said, "But one woman can't raise another woman's child. I found that out." She could imagine Lannie swallowing the pills and almost broke into tears again. "Oh, Barney," she said. "Why didn't we have a baby of our own?" Barney dropped her hand and covered his eyes.

"Don't, Iris," he said. She sniffed and blew her nose. They both fell silent, Iris wiping her eyes now and then. After a while Barney pushed back his chair and went outside.

His feet led him across the yard to the shop. This morning, he could tell that spring, the season of hope, was almost over. Summer was about to begin. The sky was clear and pale. Soon it would seem to rise, there would be a greater distance between sky and earth, the ground would dry and turn to powder underfoot, the heat would make the hills shimmer and dance, and the heavy scents of flowers and grasses in the air would fade and disappear, be replaced by the faint smell of wheat ripening in the vast yellow fields, by the peppery odour of sage and dust and the hot sun.

He had finished all the spring work: the seeding, the summerfallowing, the machinery repair. He should be in the house doing books. But when he was troubled, he couldn't concentrate on bookkeeping, then he needed to be outdoors where he could find small jobs to keep himself busy, and look up at the sky now and then.

Pigeons swooped out of the shop when he entered, their wings beating the chilly air. He felt the dampness on his back and shivered. He walked around the combine once, speculatively. No, too soon to worry about servicing. He checked the seed boxes on the drill. Clean. He had cleaned them out right after seeding. The shop was neat, his tools in place. He sat down on his workbench, his brown workboots set apart on the smooth grey cement floor. Putting his hands on his knees he leaned back. His machinery loomed over him, monstrous in the dim light.

This morning he kept seeing her as a little girl, and that was odd because it seemed to him that she had always been more like a grown-up than a child. She had never chattered, never skipped around a room or been caught jumping on the furniture or giggling till midnight with a friend in her room. Iris often seemed more like a child to him than Lannie. Iris could get a certain look on her face that was just like a child. Lannie never did. He had always thought of them as his women. He put his hand over his eyes and then lowered it wearily. Maybe that was where he had gone wrong. Thinking of Lannie as one of his women, forgetting, because of the way she always sat unsmiling, watching, with that air of waiting, that she was only a child. He stood up and walked around his combine again.

But why was she that way? Why? Howard, the answer came, she

was waiting for Howard. He stopped short, breathing in the realization with the smell of oil and gasoline and dust, the sound of wings
beating in his ears. He took out his handkerchief and wiped his
mouth and his forehead, where beads of sweat had suddenly
appeared. He sat down on his workbench again. She was waiting for
her father to come for her. All these years and she was still waiting.
He looked down at his workboots, resting his arms on his thighs.
The toes were scuffed, almost worn through to the metal caps. He
should buy new boots.

He thought about his own father. Look how we fight, he said to
himself. Sometimes I think I hate the bastard and he sure acts like
he hates me. But at least I know where he is. I know how he feels
about me. And I know that if I went back home this morning, just
like that, gave everything up, he'd take me in.

And Lannie doesn't know anything, she just keeps hoping. He
felt as though someone had punched him in the gut. He tried to
relieve the pain spreading upward to his chest by stretching his torso
and taking deep breaths.

It wasn't right, it wasn't natural. But then, he thought, how the
hell would I know. I'm the man who gave up his family when I saw
something that I thought looked better. So who am I to talk about
what is natural? She wanted her father, that was all, and she had
finally given up waiting. He walked to the door of the shop and
stood staring out across his fields.

Again he saw her body, shining white, in the doorway of her
room, that morning years ago. All right, he said to himself, all right.
He had never touched her. He never would. He hadn't done any
harm that way. He would never do her any harm. Everyone has a
secret, he thought. Everyone, and this is mine.

When he came in for lunch, Tim was in the kitchen with Iris.
He had turned one of the kitchen chairs around to face Iris at the
counter and he was sprawled on it, his long, blue-jeaned legs
stretched out in front of him, his feet in boots, his faded blue

denim shirt wrinkled and the collar turned inside on one side. As the door swung shut behind Barney, Tim rose to his feet, brushed his hair down nervously with one hand and put the other out toward Barney.

For a split second Barney wanted to hit him. He put his hand out and said curtly, in reply to Iris's introduction, "Hello." Then he went into the half-bath and shut the door. When he came out, he felt calmer. Iris, passing him with a dish of food, stretched upward and pecked his cheek. He didn't respond. He wanted to, but couldn't in Tim's presence. The boy's height, and long arms and legs, seemed to take up too much room, to fill the kitchen, and his nervous quietness only irritated Barney more.

They began to eat. Tim ate slowly, politely. Barney kept stealing glances at him. He looked tired. There were blue smudges in the pale skin under his eyes and there was something about the way he cut his meat and lifted his fork that told Barney he was upset, not noticing what he was doing. He felt sorry for the boy suddenly, and was surprised at himself.

He was surprised too, now that he noticed, that Iris had cooked a roast for their noon meal. She didn't usually do that, he didn't think. As if she knew what he was thinking she said, "I had it out to thaw for supper last night. Then nobody ate supper." She gave a small, nervous laugh, and touched her fingers to her throat. It occurred to him that she always made that little gesture, especially when she was nervous. He had never noticed that before.

"You go to school?" he said to Tim.

"Yes," Tim said. "I take an English class with Lannie. That's how I met her." His eyes met Barney's and both men looked away quickly. Barney saw that Lannie's shining hair, her fine-boned face, her pale skin, had flashed in front of Tim too. He could barely swallow.

"What are you going in for?" he asked. Tim didn't reply for a moment.

"Well, my father has a service station." He set his fork down.

"But there's no future in that," he said. "He leases it from one of the big oil companies. You know how that is. He could be wiped out tomorrow. I try to tell him to get out . . ." His voice was growing louder, tighter. He picked up his fork again. Barney watched him.

"You studying to be an engineer?" he asked.

"No," Tim said. "I guess I'm not studying to be anything." He laughed as if he were near tears and blinked several times. Iris was silent, listening. There was a gopher in the yard nearby and they could hear its shrill whistle. "I'm a writer," Tim said finally. "A poet." No one spoke. Tim seemed to be waiting. He kept his eyes on his plate, his fork poised above it.

"A poet?" Barney said, as though he wasn't sure what this meant.

"Yes," Tim said. He made a gesture with one hand and opened his mouth and then closed it again. He had given up pretending to eat. He put his arm on the table and shaded his eyes with his hand as if the sunlight in the room were too bright. Barney was silent.

"How do poets earn a living?" he asked at last.

"They work in service stations," Tim said. "They teach." He laughed without mirth. "They starve." Barney poked at his mashed potatoes.

"Well," Iris said. "I guess money's not that important."

"How the hell would you know?" Barney said, and then, seeing her hurt, surprised look, he brushed his hand across his face and then touched hers, the one that lay innocently by her plate and said, "I'm sorry, Iris. I'm upset today. I didn't sleep too well." She forced herself to smile.

"That's all right," she said. "We're all upset." Soon she was picking up the half-full plates and taking them to the counter.

"I baked a pie," she said. "Anybody feel like a piece? It's cherry."

When they had finished eating, Barney and Iris drove to the hospital with Tim following behind in his father's old green station wagon. In the hospital parking lot, Iris opened her door and started to climb out. Barney hadn't moved or shut off the motor.

"Tell her," he said, and hesitated, "tell her I had to pick up some parts. I'll come later." Iris held the door open.

"All right," she said quietly, and climbed out. She knew Barney had no parts to pick up.

Tim was already waiting for her at the door. She watched Barney turn toward downtown. Maybe he would drink a few cups of coffee in the cafe, chat with the men he'd known all his life, and then he would be able to come back and sit with Lannie. She looked at Tim, hoping he hadn't noticed that she was worried, then suspected that he already knew.

"I'll just see how she is before you go in," she said to Tim. He nodded gravely.

She found Lannie propped up with two large pillows. She was staring straight ahead and barely turned her head when Iris came in. Someone had brushed her hair and it lay spread out around her face on the pillow like a halo. There was a little more colour in her face today.

"Hello, dear," Iris said. She walked to the bed, bent over and brushed Lannie's cheek with her lips, then uncertainly backed away a few steps. It was a big room, empty, and its size and emptiness made the bed with Lannie in it look small. Lannie smiled faintly at her. "Angela phoned from the hospital this morning out to the farm. She wants me to say hi to you. The nurses wouldn't let her in to talk to you so she says she'll be in as soon as they'll let her." Lannie didn't speak. "She had a girl," Iris said. "Seven pounds, nine ounces." Perhaps she shouldn't have mentioned that. "Oh, I'm sorry," she said. Sometimes she was so thoughtless. Lannie made a disparaging noise.

"None of this is your fault," she said softly, without looking at Iris. For a moment Iris couldn't speak.

"Yes," she said. "It's my fault all right." She spoke quietly but with absolute certainty. Lannie didn't respond, as if she might not have heard. Iris took a moment to steady her voice. "Tim is here, dear," she said. "He wants to see you."

"Oh," Lannie said, startled. "I forgot I asked him." She seemed to sink deeper into the pillows.

"Does he know?" Iris asked. "Does he know about the . . . pregnancy?" From now on she would not say 'baby.' Lannie turned her head sharply toward Iris.

"Barney told you?" she asked.

"No," Iris said. "Not Barney. Angela. It doesn't matter, Lannie. I just want to know if Tim knows or not."

"No," Lannie said. It was the old silent Lannie. "I was going to tell him."

"Don't," Iris said. "Don't, Lannie." Lannie was watching her again, puzzled, almost frightened. "I . . ." Iris began. "I don't think you should have this baby." Lannie was still watching her. "Lannie, maybe this isn't the best time to talk about this, but Tim is waiting to see you, and I'm afraid. We've got to settle this now. I don't think it can wait." Lannie had lifted both long-fingered white hands and put them over her face. Then she took them down and in a gesture of resignation let them fall by her sides on the bed.

"All right," she said. She was looking at the wall again. Iris came closer to the bed and, taking the straightbacked metal chair that had been pushed against the wall, brought it closer to Lannie's bedside and sat down.

Now she felt sure of herself. Lannie couldn't make a decision. Barney was so inexplicably disturbed that for the first time in their relationship she couldn't depend on him. The responsibility had fallen into her hands, she had to take control and this afternoon she felt able to handle things herself. There was Lannie, her arms at her sides, her wrists turned up, her palms open, waiting to be told what to do. Iris took a deep breath and then slowly expelled it.

"I think you should have an abortion," she said. "Dr. Williams will make the arrangements for you to see the right people. He says if there aren't any hitches, and in this case he says he doesn't think there will be, it could all be over as soon as two weeks from now."

Lannie moistened her lips and grasped the bedspread with each hand, then released it. Iris began again.

"There are good reasons." Lannie closed her eyes as if each word were a blow. "You have to hear this, Lannie," Iris said, close to tears herself. "You aren't ready to be a mother yet. You're too young. You aren't married." Lannie didn't open her eyes. "The child might be . . . it might be . . . damaged," Iris said. She didn't dare leave this out of the argument for fear that what she had already said wouldn't be enough.

Her words hung in the air between them. A tear slid down the side of Lannie's face and trickled into her hairline. Iris reached into her purse for a tissue and wiped Lannie's temple. She said more gently, "You don't want it, do you?"

"No," Lannie whispered. "I don't think so." She began to cry, hard, silently, her mouth distorted, her breathing quick, tears squeezing out from under her shut eyelids. Iris put a tissue into Lannie's hand and closed the fingers around it.

"I know, dear, I know," she kept saying. When Lannie's crying subsided, Iris said, "Tim is waiting, dear. You won't tell him?" Lannie shook her head. "I'll give you a few minutes," Iris said, "and then I'll send him in."

She went out, closing the door behind her. In the hall she stood for a minute. Her stomach had suddenly gone queasy. What had she done? It was, it felt like, her own flesh and blood she was killing. That's what it was—killing. If it was the wrong thing to do, and how did she know if it was or not, she, Iris, had to take the responsibility for it. But then, she thought, Lannie tried to kill herself over this. Somebody has to take the responsibility. She had begun walking toward the waiting room, where she knew Tim would be sitting, listening anxiously for her footsteps. A new weariness overcame her, and she could barely lift her feet to move forward toward him.

She found Tim sitting on one of the old green vinyl couches, a magazine open on his lap. In the light from the window, she saw a depth in his eyes she hadn't noticed before and she was touched, seeing him as a man for the first time. She hesitated, uncertain again, but no, she couldn't take the chance. Lannie came first. She couldn't have a baby. It was unthinkable.

"Tim," she said. He jumped to his feet, knocking the magazine to the floor.

"Can I see her?"

"Yes, but Tim," and then she didn't know what she had been going to say.

"It's all right," he said. "I'll be careful what I say to her." Iris smiled back at him. So Lannie had found someone who cared about her in spite of herself. The complexity of life, this knowledge that was new to her, loomed up and she sank onto the couch in Tim's place and closed her eyes.

Lannie lay listening to the clatter of visitors' heels and the rubber squish of a nurse's feet on the tiled floor of the hall outside her closed door. Occasionally she could hear a fragment of a sentence, only to have the rest fade out as the speaker entered the room across the hall or moved away down the hall. Rubber-tired carts went by and trays rattled and sometimes the vacuum cleaner whirred. It was slowly coming home to her that she was alive. She had a picture of the rest of the hospital as life, especially the hall, and her room was closed off and silent, not part of it, but whenever the door opened and a nurse or the doctor or a visitor came in, life came in with them. Soon they would make her open her door and go into the hall. They would not let her stay safely in this room forever. She would have to step back into life again, like it or not.

She did not know how all this happened, how she came to be here. But when she woke in the hospital the world did not seem the same. The colour had returned to the things she looked at, the light seemed clearer. The great weight that had been pressing down on her, preventing her from moving, seemed to have been lifted.

And her pregnancy, which had been a living nightmare, a monster that followed her everywhere, she did not know how it had gotten so big, was now reduced to the shape of a problem. It was bad, but it had retreated into the realm of ordinary things that happened to ordinary people and she could face it. Why this should be she could not say. It was as if by her act of utter renunciation she had somehow expiated some of her guilt, lost some of the load she carried that made her see the world differently from other people. The bad things in her life hadn't changed, but safe here in her hospital room, she could keep them at a distance. At least for a while, at least for now.

The heavy, white-painted door to her room opened slowly and Tim came in. She felt a rise of pleasure at the sight of him and was astonished by this. He came and stood by her bed.

"Hi," he said. She could see that he didn't know if he should kiss her or not. She put her arm up toward him and he bent over and kissed her lightly on the mouth and then straightened.

"Sit down," she said, indicating the chair that Iris had vacated. He pulled it around and sat down, leaning on his crossed arms, which he placed on the bed beside her. They looked at one another.

"You okay?" he asked. He was speaking so softly that she could hardly hear him. He ran his fingers lightly down her arm. When he reached her wrist she moved her hand and took his in it. He smiled.

"I love you," he said. It was the first time he had said it. She had the vision again, the one of life entering her room from the hall outside.

"I'm sorry," she said, meaning about worrying and frightening them all. He made a noise, a quick expulsion of breath, and closed his eyes.

"It was close, I guess," he said, opening them again.

"Was it?" Tears sprang up. She held them back. "Well," she said, trying to be gay. "No death experience, no long tunnels, no heavenly afterlife."

"Shucks," he answered, smiling down at her. They looked at one another again.

"Comb your hair," she said. She was smiling too, she couldn't help it. He thrust both hands upward, and tried to smooth it down.

"Oh, Tim," she said, and was crying again.

"Marry me," he said. "Live with me." The room was very still. Her tears ceased and she looked away. After a long pause she said, "I would make a terrible wife."

"I don't care," he said, leaning toward her. "I don't care." They were looking at one another again. She sighed and wiped her eyes with the tissue Iris had given her.

"I can't even think about it," she said. "Not yet. Not yet." She was thinking about the abortion, about what she would do after that. She wanted to tell him, but she knew she might have done something terrible to the baby, she might have made it into a monster, . . . no, she would spare him that. She caught herself. She had been thinking as if the baby was his, forgetting that she didn't know whose it was, and for a second the old horror leaped up and threatened to overwhelm her. She pushed it away.

"I'll wait," Tim said. "I mean, I love you. I'll wait." She watched him, trying to keep the nightmare back by memorizing his face, his pale blue eyes, his thick, creamy-coloured eyebrows and eyelashes, his generous mouth. "I mean, not forever," he said. "But I'll wait quite a while. Quite a while." She was beginning to see that the baby was a burden she would carry all her life, that from some things there was no escape. Not ever. It seemed to her that the room grew quieter, that time came to a stop and for a second she couldn't get her breath. Her body was sinking. Not ever.

"I'm going away for a while," she said. She didn't know where those words came from, what made her think them, but she didn't take them back.

"Good," he said. "Stay away as long as you like. As long as you need to." She should tell him no right now, tell him that it was impossible, that she would never marry him, or anyone, that he shouldn't wait. She should send him away. She couldn't understand why she didn't. It was like all the times she had let him make love to her, she still couldn't end their affair. There was something there, and now she caught just a glimmer of it. It was like a light, a bright clear light had shone on her briefly, illuminating everything, and then suddenly faded. She wanted it back, she wanted to see again. For no reason, she remembered Angela asking, what do you think life is for? And her answer, I don't know. I don't know what life is for. That seemed so long ago, as though a different Lannie had thought that. She turned to Tim again, wanting to speak.

Behind them there was a light knock and the door opened. Iris stood in the doorway, looking embarrassed. She was wearing the green dress again, the one with the little buttons down the front, Lannie hadn't noticed it before, and, seeing again in the light of the second before, she forgave Iris completely for James.

"I was just leaving," Tim said. He rose and stepped back, catching his foot on the chair and setting it right almost in the same motion. Iris laughed. "I'll come back tonight," he said, and then looked at Iris, "if they'll let me."

"They'll let you," Iris said. Tim went out. Because of the dress, because of James, Lannie remembered.

"Barney?" she asked, drawing in her breath quickly. "Where's Barney?" How could she have forgotten?

"He's coming, he's coming, dear. He said to tell you he'd be here." Iris was close to the bed now. "James is here," she said. "He wants to see you. Will you?"

"Of course," Lannie answered. Iris went out. In a moment the door opened and James Springer came in, moving slowly, stooping, pinning her with his dark blue eyes.

"My pills, eh?" He didn't appear to be angry, only amused or rueful, she couldn't tell which.

"It's all right," he said. "I guess we all forgive you." He laughed the same wry laugh. "I forgive you," he said, and laughed again, as if he knew no one cared about his forgiveness. "Thought about it myself," he said. He patted her hand clumsily. Something warm was starting inside of her, somewhere low down, in her abdomen. Why, it's where the pain was, she thought in amazement.

"Lot of people care about you," he said. It's true, she thought. She looked at him knowing her surprise showed. He smiled slowly, squeezed her hand, then laughed that same wry chuckle. For a moment he said nothing and she knew he was thinking about the baby. Finally he said, "Well, I'll be going then." Painfully he pulled himself to his feet, patted her hand once more and started walking to the door. He was old, he was ugly, but he was alive. Lannie watched him with awe.

Iris was standing in the hall when James came out of Lannie's room.

"How's Barney taking it?" James asked.

"Not very well . . . it's upset him," she finished lamely. James leaned toward her.

"He found out about the baby," he said. She nodded. "He's pretty upset, eh?" She nodded again. She could tell he wanted to touch her, comfort her. "I don't know," he said. "What a man could do. She's his daughter, but she isn't." Iris waited. "There's some things a man don't want to get too close to," he said to her. She nodded once, uncertainly. She did not understand. His words were landing like separate thuds in her chest. She brought her fingers up to her throat. She could not think how to handle this, watching James as they stood facing each other in the hospital corridor. With part of her mind, she recognized a soap opera playing on the television set in the sun room, and a nurse hurried by carrying a metal gadget in her hand. How wise he is, she thought.

"Leave him be," he said, finally, touching her shoulder, and starting to move on. "Come when you can," he said softly into her ear as he passed her.

"Yes, I will," she said firmly. She had come to a decision.

"Dr. Williams says you can go home tomorrow," Iris said. Lannie looked up from her magazine.

"I didn't hear you come in."

"I see you're keeping your door open now," Iris said.

"The nurses keep opening it," Lannie replied. She shrugged and set the magazine down.

"I think I'll close it," Iris said.

"Did Tim get away all right?" Lannie asked.

"Yes, this morning first thing," Iris said. "He says he'll call you as soon as you're home again." Lannie sighed and closed the magazine slowly, thoughtfully.

"Are they going to make me see a psychiatrist?" she asked.

"Yes, dear," Iris said. "It's all arranged. In Swift Current next week. Dr. Curtis-Mann." The colour drained from Lannie's face. She looked as if she were shrinking, drawing back inside herself.

"Lannie," Iris said, frightened by the rapid change in her, "I know it's for the best. I know it is. And anyway," she walked to the window on the far side of Lannie's bed and stood looking out over the neatly clipped, green lawn and the border of gnarled old poplars to the school grounds beyond. "You have to see one before you can have the abortion." Her hands clenched on the windowsill.

A bell rang faintly in the distance, or was it only in her head? No, children began to pour out the door of the red brick school. There was no sound from Lannie. "And one more doctor. A gynecologist," Iris said. Lannie might as well know it all.

Two boys, perhaps eight years old, had broken out of the crowd of children and crossed the playground, running as fast as they could, one ahead of the other. "It's arranged for the next morning," she said. The second boy was trying to catch the first. Now and then he would get a hold of the first boy's jacket and the first boy would twist his torso and yank himself free. Then they would run some more. When they were on the road in front of the hospital, just

beyond where she was watching from the window, Iris noticed that
the second boy had red hair. She turned back to Lannie.

"All right," Lannie said. "All right." She was lying on her pillows
with her eyes closed. "Maybe I am crazy," she said. "I think I was
crazy."

"Oh, Lannie," Iris said. "Don't think that. Nobody thinks that."

"You have no idea," Lannie said, "how I dread going out there."
She gestured with her head toward the hall. "Everybody talking
about me." Iris turned away from the bed. She was restless today,
couldn't stand still.

"They'll talk for a while," she said, "and then they'll forget about
it. They always do." Lannie pulled herself up to a sitting position and
bent forward, her hair falling downward so Iris couldn't see her face.

"No," she said softly. Through the fall of hair Iris was not sure
she was hearing correctly. "They never forget." Iris had gone back
to the window. At this she turned, placed her elbows on the sill
behind her and faced Lannie squarely. Lannie was still leaning forward, her hands on her thighs, just above her knees. "They never,
never forget."

"What do you mean?" Iris asked.

"Me," Lannie said, straightening, tossing her head so that her hair
fell back behind her shoulders and her white throat was exposed.
"Me!" she repeated. "Don't you see that I'm marked? I'm marked for
life here. As long as I stay here, I'll always be the one whose mother
died, the one whose father deserted her." Her words repeated themselves in the quiet room. Iris stared at her, frozen.

"And now," Lannie said, "and now, I'm the one who tried to kill
herself."

"Oh, Lannie," Iris said. "It's not that bad. It won't be." But she
wasn't sure.

"Iris," Lannie said. "You don't know. You just don't know." Iris
said nothing, seeing clearly for the first time the gulf between her
experience and Lannie's. It seemed she could never cross it. Lannie

fell back against her pillows. "You come from one of those good families," she said wearily. "You're a Thomas. The Thomases are respectable people." She said the words as if their taste was bitter on her tongue. "Pillars of the community. If you're a Thomas all you have to do is walk down the street and everybody likes you, everybody respects you." Iris flushed, then shrugged her shoulders, a small, baffled shrug and said, "We have our scandals too, just like other people."

"Sure," Lannie said. "Me."

"I was thinking about my Aunt Catherine," Iris said. "Did you know that she once ran away with an insurance salesman? And then came back again when it turned out he drank?"

"But it doesn't matter," Lannie said. "Don't you see? It never seems to matter what your family does. People forgive you."

"And your second cousin, Susan. She was seven months pregnant when she got married." Iris had walked around the bed to Lannie's side. Now she walked back to the window again and stood looking out.

"I'll always be a walking scandal in this town." Iris turned to her. "Why is that, Iris? Why is that? Why can't I be like you?"

Iris weighed Lannie's words. It was true. No one would ever forget Lannie, she would be used as an example to the young people of the town for years to come, just as everyone had politely forgotten Aunt Catherine's mad spree and Susan's deviance from the straight and narrow. Lannie was like James. People talked about the things he'd done fifty years ago as heatedly as if he had done them only yesterday.

She had not thought about the town, about the people in it. They had never done her any harm, she had always been part of it, she had just assumed their underlying benevolence. But she could remember times when people had been malicious, petty, not kind, when they had acted to hurt others, to destroy them if they could, and she wondered how all her life she could have been so utterly blind.

"I guess it's true," she said, "There are differences in the way people are treated. It seems like some people suffer more, or more easily, and people see that. It's a . . . a quality of soul, I guess."

"What does that mean?" Lannie asked.

"I guess," Iris said, "I guess . . . I don't know."

Chapter Eleven

IT WAS EARLY AFTERNOON. Iris was sitting in a flow-ered armchair in the living room, her elbows on the chair arms, her hands clasped on her stomach. The big house was quiet and she sat motionless, grateful for its silence and its emptiness. She had no energy anymore it seemed; the feeling of buoyancy she had always felt in her limbs, as if she might some day fly, had left her. She could not feel glad that Lannie was on her way home. She couldn't remem-ber what it felt like to be glad, or imagine ever being glad again, not since the day she had found Lannie, since she had walked the streets of the town alone, sat in the cafe by herself. She stirred in her chair and turned toward the big window, still hung with her mother's sheer white curtains. They made the view of the driveway, the lawn, the pines, look grey and indistinct as though there was a perpetual mist outside. She had often thought of taking the curtains down so that she could see the view clearly, but now the view no longer mat-tered, nor the smell of her garden in the sun, nor the closet upstairs full of the clothes that she had loved.

Barney stood outside the door to Lannie's hospital room, holding her small, salmon-coloured suitcase in one hand. The suitcase was empty and it felt awkward, too large to carry under one arm, but too light to feel right when he held it by the handle. He hoped he would know the right thing to say. He hoped Iris was right not to come herself. He hefted the suitcase with one hand as if testing its weight one more time, and then he pushed open the door and went inside.

Lannie was standing by her bed, her back to him, bent over, gathering the magazines that were scattered across the sheet and piling them in front of her. She was dressed in beige corduroy slacks and a light blue shirt. She looked over her shoulder when she heard the door open, pushing her hair back with one hand. There was a delicate pinkness to her skin now, like that of an infant.

"Oh," she said. "Oh, good. You brought a suitcase." He held it out to her and she took it from him. It was the first time they had been together without Iris since Lannie's first day in the hospital. "Where's Iris?" she asked. Her voice was unsteady and she tried to cover this by clearing her throat. Barney perched on the arm of the big chair at the foot of the bed.

"Waiting for us at home," he said.

Lannie moved the magazines over, set the suitcase on the bed and flipped it open. She began to fold her dressing gown with elaborate care and Barney could see a barely perceptible tremor in her hands. She opened the night table and took out a hairbrush, a hand mirror, a small blue satin zippered case. He could feel her nervousness. He wanted to help her, to tell her that he understood. She turned quickly and her hair fell back on her shoulders, the bronze gleam as vital and rich as it had always been, as though nothing had changed. He saw the open doorway, felt the chill of the early morning air.

While Lannie put the few small items one by one into the case, Barney stood and went to the window, where he leaned against the frame and looked out at the empty schoolyard, at the lawn below the window and at the hospital caretaker who was clipping a bush.

"I guess," he said, "I guess . . . we have to write Howard off." He heard no sound from Lannie and when he turned to face her, she was staring at him, her hands poised on the suitcase lid, her eyes wide. She moistened her lips.

"That may be," she said in a tentative way. She closed the suitcase, moving more slowly now. In a different voice, one carefully lighter, she asked, "Why didn't Iris come?" Barney lounged against the window, examining the fingers of one hand.

"Oh, she . . . I figured you wouldn't mind if your old uncle came for you." He looked up cautiously. He had tried to say stepfather. She was watching him. Slowly, she smiled. He smiled back.

"I'm glad you did," she said.

Iris walked around the living room, touching things lightly, without seeing them. She could not answer for the world, she could only answer for herself. How could she have been so stupid? So wrong? How could she not have seen that what she did with James was part of the evil? How could she have thought that her behaviour was justifiable, good?

She would give him up. She had admitted to the existence of evil, but she would not be a part of it. It will kill him, she thought, and stopped walking. Her eyes settled on the picture of her parents that hung on the wall by the mantle. Her mother's eyes looked at her, warm, gentle, her carefully-waved, white hair touching the arm of her father's dark suitcoat as he sat beside her, one arm around her shoulders. Her father's eyes were more direct, so innocent, she thought, so good, so kind. And my poor mother might as well be dead for all I think of her. She felt the familiar urge to cry as she stared at the photo. But no, tears were useless. So he would die. Well, he was an old man. He would soon die anyway.

Just as Iris turned to the window, the gleaming maroon car turned off the grid road and started down the long avenue of pines toward the house.

Although Barney hadn't come with them, Lannie and Iris didn't share a hotel room in Swift Current. Iris had reserved adjoining rooms, knowing that Lannie was accustomed to solitude and that even if she chose to, she couldn't change the habit so quickly.

She had gone with Lannie to the psychiatrist's office, intending to wait for her, but the receptionist had said, "Dr. Curtis-Mann has booked two hours with Miss Christie. There's no need for you to wait."

"Lannie?" Iris asked.

"Don't wait," Lannie said. "I'll meet you at the hotel in time for supper." She hadn't seemed nervous, only reserved and haughty in the old way.

When she tired of walking in and out of stores—she no longer wanted to buy anything—she went back to the hotel, kicked off her shoes and sat on the bed, half-heartedly reading a magazine she had bought in the lobby. Once she got up and turned on the television set. A soap opera was playing. When it was over, she didn't bother to turn off the set.

Sooner than she expected, she heard Lannie's key opening the other door of the room next to hers. Lannie came into her own room, tossed her purse onto the bed and came immediately through the adjoining doors into Iris's room.

"Iris," she said. Her voice rang with tension, even the muscles and sinews of her body seemed visibly taut. Her eyes glittered, her cheeks were coloured with two spots of red. She held out a magazine.

Iris, who had been leaning back against two plumped up pillows, sat up and swung her legs over the edge of the bed, and reached for the magazine.

"Page twenty-eight," Lannie said, in a breathless, high-pitched voice. Iris began turning the pages. It was a medical magazine. Puzzled, she stopped at page twenty-eight. Lannie sat down beside her.

"Dys-men-orr-hea?" Iris said, struggling with the word.

"Read," Lannie said, tapping the page, almost smiling. Iris did as she was told.

"That's me," Lannie said, her finger on the word a few lines down the page. "That's what I've got."

"What's this . . . prostoglandins?" Iris asked.

"You'll see as you read it," Lannie said. Iris glanced at her, half-smiling herself now. The article was about painful menstruation, its causes and cure. Iris could feel her brow furrowing with the effort to understand the argument written in such difficult, technical language.

"Oh, never mind," Lannie said. She took the magazine out of Iris's hands and stood up. Her excitement quivered in the air between them.

Holding the magazine against her chest, Lannie began to walk slowly up and down the carpeted hotel room, from the mirrored wall past the rumpled bed to the table on which stood a big lamp with an ugly orange plaster base. She spoke as though she were reciting facts she had memorized for an exam.

"The psychiatrist said . . . She's a woman! Did you know that?" Iris moved impatiently, putting her feet on the floor, looking for her shoes, which had got shoved under the bed somehow. "She said there are physical causes for severe menstrual pain." She faced Iris. "Did you hear that, Iris? Physical causes!" She emphasized each syllable. "I am not crazy!" she said, lifting her arms as if she were about to launch into flight. "Can you imagine, Iris?" she asked. "Can you imagine what it's like to hurt like that and to have everybody tell you it's all in your head? That you're doing it to yourself? To believe yourself that you are doing it and to try to stop and not know how . . ." She began to pace again. Iris couldn't speak.

"Diet!" Lannie said. "I have to watch what I eat—no salt, lots of iron and calcium. Oh, and exercise, I don't get enough exercise. She's sending a report to Dr. Williams." Lannie paused in the centre of the room. Iris saw the tension leave her body, saw her shoulders drop slowly, her eyes grow distant, her expression soften. She went to the chair under the window and sat in it, turning her head to one side, letting one arm trail down the side of the chair.

"That's wonderful news, dear," Iris said, hardly daring to believe it. She wanted to say more, to ask questions, but nothing she started to say was equal to the moment. But the abortion, she wondered, what about it?

"Did she . . .?" Iris ventured, and then stopped.

"Yes."

The hotel room was dimly lit, the small windows heavily curtained, the rug threadbare and plain. There was dust on the TV set and on the table in the corner. Iris thought of her blue carpeted living room, of the heavy silver tea service on the dining room table and the luxurious master bedroom on which she had lavished so much attention. In the end, all that had not protected her, nor had it protected Lannie. Lannie meditated in the chair in front of the window while Iris sat on the bed and thought wearily about what lay ahead, hoped only that they would both have the courage to go through with it.

"Well?" Barney asked.

"Next Thursday," Iris said. Barney sat down heavily on the side of their bed without regard for the brocade spread Iris had just smoothed over it. He set his elbows on his thighs and leaned forward, resting his forehead on his clasped hands. Iris could not remember ever having seen him look so sad. She watched him, without moving, wishing she had some comfort to offer him. He said, not taking down his hands, "You take her. I can't." After a moment he rose, and began to button his shirt. He had aged. In the morning light she could see the new wrinkles under his eyes and in their corners and when he crossed the room to their dresser she saw that his walk had less spring to it and that his smile was tinged with something else, as if he were barely hiding some stronger feeling, as if a chasm had opened inside him.

"All right," she said. He held his arms out to her in a gesture that surprised her and she leaned against him for a minute feeling his warmth and his enduring solidity.

There was a week to get through before the operation. Iris did her best to keep Lannie busy and to stay beside her all the time, except at night, when they each closed their bedroom doors behind them and retreated into privacy. Each morning after breakfast, she and Lannie put on their jeans, wide-brimmed hats and gardening gloves, and spent an hour or two crouching among the rows of green vegetables and flowers. They painted Lannie's room a light peach shade, picked by Iris, hung new curtains and had a matching rug installed.

While they worked, Iris's thoughts were focused on the abortion, on getting it over with. She didn't think beyond it because she couldn't imagine what might happen afterward and she was afraid to think about it. And she could see that dwelling on the past, berating herself forever about it, would destroy her, so she tried not to think about it either. She didn't know what Lannie thought about and she didn't ask. Lannie worked alongside Iris without speaking, but her silence now had a reflective quality that Iris found less disturbing than the old silences had been.

One morning while they were weeding in the strawberry patch, Iris suddenly put down her hoe and went into the house. She dialled hastily, letting her straw hat dangle by its string from her wrist. She spoke quickly.

"I can't see you till this is over," she said to James. "I have to stay with Lannie. I have to, James," she repeated, as if he had protested. "You have to understand that I'm to blame for a lot of this." She rested her forehead against the upper cupboard. Her breath felt warm on her hand, she could feel herself perspiring. She was hardly listening to him.

"It wasn't you, Iris," he answered. "But I know you have to stay with her." His voice was sad, it made Iris remember how quiet his house was, without echoes, the air somehow warm. "Bring her to see me," he asked, but Iris knew immediately that she wouldn't, although she didn't know why.

Iris looked out the window of her room over the lights of the small city, which stretched out around her, silent, shadowed, geometric. She thought of Lannie lying in a drugged sleep in her hospital bed, saw in a flash the operation, the blood, the dead fetus. What do they do with it, she wondered, and shivered, and willed herself to be calm. She stood and watched the lights and imagined the lives of the people, each enclosed by his own house, his own fenced yard, the small measure of his comings and goings in the world. It either matters terribly, she thought, or it doesn't matter at all and I don't know which. But I love Lannie, she thought, and the baby was only a hope. Born, it too would become real and I would have learned to love it too, the way I love Lannie, and I would be just as helpless when it needed me.

Meditating at the window, she felt the touch of James's hands on her body. Without him she would lose forever that perfect matching under the skin that the two of them had. She resigned herself to the loss. She would not look elsewhere for it. She would pull into herself, become more solid, more purposeful. She would learn to be satisfied with what she rightfully had.

James would die. She imagined how he would grow quiet without her, how he would sit in his chair day after day, moving less and less, the curtains drawn, till life stilled around him, and then in him.

She and Lannie were home the next day by early afternoon. When they got out of the car, they could both hear the rumble of the tractor out on a distant quarter, growing louder, then fading, then growing louder again in a familiar rhythm. As though agreed upon, they both stopped and listened to the reassuring sound before they went into the house.

"I'm going into town for a few groceries," Iris said to Lannie, when she had settled her on the living room couch. "I'll be back at five. You rest till then." She got back in her car and drove to town.

She went straight to James's house. He was not expecting her and didn't answer the door right away. When he opened it and saw her, his face smoothed somehow, he grew younger, and he put his hand on her elbow lightly to draw her in. Iris felt her resolve weakening with the spread of her desire for him. He closed the door, then held her against him, she hadn't the heart to resist, couldn't have anyway. He put his face against her hair, his breathing was fast and shallow. They kissed, he lost his balance momentarily and then steadied himself with one hand on the door frame. They went into the bedroom and sat down together on the side of the bed. Then Iris knew that there would have to be one last love-making.

So there was a long, tender hour without words, when both she and James were immersed in that other world they had together of sensation and of something more, some rich, dark, boundaryless world where they were one person and understood one another beyond the limits of their skin. When it was over and they were lying side by side, Iris reached down and pulled the covers over her body. James looked at her and then stared at the ceiling.

"You've come to tell me it's over," he said. He had another sense, one that other people lacked. Perhaps it was because he was so old, or so near to death, or perhaps, she thought, he had always had it.

"I won't try to keep you," he said. Already, she thought, his voice was fading. "No one will ever love you the way I do," he said.

"James," she said. She turned toward him, placing her hand on his chest where the hair, now white, lay along the curve of his breast. She saw his ribs, the white skin receding between them and for a moment almost relented. "James, I love you," she said, "but . . ."

"It isn't right," he said. "For you, it has to be right." She took her hand away.

"Yes," she said. My heart is breaking, she thought, and then thought, no, mine is not a heart that breaks. And suddenly she remembered Lannie asking her from her hospital bed what she meant when she said that her family was forgiven things because of a quality of soul they possessed. Now she knew what it was. It was this. She had no passion. She did not even fully comprehend what passion was. She had only a lightness, a gentle enough, a good thing, but James was all soul, he lived by the power of his feelings. Their intensity was overwhelming, was whole, gripped him completely. He could die of love, yes, could die of love, but she could not. In that, Lannie was like James. She saw it now, and felt herself to be nothing beside James who lived, it seemed to her, as people should live.

But then, she thought, a world where everyone is like James would be impossible. There have to be people like me who can be the nurses and the teachers, the guardian angels, the spirits that bind things together.

"Iris," James said. "Iris." His voice was soft. He spoke very slowly. "You don't know what right is."

"What?" she asked, turning to him and placing her hand on his chest again.

"How can love be wrong?" he asked. "How can it be wrong to love somebody?" She could hear him crying, and wondered how soon after she left his tears would stop. "There are rights and there are wrongs," he said. "You have a husband. I know that." She knew he was trying to say more and couldn't because he couldn't trust himself.

"James," she said, surprised at how loud her voice was in the quiet house, the silent street outside. "I let this happen to Lannie because I didn't pay enough attention to her. And Barney, I missed things in him I should have seen." When she closed her eyes she saw again behind her eyelids the magical baby lying in the carriage on the grass under the trees, saw the brilliant beauty of the colours, felt the perfect harmony of living things. It was the vision again. She opened her eyes. There was a soft glow in the room.

"You're not responsible for the rightness of the world," he said. His voice had grown loud again; it was heavy with emotion. "Barney's a grown man. You didn't kill the girl's mother and you didn't chase her father away!" Iris tried to think, but there were so many things to think, her thoughts weren't clear anymore, she was confused. She rolled over against James and clung to him. He lifted his hand and rested it on her head, like a benediction.

"I don't know what to do," she said. "I thought I did, and now I don't." He stroked her hair.

"Nobody knows what to do," he said. And feeling the truth of this, they held on to one another.

"Uncle Barney," she said. "You have been so good to me. I will always be grateful to you, and to you too, Aunt Iris."

"You sound as if you're leaving forever," Iris said, trying, and failing, to keep the fear out of her voice.

"Oh, no," Lannie said. "I wouldn't do that. I know you love me." She moved her eyes to Barney. "I have to ask for money," she said. She shrugged her shoulders as if she wanted to say more but recognized the uselessness of it. Barney stood and reached for his wallet.

"I'll give you some cash," he said, "and I'll write a cheque too." He was always more confident when he was handling money. He went down the hall to the kitchen where he kept his chequebook.

"Will you be gone a long time?" Iris asked.

"I don't know," Lannie said. "A couple of months. Maybe more."

"But you'll write?" Iris asked again.

"Definitely," Lannie said. This was not what Iris had expected. Lannie suddenly taking control of her own life. But now that she could see it in front of her, Iris knew it was the best thing, the right thing. It was what she should have hoped for. Barney came back into the room and handed Lannie a cheque. He hesitated, and while he was still fighting with himself, Iris could see the struggle, Lannie reached up, put both arms around his neck, and kissed him lightly on one cheek and then on the other, formally.

"Thank you," she said, her voice soft for the first time that Iris could remember, a new gentleness in it. Then Barney bent and without touching her, kissed her forehead.

"Do you . . . where . . . are you going east or west?" Iris asked, and Lannie smiled.

"West," she said. She's going to look for her father, Iris thought. She was too shocked to comment. Lannie had moved to the doorway now and Iris got up to stand beside Barney. She put one arm around his waist. Lannie picked up her suitcase and went to the front door and opened it. The long, golden light of evening lit up the yard behind her.

"Take my car," Iris said. "You've got a couple of hours before the westbound bus leaves. Barney and I can pick it up in the morning."

"Thank you," Lannie said again, and then she stepped outside and shut the door behind her.

When Lannie reached town, she turned the car toward the old section, driving past Angela's house, not stopping till she reached the old white house with the wide verandah around it. She pulled up in front of it, got out of the car, and went up the walk. James opened the door before she could knock.

"I saw you drive up," he said. "Thought it was Iris." He laughed at himself. "Come in."

"Thanks," Lannie murmured and passed him to sit down on the couch. He followed, slowly, behind her and sat down in his armchair. The room looked dusty and uncared for.

"Iris didn't clean this week," Lannie said.

"No," James said. He had lit a cigarette.

"Is she, she's coming back, isn't she?" Lannie asked. James looked at her and a light shone in his eyes. She felt that he saw through her.

"You're a lot like me," he said, as though he had just realized this.

"Like you?" she asked. He drew on his cigarette and looked ahead, out the window. Finally, he spoke.

"Yeah," he said. "You take things pretty hard." Lannie nodded. "Things are either good or bad, there ain't no in-between for people like us." He laughed, the same wry laugh she had heard before. "It's a helluva thing," he said, and coughed once. Lannie said again, "Iris is coming back?" He drew on his cigarette and then held it protruding between the fingers of his clasped hands.

"I think she'll be back," he said, his voice so soft she could hardly hear him. "You think that's wrong?" His voice changed as he asked this question of her.

"It's not my business," Lannie said. "Things aren't all that clear to me, what's right and wrong." James smiled.

"They're not that clear to Iris, either," he said. "Or to me. But I'm old, I won't be here that long." His voice faded out in the quiet room.

"I'm leaving," Lannie said. He looked at her again.

"Oh," he said.

"Yes," Lannie said. "I came to say good-bye."

"Where are you going?" he asked. "To see the world?" Lannie laughed.

"No," she said. "I have a plan." The delight, the satisfaction in her voice made them both smile. "I'm going to Calgary first," Lannie said. "I have a brother and a sister there. I'm going to see them."

"Why?" he asked. His voice was gentle.

"I'll know when I get there," she answered. For a moment she was silent. "Because they exist. Because they are my brother and my sister. I used to think things were more complicated than they are." James nodded. "Then I am going to find my father," Lannie said. She waited for him to say something.

"I'm not surprised," he said. "I'm too old. I've seen everything." He shifted in his chair. "You know where to look?"

"I'll find out," she said. "I have an old address. I'll start there." He nodded again, and then he laughed.

"And you won't quit till you find him. I know your kind." Lannie didn't say anything. "You might not like what you find."

"That's not the point," Lannie said sharply.

"You women," he said. "Everything's always got to have a point." He shook his head. "Well, good luck. Let me know how you make out."

"I will," Lannie said. She was standing now, a feeling of gaiety growing in her. She smiled at him, a full-blown smile, and then turned and went out of his house to the car. She opened the door and pulled out her suitcase and started down the street toward the service station where the westbound bus would soon stop.

Inside the house James had not moved. He sat in his armchair, the end of his cigarette glowing softly in the darkening room. He could hear the sound of his heart beating in his chest. He could feel every beat. Every beat.

He thought about Iris. How in his seventy-four years he had never stopped to think what was right or what was wrong, but had always acted from the heart.

He looked around the dusty, familiar room. He thought of his wife, her pale blue eyes, her dark hair pulled back from her face, saw her bending to water the fern in front of the window.

"Aurora," he said, but she had faded from view.

He listened to his heart again. Still strong, thudding in his chest.